Acclaim for the
of MICHA

"Michael's talent outscaled even his own dinosaurs of Jurassic Park. He was the greatest at blending science with big theatrical concepts…There is no one in the wings that will ever take his place."
— *Steven Spielberg*

"Intricate plotting and flawless pacing…you won't be able to put it down."
— *Time*

"Crichton keeps us guessing at every turn."
— *Los Angeles Times*

"A fascinating, splendidly documented thriller."
— *New Yorker*

"One gorgeous read."
— *Boston Globe*

"Irresistibly suspenseful."
— *New York Times*

"Will keep you turning the pages."
— *Forbes*

"Compulsively readable."
— *National Review*

"Completely brilliant."
    —*Daily Mail (UK)*

"An exciting story…in the hands of a master storyteller like Crichton, it's good entertainment."
    —*Sunday Telegraph (UK)*

"Wonderful…powerful…"
    —*Washington Post*

"[Crichton] marries compelling subject matter with edge-of-your-seat storytelling."
    —*USA Today*

"Crackling…mysterious…"
    —*Entertainment Weekly*

"Every bit as informative as it is entertaining. And it is very entertaining."
    —*Wall Street Journal*

"One of the great storytellers of our age…What an amazing imagination."
    —*New York Newsday*

A silent crowd waited in front of the Carlton Hotel, watching as cars came up the elevated ramp. Several people in the crowd held binoculars, which they used to scan the upper windows of the hotel; others kept cameras poised.

Across the street, on the sidewalk above the beach, people were clustered against the rail. Something seemed to be going on. He pushed his way through the bystanders and eventually managed a view down over the sand.

It was a photographic session for a fashion magazine. The model, a skinny girl with a dark tan and large, brilliant eyes, reclined on a striped beach mattress.

"Who is it?" a navy sailor asked, as he elbowed his way to Carr's side.

Carr walked on.

He absorbed it all—the gray ships of the Sixth Fleet, anchored in the harbor; the private beaches, swept smooth until they resembled well-tended lawns; the groups of Germans, wearing shorts and sandals, burned a painful red. And he looked at the girls.

He saw one who was really remarkable. He could not see her face; it was covered by a broad straw hat, and only a few strands of blond hair were visible at the edge. Alongside her was a half-finished drink, a pack of cigarettes, her sunglasses, a paperback book. And her purse, a large alligator handbag, with gold initials that gleamed in the sun: AC.

He decided to say hello…

Scratch ONE

by **Michael Crichton**

WRITING AS JOHN LANGE

A HARD CASE **CRIME NOVEL**

A HARD CASE CRIME BOOK
(HCC-MC2)
First Hard Case Crime edition: October 2013

Published by

Titan Books
A division of Titan Publishing Group Ltd
144 Southwark Street
London SE1 0UP

in collaboration with Winterfall LLC

SCRATCH ONE™
by Michael Crichton writing as John Lange™

ISBN 978-1-78329-119-9

Design direction by Max Phillips
www.maxphillips.net

Typeset by Swordsmith Productions

The name "Hard Case Crime" and the Hard Case Crime logo
are trademarks of Winterfall LLC. Hard Case Crime books
are selected and edited by Charles Ardai.

Printed in the United States of America

Visit us on the web at www.HardCaseCrime.com

Chapter I

Monday: Principauté de Monaco

Victor Jenning, tanned and very fit, walked down the steps of the Casino into the cool night air. They were already bringing his blood-red Lamborghini around from the lot. It was a new car, and Jenning was pleased with it—Carrozzeria Touring body mounted over a 3.5 liter V-12 engine that ran smoothly at 240 kilometers an hour. It was a hardtop, of course. Jenning loathed driving fast in an open car—unless he was racing—and he had rolled enough cars to have a healthy respect for solid protection overhead.

People were gathering to admire the car as he came to the bottom of the steps. It was only natural; the car had never been produced prior to 1965, when old Ferrucio Lamborghini, the tractor and oil burner tycoon, had established a limited production shop in Cento, just a few miles from Ferrari's plant at Maranello. Three hundred Lamborghinis were made a year, so it was still quite a rarity. It had cost him $14,000.

As he made his way around the crowd, he answered their questions with smiles and a slightly bored voice, then got in behind the wheel. He was a jaded man, and so felt only mild pride, but it was sufficient to make him forget—momentarily at least—the ten thousand dollars he had just dropped that night at baccarat, in a particularly poor run of luck.

He started the engine, listening with satisfaction to the bass growl from the twin exhausts. The crowd parted, and he reached down for the lights. His hand flicked on the windshield wipers, and he had a twinge of embarrassment. Damn!

It was painfully obvious that he'd owned the car just a week. He bent over to peer at the switches.

At that moment his windshield shattered in front of him.

The crowd gasped; somebody screamed. Another shot, and Jenning, who had immediately dropped as low as he could, felt pain in his right shoulder. He turned on the lights, released the brake, and put the car quickly into reverse. Still hunched over, he roared backward, sat up, spun the wheel around, and tore off into the night. Air blew through the gaping hole in his windshield, and he swore to himself.

Victor Jenning was a man accustomed to attempts on his life. There had been four in the last two years. None had come close to succeeding, though he had a slight limp as a result of the second. In a strange way, he did not mind the assassination attempts—they were part of the game, one of the risks in his line of work. But he hated to see his new car damaged. It would take weeks, now, to get a new windshield fitted properly.

As he drove through the dark streets of Monaco toward the doctor, he was so furious that he did not bother to reflect that, had he known how to work his lights, he would probably be dead.

Tuesday: Cairo, Egypt

One of the Arabs held a gun. "It will not be long now," he said pleasantly.

In the back seat of the taxi, the European stared at the gun, at the Egyptian holding it, and at the back of the neck of the driver. They sped through the dark streets of the city.

"Where are you taking me?" he said. He was French, and spoke Arabic with a slurred accent.

"To a meeting. Your presence is desired."

"Then why the gun?"

"To assure...punctuality."

The Frenchman sat back and lit a cigarette. He remained cool; it was part of his training. He had been in tight situations before, and he had always managed to escape safely.

The car left the city and headed south, into the desert. It was a moonless May night, black and cool. The Frenchman could see the outlines of the palm trees that lined the road.

"Who is this person I am meeting?"

The Arab laughed softly: "You know him."

They drove for ten minutes, and then the Arab with the gun said, "Here."

The driver pulled off the road, onto the sand. The Nile was a few hundred yards away.

The car stopped. "Out," the Arab said, motioning with the gun.

The Frenchman got out and looked around. "I don't see anybody."

"Have patience. He will be here soon." The Arab drew a pair of handcuffs from his pocket and handed them to the driver. To the Frenchman, he said, "If you please. Our man is rather nervous. This will reassure him."

"I don't think—"

The Arab shook his head. "No arguments, please."

The Frenchman hesitated, then turned and held his hands behind his back. The driver clicked the handcuffs shut.

"Good," said the Arab with the gun. "Now we will go to the river, and wait."

They walked silently across the sand. No one spoke. The Frenchman was worried, now. He had made a mistake, he was sure of it.

It happened with lightning swiftness.

One of the Arabs tripped him, and he pitched forward on

his face into the sand. Strong hands gripped his neck, forced his head down. He felt the grainy sand on his lips, in his eyes and nose. He struggled and kicked, but the Arabs held him firmly. His mind began to reel, and then blackness seeped over him.

The Arabs stepped back.

"Stupid fool," one said.

The driver removed the handcuffs. Each man took one leg, and they dragged the body to the river. The Arab put his gun away and held the body underwater with his foot until it sank. It would rise to the surface later, when it was bloated and decomposing. But that would not be for several days.

The body sank. A few final bubbles broke the calm water, and then, nothing.

Friday: Estoril, Portugal

The man walked across the rocks in his bare feet, looking into the setting sun. The waves of the Atlantic crashed into the rock. He was an American, a minor consular official attached to the office in Barcelona. He had received news of his transfer to Nice just three days before, and had decided to relax for a few days before moving. He was accustomed to traveling, and did it easily, so there were no major preparations to look after. Lisbon had been the perfect choice for a short break. He had been here during the war, and loved it deeply. Particularly this stretch of coast, west of the city, past the point where the Tagus River emptied into the ocean.

He smiled, breathed deeply, and reached in his pocket for cigarettes. To his right, the rocky shelf leading up from the sea ended in a sloping pine grove; to the left, the water rushed up against sharp, eroded stone. He was alone—few people came here at evening, this early in the season. He felt relaxed and cleansed after the bustle of Barcelona. The match flared in his hand, and he touched it to the cigarette. What the hell was he going to do in France, where cigarettes were so expensive?

Offshore, a fishing boat started its motor, and he listened to its faint puttering as it pulled away. He would have lobster tonight, he decided, in a little place in Cascais. Then he would return to his hotel and compose a letter to his girl in Barcelona, explaining that he had been sent away, suddenly, and was returning to the United States. The Spaniards were accustomed to hush-hush, sudden maneuverings among any kind of government officials; Maria would take it well. And although he would miss her, he was confident he could find a suitable replacement on the Riveria. Hell, if you couldn't find a girl there, you couldn't find one anywhere.

Behind him, there was a sharp *crack!* It was a sound he did not hear, for by that time, the bullet had entered the back of his head, smashing the occipital bone and burying itself deep in his cerebellum. He felt a momentary twinge of pain, and was pitched forward onto the rocks. His face smashed down hard, breaking the bones of his nose and jaw. Blood flowed out.

Two other men, neatly dressed in sport clothes, viewed the fallen body with satisfaction. The tide was coming in; within an hour, these rocks would be submerged, and the body carried out to sea. It was a good, clean, neat job. They were pleased.

Chapter II

Saturday: Köbenhavn, Denmark

Per Bjornstrand, a Norwegian, checked into the Royal Hotel at 4:00 P.M., and went immediately to his room to shower and change. He had just arrived at Kastrup Lafthavn on a direct flight from Oslo, and it had been a tiring trip—the plane was delayed in Oslo, and there had been considerable turbulence for over an hour in the air.

He felt better after cleaning up, and went down to the sleekly modern lobby. He dropped into one of Arne Jacobsen's egg chairs, and ordered a martini. They were a bad habit, martinis, which he had picked up from his British business associates, and they, no doubt, from the Americans. So many of the world's habits were American, these days. He lit a Lucky Strike filter cigarette and looked across the room at the slim blonde behind the reception desk. She was a rather elegant creature, with hair upswept, and high cheekbones.

Whenever Per Bjornstrand came to Copenhagen—which was often, since his business demanded it—he stayed at the Royal. He could, of course, stay with his sister-in-law in Hille-röd, but he always told himself that this was too far from the center of town. The truth was that he loathed his sister-in-law, a mindless child-bearing creature. And besides, the Copenhagen girls were too much to pass up.

He sat back in the chair, which encircled him like a womb, and puffed on his cigarette as he ran over his schedule for the next two days. Tomorrow he would be relatively free and would have lunch with Jörgen, an old friend from the war. On Monday morning he must see the shipping agents and arrange for transfer of the consignment from Copenhagen to Marseilles, and for storage there. He should, of course, spend Monday afternoon shopping for anniversary presents for his wife; the smart shops along Amagertorv would be filled with things she'd adore. But it was still cold; outside, along Hammerichsgade, the wind whistled bleakly, pounding rain against the glass walls of the lobby, and he couldn't imagine he'd feel much like shopping, even by Monday.

His thoughts were interrupted by the arrival of a new girl, dark and long-limbed, dressed in a tightly belted trench coat which emphasized her fine legs and narrow waist. She had very blue eyes, and a wide smile which she lavished upon Bjornstrand as she passed. He smiled back, let his eyes flick quickly over her body, and observed that she was alone. That was significant. He would ask at the desk about her later, and phone up to suggest she join him for a drink. There was no sense being alone on a cold, rainy evening. After all, he thought, breathing deeply to expand his chest, he was only forty-five, still virile and still handsome. It wouldn't last forever.

His mind, reluctantly, returned to business. He was a dealer in armaments, and—in a small way—a manufacturer. He now had a surplus of automatic rifles and assorted small arms which the Norwegian Army was selling as it upgraded its own issue, and a buyer in southern France had contacted him. The shipment was required quickly, so Bjornstrand had come to Copenhagen to manage the details himself. It was a lucrative business, and very enjoyable.

The waiter came with a small bowl of hors d'oeuvres, and the martini. "Your check, please."

He signed, adding the tip.

"And your room number?"

He scrawled it, and returned the slip. The waiter left him, and Per Bjornstrand picked up the martini. The outside of the glass was suitably frosted. He took a tentative sip. Very dry, pleasantly cold—the liquid ran down his throat, and caught fire in his stomach. But it was also bitter, strangely bitter.

For a moment, he wondered why. Then a giant hand gripped his innards, choking him. Per Bjornstrand coughed once, and made gurgling sounds as he fell back in his chair and died.

Saturday: Paris, France

Inspector Edgar Duvernet followed the doctor down the aseptic white corridor. Duvernet was a short man, and he resented the doctor's long, easy strides; it was unbecoming for a member of the police force to puff along at a taller man's heels. They came to the door.

"I warn you, he does not look pretty," the doctor said. Duvernet thought he caught a hint of condescension, an anticipation that he, Duvernet, could not take what was coming.

He snorted. The doctor opened the door. The patient was alone, on his back in bed. One arm was extended, strapped to a board; a bottle of liquid was dripping into the hand, through a needle inserted in a vein. The hand was swollen, the veins bulging. For a moment, this was all Duvernet could see, and he did not find it alarming. He stepped closer.

Then he saw the face. It was covered with a plaster guard, to protect it, but much of the flesh of cheeks and jaw were visible. It was horrible, and despite himself, Duvernet gasped. The skin had the color and texture of a half-deflated football. The purple-black eyes were puffed shut, and a neat suture ran across the nose, then around one eye, terminating in a straight line down the cheek.

"You should have seen him before," the doctor said.

"Bad?" Duvernet asked, still looking at the patient. He did not trust himself to face the doctor just yet. *Mon Dieu,* it was stuffy in here! He was feeling suddenly nauseous.

"The whole right side of his face was caved in, and his right eye nearly scooped out of the socket. It was an inch lower than his left, when we got him. His jaw was broken and his nose crushed, his upper lip torn badly in two places, several teeth gone. We had to—"

Duvernet wobbled, and tottered over to a chair. The doctor quickly opened a window, and passed smelling salts under the policeman's nose. New to the job, he thought. "I don't mean to bore you with technical details," he said.

"Not at all," Duvernet said, jerking his head up from the ammonia odor and looking quickly at the doctor, searching for signs of amusement. He was relieved to find none. It's because I am new to my job, Duvernet thought; only that. In a month or two, such things will not bother me.

"Is he all right?" Duvernet asked, looking at the floor.

"He'll survive, though he's lost a lot of blood. We're trying to see that he doesn't develop meningitis, that's the big worry." When the man broke his nose, he had shattered his ethmoids, exposing the dura mater covering the brain. It made things very touch and go, the doctor knew, particularly when resistance was severely lowered. He frowned. "Any idea how it happened?"

Duvernet shook his head. "None at all. We were hoping he might be able to tell us."

"Not for weeks, I'm afraid. He'll be under heavy sedation for some time, and his jaw is wired shut. Do you have everything you need?"

"Yes. Just tell me: where is the nearest telephone?"

"At the end of the hall. In an emergency, the desk will give you an outside line."

"Bon. Merci." Duvernet stood, shook the doctor's hand, and sat down again, very shaky. He looked for a long time at the patient's feet, and then at the bottle of fluid, with the tube going down to the hand. He breathed deeply, and shortly began to recover.

This man was Jean Paul Revel, an exporter from Marseilles. Perfectly straightforward and honest. He had come to Paris on business—his wife had verified that, in a telephone call—and had arrived on the 7:14 train at the Gare d'Orleans. He had left the station, and entered the Metro station, carrying a small suitcase. Somehow, M. Revel fell forward from the platform into the path of an onrushing train. Observers stated that he flailed his arms to regain his balance, and some quick-witted person grabbed his coattails. Probably he would have escaped injury entirely, had not the train come along at that moment and smashed into his face and chest. He suffered a broken collarbone, two cracked ribs, and a badly battered face which had been immediately operated on.

The police were interested in questioning him, and normally would have been content to wait until he had recovered. There was, after all, no indication of foul play. But the call from the Deuxième had been put through that morning, and so here he was, Edgar Duvernet, on the job.

He reached into his pocket and withdrew his pistol. He flicked off the safety and placed it carefully in his lap. He had five hours before the second shift went on. Duvernet looked around the room, hoping for something to read, seeing nothing. Outside, it was raining, the chilly drops falling slantwise against the window, streaking the view of the newly green trees.

Saturday: Nice, France

Dr. Georges Liseau, looking slim and elegant, strode into the room. The five men collectively known as the Associates stood as he entered. Like himself, many had the swarthy complexions which betrayed an Algerian birth; one or two had knife scars on their faces, but otherwise they were unexceptional, respectable-looking. One would never suspect that they were all Arab agents.

"Sit down, gentlemen. This isn't a board meeting." Dr. Liseau's voice was mildly sarcastic. As usual, he took his seat at the head of the table, and did not remove his sunglasses. He surveyed the men in the room, then said, "Any explanations?"

There was a general rustling of paper and shifting of position, but no one spoke.

Liseau sighed. "Our record," he said, "is not very good. The Jenning business was executed quite badly. The attempt in Paris was amateurish. I understand the man is alive, and expected to recover with nothing more than a few scars on his face. The arms shipment may not be delayed. We shall have to improve our efficiency."

Liseau sat back, and allowed his words to sink in. The five men were staring at their hands. Well, what did they expect? Congratulations?

"It is true," he continued, "that the efforts in Lisbon and Copenhagen were satisfactory, but there have been too many mistakes. The use of strychnine on Bjornstrand was inane; the autopsy will certainly show he was poisoned. Gallamine would have been far preferable." Gallamine was like curare, a potent muscle relaxant. Overdoses produced such severe relaxation that the patient could not breathe, and went into shock. But it looked natural, that was the point—it could be heart failure, anything. Liseau sighed.

"Time is running out, gentlemen, and we cannot afford more bumbling. There are two new developments about which you should be informed. First, the assassin from America is coming, as expected. He left New York yesterday, and is now in London. Presumably he is being briefed by the Paris head, a man called Amory. We know Amory left for London this morning. The Consulate here is expecting the American to arrive in Nice tomorrow. He must be dealt with."

Liseau paused to light a cigarette.

"Second, I have called in outside help—someone who will, I hope, make no mistakes. The man is Ernst Brauer."

The reaction to this was immediate. The men looked up, puzzled, concerned. And with good reason—Herr Brauer was widely known as a cleanser of organizations, a ruthlessly efficient hunter of traitors.

"You are displeased?" Liseau asked mildly.

The balding Italian answered. "It is not that," he said, gesturing helplessly with his hands. "But there is some question of Brauer's activities in Berlin in '58...."

Liseau waved a slim, impatient hand. His hands were beautiful, one of the first things one noticed about him. They moved gracefully when he spoke, skillfully when he held a scalpel. The fingers were long and strong, and beautifully groomed. "You are too polite," Liseau said. "What you mean is that he may have gone double in Berlin."

The Italian shrugged, noncommittal. "It was a rumor."

"It was a fact. Herr Brauer is motivated only by money. In our case, we will see that he is amply paid."

"Have you met with him?" another man asked.

"Yes," Liseau lied. It was better to present these men with a *fait accompli.* "Yes, I met with him yesterday."

"So long as you are satisfied."

"I am." It was a quiet statement, but definite. Nobody questioned him further.

"What about this American killer?"

Liseau smiled. "He will not trouble us, I assure you. A reception for him has been planned, a quite satisfactory reception. He will never get off his plane."

I wish I could be so confident, Liseau thought. And I wish I knew what was being discussed at that briefing. He glanced at his watch, and stood. It was almost time for his appointment with Brauer.

Saturday: London

They met for dinner in a private room above a restaurant off Tottenham Court Road. Amory, the Paris man, arrived first, and viewed Morgan with deceptively casual interest as he came in. They shook hands.

"Drink?" Amory asked.

"Fine," Morgan said. "Dry vermouth on the rocks."

Amory ordered. It was an interesting drink, he thought—alcoholic, but weak. It fitted a man whose business was killing. When they were alone, he said, "It could be messy, very messy."

"I expect so. It usually is." Morgan had a childish, pudgy face. He looked rather cherubic—not like an angel, really, but more like a satyr or a practical joker. There was a disarming air of amusement about him which made his hard, flat statements incongruous. He doesn't talk the way he looks, Amory thought. Not at all.

Amory was interested in Morgan; he was a rare type—an American killer with none of the cheap gangsterish qualities of so many American hired men. There was something about the American personality which precluded the possibility of a cool, sophisticated murder. The Europeans were much better at it, and Amory, in his work, generally relied on Europeans.

"I'm afraid this briefing will be rather lengthy. It's a woefully complicated business. How much have you got already?"

"Just the bare outlines. A shipment of guns that Washington would like to see delivered, and that some others are anxious to stop."

Amory nodded. "I wish it was that simple. The guns are automatic rifles and small arms, Norwegian surplus. The Norwegian army is updating its issue, and these weapons were auctioned about three weeks ago. The whole lot was bought up by a man named Bjornstrand. I just received a call that he died four hours ago in Copenhagen."

Morgan did not seem startled. "Any details? Autopsy?"

"One is being performed, and we are trying to get a preliminary summary. But it has to go through the Danish and Norwegian governments before we can get our hands on it, and I don't think we'll know for two weeks. It might have been natural—he died right in the lobby of his hotel—or it might have been very daring."

The drinks came, and conversation broke while the waiter was in the room. When they were alone again, Amory said, "Maybe I had better start from the beginning." He took out a pocket notebook, and thumbed through it. "I couldn't bring the file, so I won't be able to give you all the minutiae, but basically it goes like this: in March of this year, the Israeli government approached several people about the availability of new automatic weapons. It was a panic move, initiated by a leak that Czechoslovakia was supplying automatic stuff to Egypt and Syria. At that time, in March, nothing was around. Then, very conveniently, the Norwegians decided to unload all their equipment. An arrangement was set up through a fellow named Victor Jenning. He's an American who lives in Monaco and has been supplying armaments for years to everybody. Did it for Sukarno; did it for the Turks, and the Venezuelans. He's a strange type, purely an intermediary— he has no stock of his own, he simply buys and resells. His passion is automobile racing, and fast women, and he's been married—"

"I've heard of him."

"Ummm. Well, anyway, Jenning was to arrange for a shipment from Copenhagen to Marseilles, and from there to Israel. All hush-hush, since the Arabs would go through the ceiling if they found out beforehand. We initially favored— unofficially—this transaction. We even put up some of the capital," Amory added, slightly embarrassed.

Morgan sipped his vermouth slowly, and lit a cigarette.

"Now it gets sloppy," Amory continued, consulting his little notebook. "Monday night an attempt was made on Jenning's life. Then on Tuesday the Egyptian police recovered the body of a French businessman outside Cairo. This fellow's job, actually, was to discover if the Egyptians had any inkling of the impending arms sale. He was being paid a per diem rate."

Morgan knew what Amory was saying. The Frenchman had taken on a very risky job.

"Then we had a bad day yesterday: a man in our organization was being transferred to Nice, to help out. He was killed in Lisbon. No details. Now the Norwegian intermediary dies in Copenhagen. Very messy, and it gets worse.

"This morning I got a panic memo from Washington. It seems that a visiting committee from the International Atomic Energy Commission has been looking over the new Israeli reactor, the one we helped build, the only one in the Middle

East. It was supposed to be a research reactor. But it is now geared for making plutonium."

"I don't think I follow you."

"It's really very simple, and very serious. The Israeli reactor is churning out the raw materials for an atomic bomb."

"I see. And the Arabs haven't got a reactor?"

"No. There are only sixty-eight reactors in the world, and only ten countries have them. The United States has the largest number, twenty-four; Russia has eleven. There's no point in worrying about the big countries. It's the little ones we have to sweat."

"Is Israel actually making a bomb?" Morgan asked.

"Now *that*," Amory said, "is anybody's guess. They're certainly going to be hard put to find a test site. But they might, that's the point."

"And the Arabs are shaken up?"

"To put it mildly. Look at it from their position. They see that we've helped finance a reactor for Israel. We say we didn't know they were going to use it for a bomb, but you can't expect them to believe that. Now, they hear of a big arms shipment. Their panic and mistrust could explode into a war."

"What's Washington want done?"

Amory threw up his hands in irritation. "Well, we've screwed it up already. Washington is committed to the arms shipment. We can't back out without appearing to let down our ally, Israel. And we can't go forward without appearing to be engaged in a subversive plot against the Arab world. Washington has decided to push forward with the shipment anyhow, and try to present it as a *fait accompli* to the Arabs, who have not yet formally announced that they know of the shipment. In fact, they don't seem to intend to announce it—they're going to try to stop it on the sly. They've got a group in Nice working on it. We have to knock out that group."

"Arabs?"

"In Nice? No. Frenchmen—old Algerians, I think. Pro-fessional people. Their leader is a surgeon."

"Sharp?"

"Very sharp."

"You want him killed?"

"Yes."

"And the others?"

"If possible." He handed Morgan a packet. "This is our file on the group, the Associates. It has pictures. All you'll need, I think."

Morgan did not open it.

"Do they know I'm coming?" he asked.

Amory folded his hands in his lap and smiled grimly. "I wish I knew," he said.

Saturday: Nice

Liseau, wearing his sunglasses, examined his visitor. God, he's ugly, he thought. He looks just like a pig, with that round face, upturned nose, and narrow, squinting eyes.

"You have impressive credentials," Liseau said, picking up a scalpel from his desk. As a surgeon, he enjoyed scalpels. He liked to have them in his hands, to play with them, to sense their sharpness. He watched the pig-faced man, Ernst Brauer. Brauer did not blink, though his eyes followed the scalpel.

"Your nerves are good, *deutsche schwein*."

Again, the man did not blink. You could not startle him, Liseau saw, you could not insult him. He was entirely im-passive, a great blond murder machine. The surgeon looked at the body, the bunched muscles in the shoulders and fore-arms, the heavy, bulging calves and thighs. There was power and endurance in him, no doubt of it. If there was discipline as well, he might be ideal.

"You speak languages?"

"French, English, Spanish, and German."

Liseau smiled thinly and drew a cigarette from an inlaid box on his desk. He did not offer one to Brauer, nor did he light his own. He waited.

"Is there anything you do not do?"

"Yes. I do not kiss my employer's ass."

"Very wise." Liseau lit his cigarette.

So the insult had shown through, after all. This man had a limit, a final point beyond which abuse was intolerable. That was reassuring: Liseau did not want a totally unfeeling automaton around him. Somewhere, there must be an end to detachment and efficiency, and a beginning of passion.

"How is your tongue?"

"Silent enough," the German grunted. When he grunts, he is even more like a pig, the surgeon thought. Liseau stood up from behind his desk, looking slim and dark—just the reverse of the blond chunk of muscle he faced.

"Good. I believe we can do business."

Ernst Brauer nodded. He knew that Liseau regarded him as an animal. Most people did—Brauer had long since grown accustomed to the reaction of people to his physical appearance. But he knew something about Liseau, and what he knew disturbed him.

Liseau was very good at his job. In appearance, he was elegant and imperturbable; his manner precise, his movements calculated and economical, his speech careful. He gave the impression of a man who makes no mistakes, and that was a good impression for a surgeon to give.

But Brauer knew some less elegant and aristocratic facts about Liseau. He had been born in Algiers, the son of a French doctor and an Algerian beauty—which no doubt accounted for his dark skin and his ascetic face. During the Algerian War, he was rumored to have helped the OAS, as a torturer. Brauer loathed torture. In his own direct manner, he found it repellent. He was willing to kill a man, if he was paid enough, but he would not prolong the agony for any reason. His every instinct was toward swiftness, sureness. He was not a sadist, though God knew he looked it.

But this one, he thought, smiling blandly at Liseau. This one is dangerous. He never loses his temper, never speaks loudly, never falters in his control. It is the legacy of his training, and the inclination of his personality.

He is like a cobra, Brauer thought. Haughty and aloof, able to strike with startling precision. I am sure, he thought, that he does not trust me. We are too different.

"But you would not object, I hope, to a small demonstration of faith?" Liseau asked.

Brauer shrugged. It was, for him, a massive gesture. He barely listened to the conversation; he was wondering why Liseau wore sunglasses all the time. Perhaps he had weak eyes. Perhaps it was a trick, a way to disconcert people, to draw their attention away from other aspects of him. It was effective, Brauer had to admit that.

"Good," Liseau said. "There is a man named Revel in Paris, in a hospital. I do not care how you do it, so long as you are not caught. Shall we go over the details?"

"All right."

Liseau sat down again, and offered Brauer a cigarette.

Chapter III

Sunday: Paris

It was three in the morning, and most of the lights in the hospital corridor were out. Brauer padded down the hall in crepe-soled shoes. The doors into the various rooms were all open; he could see the patients, snoring and wheezing, in the glow of the dim night-lamps.

He came to one door that was closed. That would be Revel's room. But was he alone? Brauer put his ear to the door, and listened. He heard the faint scratch of a match, and the sound of feet shifting position.

So there was a guard.

He reached in his waistband, and withdrew the Luger 9mm. It was a gun he favored, despite its weight and the difficulty in obtaining ammunition. It fired a special eight-round cartridge called the Parabellum, and would not handle ordinary 9mm ammunition. And, of course, it had been discontinued since 1942, when the German Army switched over to the Walther P-38. But he was attached to it, and it had never jammed on him yet. That was something.

Brauer never used a silencer. To be effective, they had to be ponderous things, ruining the balance of a pistol; they were a waste of time, a superfluous precaution. So few people were familiar with the sound of a gun that it was rare for a listener to associate a loud noise with a gunshot. He had many times fired guns in houses and hotels, in the dead of night, and nobody had ever complained, or investigated.

A hospital might be a different matter, however. Any loud sound would be checked—a nurse would probably conclude that a patient had fallen out of bed. He would fire the Luger here only as a last resort.

He listened again at the door, trying to decide whether the guard would be to his left or right as he entered. It was impossible to say; he could hear nothing.

With the safety still on, he put the Luger in his left hand and opened the door with his right, very quickly.

He took in the whole room in a glance. A little fellow was seated in a chair to the left, a gun in his lap; Brauer struck him viciously across the face with his Luger barrel. The man groaned and fell over. Brauer picked him up and drove his fist into the pit of the man's stomach. Then he dropped him like a wet rag.

Revel lay on his back, on the bed. He had not stirred; probably he was under heavy sedation. So much the better, Brauer thought. He placed his fingers on each side of Revel's windpipe, feeling for the pulse of the carotid arteries. Then he squeezed hard, knowing that it would have the dual effect of stopping most blood supply to the brain, and also slowing heart rate through reflex action. Ernst Brauer knew a good deal about anatomy and medicine—it was part of his job. He was aware that he must pinch off the arteries for several minutes to be sure of success. In five minutes, even if Revel were not killed, his brain damage would be so severe that he would probably never utter another coherent word in his life.

Brauer squeezed. Revel began to stir, and he put his hand over the man's mouth. He kept one wary eye on the door; at any minute, a nurse could walk by, making evening rounds.

But nobody came. And nobody saw Ernst Brauer leave six minutes later, silently, a great hulk in the night.

Sunday: London

The telephone rang. Morgan did not move, but his eyes opened wide. He always awoke that way, instantly alert, catlike. His eyes roamed the room cautiously, and then he sat up to answer the phone. It would be the desk, awakening him in time for his flight.

"Mr. Morgan? Long distance from Paris. Please hold the line, sir."

That was a surprise. He waited impatiently.

"Hello. Morgan? Amory here." He sounded tired and depressed. "Afraid I can't make it today, so you'd better not come. A dear friend of mine, from Marseilles, was killed last night in his hospital bed. Very bizarre, and I've got to do what I can, as a friend of the family. Perhaps we can postpone our plans?"

"I hope so. That's distressing news," Morgan said, lighting a cigarette. "What do you suggest?"

"Well, I think we could proceed as scheduled in a day or so. Suppose you put off things for twenty-four hours. I'll call you if there will be a further delay. All right?"

"All right. Sorry to hear the news."

"Very messy," Amory said.

When Amory had hung up, Morgan lay back in bed, stared at the ceiling, and finished his cigarette. Then he got up, showered and shaved, and called Air France to cancel his ticket to Nice that morning.

On the second floor of the same hotel, the telephone rang. Groping for the sound, Roger Carr reached out and clutched a firm breast. Surprised, he opened his eyes.

"Ouch!" the girl said, sitting upright in bed. "What was that for?"

Carr groaned. The telephone was still ringing. Dazed, he

looked around. It was over there, on the night table. "Sorry," he mumbled, and picked up the receiver.

"Nine o'clock, Mr. Carr."

"All right." He replaced the receiver.

The girl was annoyed: "Was that your idea of a joke?"

"No," he said, rubbing his eyes. He felt absolutely stinking aching horrible. "Just a mistake."

"Some mistake." She rubbed herself gingerly. She was a well-built girl, he thought, looking at her as she sat naked, the sheet fallen to her waist. Where the hell had she come from?

Then he remembered. The Green Dragon Pub. She was the one with the aloof air and the tight sweater. And those black boots. She had smiled at him, and he had picked her up. Or was it the other way around? He couldn't remember.

He stood up cautiously, then lurched into the bathroom and started the shower. Cold: it was better that way. Snap yourself awake. Rinse off the booze feeling. He shivered, and sighed.

In an hour and a half, he'd be on an Air France flight to Nice. He was ready for the sunny Riviera. He'd had it with London.

Roger Carr had spent the last twenty-four hours in London, doing some minor business for his law firm, Harrison, Bentley and Reed. Carr always did minor business for them; in fact, he would never have been hired were it not for his connections. Roger Carr had excellent connections.

First, there was his father, the distinguished Senator Carr. He had been a partner in Harrison, Bentley and Reed for many years before running for the Senate at age fifty-nine. The firm kept his son as a gesture; the senior partners regarded the younger Carr's salary as a business expense, nothing more.

Then there was the Governor. Roger and the Governor

got along famously, and the Governor was one of the biggest clients in the firm. The Governor had met Carr one afternoon when Roger was carrying some papers over to him; the two had struck it off instantly, and were now fast friends. The Governor claimed that all lawyers bored hell out of him. Roger was an exception. Slightly debauched with a cherubic face and a mildly satyric air, he reminded the Governor of his own hell-raising youth. The Governor appreciated that.

And so, when it came time to send a lawyer to southern France to purchase a villa for the Governor, Roger Carr had been the obvious choice.

"You have taste, goddammit," the Governor had said, chomping down on his Havana cigar. "I want something tasteful. Take your time about it—four weeks, six weeks if you want to. And see that you don't waste all your energy working for me."

"I will carry out your instructions to the letter," Carr had replied.

And he intended to.

He smiled at his lathered image in the mirror as he shaved. He was a likable, engaging man who was both intelligent and perceptive. He enjoyed his work—what there was of it— and principally attributed his failure to go farther in the firm to an overriding sense of boredom with the law. It was a feeling which had afflicted him since his graduation, at the bottom of his class, from the Harvard Law School. On principle, he was opposed to stuffiness, weekends in Connecticut, suspenders, and waistcoats. Unfortunately they were *de rigueur* in his profession, a fact which he accepted rather gracelessly.

Friends were always urging him to "get hold of yourself" and "make something of yourself." He found such solicitousness embarrassing; he did not want to make something of himself if it meant he must wear suspenders and clear his throat judiciously whenever he met a client. He had always felt that there was another road to success, another sort of impetus.

And, in his own peculiar way, he had always felt that the impetus would someday come to him.

He caught an early cab, and arrived at the air terminal on Cromwell Road thirty minutes before the flight. He got out on the ramp, engaged a porter, and went inside through the automatic doors.

This terminal was depressing. The girl at the Air France desk was a welcome relief. He handed over his ticket, and his passport, and she dug into a clutter of forms, hunting his name. Carr leaned over the counter and tried to get a look at her legs.

When she straightened, so did he.

"Fine, sir," she said in a soft accent. "The bus to the airport leaves in twenty minutes. Do you have any luggage to check through?"

"Yes, I do," Carr said, and suddenly realized that his porter had not arrived. He looked around, but did not see the man. "It's coming," he said.

"Very good. I'll just fill out your embarkation form." She thumbed through the passport, looking for the rectangular entry stamp. "You have been in England only since yesterday?"

"Right."

She scribbled on the yellow card. "Flight 703, to Nice. You'll have to sign here."

Carr took the form and the offered pen, and signed. He put the card in his passport, and they both looked at each other.

The porter had not arrived.

"I'm sure he will be right here," the girl said, echoing his own thoughts. "It's a new building, and they sometimes get confused."

"I understand." He reached in his pocket. "Cigarette?"

"No thank you." She had a nice smile.

Carr lit a cigarette, blew a stream of smoke upward, and checked his watch. He had been here five minutes. "Maybe I could go look—"

"No, no. It's better if you wait here."

"Okay." He put his hand in his pocket and jiggled his keys, then stopped. There was no sense in getting impatient. The girl smiled at him, and he smiled back. He wondered if he had locked his suitcase; he thought he had, but he couldn't remember for sure.

About that time the porter arrived, looking chagrined. "There you are, sir. Bit of confusion, you know, sir. Thought you'd said BEA desk. Sorry, sir. Accent, you know." He seemed to grow even more embarrassed, and would not look at Carr as he swung the bags onto the scale. Feeling magnanimous, Carr gave him five shillings. It occurred to him as he did this that, had he been in New York, he would have chewed the porter out.

The man blushed, touched his cap, and disappeared.

"Twenty kilos exactly," the girl said, reading the scale. She put a tag on the handle. Carr went downstairs to get his bus, feeling strange. He could have sworn his suitcase wasn't that heavy when he had checked in at New York the day before. But he wasn't sure, and it didn't matter. He shrugged, and stopped at the gift shop to buy a paperback book. He wanted something light and amusing, of no consequence.

The copilot of Air France Flight 703 had just spilled hot coffee on his pants, as a result of sudden turbulence. He was swearing loudly, so the pilot could not hear the message that was coming direct from Orly control, relayed from Heathrow, London. Static was bad; the pilot asked for a repeat, turned aside, and told the copilot to shut the hell up.

The rest of the crew became instantly alert, and pulled on their headphones. Their faces were grave as the message was repeated. The pilot began to sweat.

"What is your ETA Nice?" Orly asked, with maddening calmness.

"Screw the ETA. Do you have confirmation of this message from London?"

"Affirmative. What is your ETA?"

Angrily, the pilot broke contact and turned to the copilot. With a curious kind of relief, he noticed large drops of sweat on the man's brow, "When do we go into the pattern?" As he spoke, he realized that this was the wrong man to ask. He felt foolish.

The navigator answered. "We are two minutes past Lyons. Three minutes before we go into the Nice landing pattern."

The pilot nodded sadly. There was no decision to be made, no alternatives, no choice. It would take too long to arrange an emergency landing at Lyons, and Marseilles was too far away. "We have to ride it in," he said. *"Merde!"*

Meticulously, the copilot was brushing the dark stain on his trousers with a handkerchief. His fingers were trembling.

The pilot understood the reaction; it was an attempt to act normally, to proceed with little things, to pretend nothing was happening.

"Call up Nice control," he said. "And get Adrienne in here." Adrienne was a very stable, unperturbably sexy stewardess. At least, thought the pilot, she won't go to pieces.

He had a sudden vision of everything going to pieces, in a great burst. It was a nightmare vision, and he shook his head to clear it.

*

Adrienne walked down the aisle, checking passengers to be sure their seat belts were fastened and their cigarettes out. Her smile was rigidly fixed, but she was confident it would do.

"We're ahead of schedule," one man said, glancing at his watch. "What a nice surprise."

Adrienne nodded, and said nothing. The aisle was beginning to tilt sharply as the big Caravelle jet came down. Through the window, she glimpsed blue water and the curving four-mile beach of Nice. The apartments along the waterfront were familiar and white, safe-looking.

A little American boy with freckles plucked at her sleeve. "Don't I get any gum? I want some gum—or candy. Candy."

"I'm sorry," she said. How could she worry about gum at time like this?

"I always get gum," the boy insisted, "whenever we land."

She had to move on, to check the other passengers.

"We don't have any more," she explained, looking down the aisle. His small hand still clutched her Dior-designed uniform.

"You're mean."

"I'm sorry."

"Rat."

Wrinkling his nose, he released her, and she continued down the aisle. One bluff woman, old and heavy, was still smoking a cigarette. Adrienne requested in English that it be put out, and the woman answered, haughtily and deeply insulted, in French. But she put out the cigarette.

Roger Carr had slept through most of the flight. He awoke when he felt fingers in his lap, and opened his eyes to see a very lovely girl bending over him. Say, he thought, this is service.

He realized that the plane was tilted down; they must be

landing. And then he saw that the stewardess was only tight-ening his seat belt. Oh well.

She cinched it rather tight, almost painfully. He winced and began to loosen it.

"It's for your own protection."

It was then that he noticed how nervous she was. Probably her first flight, he thought. But if it will make her happy... He left the seat belt the way it was, and watched the girl walk forward, swishing her hips in a subtle, interesting way. Do girls become sexier when frightened? He wondered.

Moments later, the wheels touched down with a shriek of rubber. It was a sloppy, bouncing landing, very unprofessional. If he had been an old lady, it would have made him nervous.

The moment the plane came to a halt, the stewardess was up, marching down the aisle. "Everyone out, please," she said. "There is no cause for alarm, but please leave your coats and hand luggage inside the aircraft."

Carr saw daylight behind him. The ramp had already been lowered. That was awfully quick. Looking out the window, he saw that the plane was stopped on the runway, a good half-mile from the airport itself.

"We're stopping *here*?" an annoyed British voice asked.

"All out, please. This way. Your luggage will be collected for you, and brought to the baggage-claim area." The stew-ardess was losing her control; her voice was rising.

"What's wrong? Is something wrong?" A woman.

"Everyone out, please. Toward the rear, please. Thank you. That way, please."

Confused and tense, the passengers were filing out. Carr, seated toward the rear, was one of the first to step onto the concrete of the runway. He saw, parked in a line several hun-dred yards from the plane, three vans for carrying passengers to the main building. Why weren't they closer?

A uniformed man stood at the end of the gangway, pointing toward the vans. "That way, please. Move along, if you will. That way." He was obviously nervous, and his face had a twitching smile.

Why didn't they bring the vans right up? What kind of a bush racket was this, anyway?

And then Carr saw the fire truck, racing across the pavement toward them. The other passengers saw it, too. A sudden sense of urgency seemed to strike them all, and many began to run toward the vans. Carr, vaguely sensing what was happening, began to run, too.

And then, behind him, there was an ugly sound, and he was knocked flat on his face by a rush of hot gas. He picked himself up and looked back to see the tail of the aircraft hidden by boiling flames and dense black smoke. There was another muffled roar. More smoke, then shouting, and sirens. Men in white asbestos suits appeared. Carr was hustled into a van by a frantic airport official. Looking around him, he saw that many of his fellow passengers had singed eyebrows and hair, and several had bad cuts. One man was wrapped in a blanket, unconscious. People were trying to prop his feet up. The van rumbled off toward the airport, and nobody spoke except for one little boy, with freckles, who kept his nose pressed against the glass window as he watched the fire.

"Wow," said the boy, in an awed voice. "Wowie."

Chapter IV

In a small, windowless room of the Nice Airport, five policemen sat hunched over desks going through the passports of every person, including the crew, who had been on Flight 703. It was a painfully slow business of checking through phonebook-sized directories, check sheets, number lists. Most of the passengers were British, on early holiday; there were a handful of Frenchmen, back from business in London, and an occasional Dutchman, German, and American. Mostly men, mostly impeccable.

One policeman, at a corner desk, came to an American passport. He gave it a routine check—looking first for obvious signs of forgery, evidence that the punched number had been altered (making a 9 or a 6 into an 8 was a favorite), or indication that pages had been removed or substituted. That finished, he checked his lists. The number, D099177, was okay as far as he was concerned. He fed it through the direct teletype line to Paris, to see if they had anything, then continued his own examination.

Roger Alan Carr, born in New York, U.S.A., on October 23, 1928. Height six feet, hair brown, eyes brown. Passport issued April 4, 1964. The picture showed a youngish-looking man, who appeared amused. The officer smiled as he looked at the picture, then he frowned. There was something about the face…

"Henri."

Another man looked over.

"You recognize this man?"

A frown. "I am not sure. Is it the one?" To answer his own question, the second man thumbed quickly through the entry stamps. Not much there: entrance and exit stamps for England, within the last twenty-four hours; entrance stamp from Orly airport on an earlier trip, 6 June 1964; some Greek stamps which he couldn't read; an embarkation stamp from Roma Airport, 15 July 1964. No entry into Italy, or exit from France, which meant that he had probably crossed the border by car. He checked the last page of the passport to satisfy himself that Mr. Carr had entered Greece with an automobile in 1964. The Greek customs stamp was there.

It did not look much like the passport of an agent. There was nothing, really, except for the picture. "The resemblance is striking. What does Paris say about the number?"

The first man consulted the clattering teletype, feeding back cleared numbers.

"It's okay."

The policeman shrugged. "He looks the same, that's all. All Americans look the same." He glanced again at the picture, critically. "He is smiling so much, he must be sleeping with the boss's wife."

There was coarse laughter in the room. The passport was tossed onto the "cleared" stack.

To Roger Carr, it seemed to take hours. Questions by the police, forms to fill out, claims and statements of damages, prodding by reporters, obsequies from white-faced airline representatives. The whole proceeding reminded Carr of his induction into the army, and it was not an experience he recalled fondly.

From the gossip and rumors running wild among the huddled passengers, he was able to determine that a bomb had been planted on the airplane; one blazingly angry woman announced that they knew, the pilots *knew,* and yet they went through with the flight. It was absolutely criminal, and she intended to sue. It would be her last experience on a European airline, she could tell you *that* here and now. Carr listened and said nothing. He felt peculiarly passive about it all, and could detect only detached curiosity in himself. That, and the desire for a drink. It was nearly four o'clock when he was released by the last cop, and allowed to make his way through the broad glass doors, past the sign that read: "Welcome to Nice, Capital of the Côte d'Azur."

Two men lounged in the comfortable leather chairs near the entrance doors to the airport. They had been there a long time, reading magazines, not speaking. Nobody paid any attention to them, for they were well-dressed and unobtrusive men. Perhaps a porter might have noticed that they did not seem interested in the explosion aboard Flight 703; in fact, they almost gave the impression that they had expected it, they were so calm.

One man was heavyset, with blond hair and florid skin, and very small blue eyes. He looked Germanic, rather ugly, with a studied neatness about him. It was a businessman's look, efficient and collected, totally self-assured. He was reading a copy of *Der Spiegel* magazine.

The other was slim, dark-skinned, dressed in a dark blue suit. He wore sunglasses which he did not remove, even to read *Réalités.* He looked like the kind of man who would enjoy such a magazine, the kind of man who could comfortably dabble in art and minor expensive fads, the kind of man who lived graciously, intellectually, and very fashionably.

On occasion, the two men would look at each other, questioningly, as a man left the airport. Their eyes would meet, one would shrug, and they would resume reading.

Liseau, lighting a cigarette, admitted to himself that he was tired. He marveled at Brauer—the German had gone to Paris the night before, killed a man, and returned. He couldn't have managed more than a few hours' sleep, yet he was alert and awake today. His endurance must be incredible, Liseau thought. He tried to read an article on the Countess Barsini's redecorated villa, but he could not concentrate.

He had begun the morning in a blind fury. The bomb hadn't worked; the people in London had fouled it up miserably. It had been all he could do to control his face as he sat in the airport. But later, upon reflection, it seemed a blessing in disguise. They would follow Mr. Morgan, and pick him up. Then they would discover just how much the American knew about the plot. Torture would be necessary, of course. Liseau smiled slightly.

Brauer nudged him.

"What do you think?" he asked, in French.

"I must admit…" Liseau hesitated. "I am not sure."

They watched the American pass through the doors.

"It might be he," Liseau said thoughtfully.

The American hailed a cab, and got in quickly.

"I think he is not our man," Brauer said. "He does not look it."

"Do you really expect him to look it? To show it on his face, or in his manner?"

The blond man flushed. "I meant, he does not appear tough. He is too much the dandy."

Liseau frowned. Brauer waited in silence for an opinion, but none was offered. He lit a cigarette, holding it cupped in his hand, like a soldier.

"I am actually surprised," Liseau said, as if it were a rare occurrence. "I expected to recognize him instantly." He frowned:

it would not do to pick up an innocent man—that was a waste of time, and a dangerous complication. "We will observe him. There is a certain question in my mind."

He got up, and Brauer followed him out of the airport, into the warm midafternoon sun of the Riviera. Bright flowers were planted around the taxi ranks, scenting the air. It was a colorful, holiday atmosphere, but Liseau was depressed, and Brauer could sense it.

A third man had watched the American leave the airport. This man was short and stocky, with a Mediterranean build and coarse, bristling hair cropped close to his round head. There had been no question in his mind about the American, but to be absolutely safe he followed the taxi to the Negresco Hotel, where he saw the American get out and go inside. That settled it. The American was the one he was after; the American would be of great use, and great value.

A fourth man was at the airport, conservatively dressed in a dark suit cut in the American style. He watched Carr leave, consulted his watch, and stepped into a phone booth. It was rather strange—most Americans, when in France, regarded the French telephone as their ultimate enemy. But this man did it so calmly, he might have been in Chicago or Washington.

"A great tragedy," the concierge agreed, as Carr signed in. "You are lucky to escape alive, monsieur. I have just heard on the radio that two people were killed, and three are badly injured. It is a terrible business, all these bombs. For the insurance, *n'est-ce pas?*"

"I suppose," Carr said. He pushed the register back across the desk. "I would like two very dry vodka gimlets sent up to my room immediately. Then I need your advice on where to buy some clothes."

The concierge bowed slightly. "Of course, monsieur. At your service, I assure you."

Carr went up to his room. He realized that he was finally beginning to react to his experience; his knees were wobbly as he turned the key in the lock, and flopped down on the bed. He wished to hell they'd hurry up with those drinks.

In the American consulate in Nice, Ralph Gorman replaced the scrambler telephone and looked across at his assistant, a fresh-faced kid with a crew-cut and a beaming, innocent smile. Gorman himself looked compactly grim as he filled his pipe and struck a match.

"I don't understand," the kid said. He had listened in on the conversation from an extension.

"I wouldn't expect you to. It's a hell of a complicated game. We know what's going on, and we know that *they* know we know, but there's no leverage, man, no *leverage*. We need a wedge, something to get our fingers on." He drummed his fingers on the table and looked at the kid. There was hardly any point in telling the truth to a new recruit; he wouldn't grasp it at all, and even if he did, it might be a nasty shock. They were all so idealistic, right out of college.

"This goddamned thing is tricky," Gorman went on, "and it calls for diplomacy. Tact. Velvet-covered iron, that kind of thing."

"Isn't that your specialty?" the kid asked.

Gorman smiled sadly. "Get me the CORTEX file," he said. The kid left the room.

Gorman turned to his doodle pad. He always used it in times of stress, scribbling nonsensical figures which somehow made him feel better. Then he saved all the doodles and took them twice weekly to his psychiatrist, a tremendous fellow in Cannes. The vice-consul had recommended him, after he had done such wonders for the vice-consul's wife. He was Viennese, trained at Western Reserve in Cleveland. But the accent was so authentic, so reassuring. His pen scratched away on the pad. He frowned. The call had come from Amory, the chief of section in Paris, a message delivered in the chief's inimitable style—wandering, pompous, quietly needling. The chief wanted Gorman to know that Morgan's cover had been blown, and that he was staying in London for a day or so. Gorman would just have to get on without him. The chief didn't understand the problems of the Nice office, and didn't care to understand them. He just wanted the job done.

Goodbye.

Well, somehow Gorman would straighten things out, though he badly wished Morgan were here. That was one thing about Morgan: he was a killer. You could just pop him into a car, give him Liseau's address, and in a day or so, *presto*! No more Liseau. No more plots, no more problems.

As it was, the chief seemed to expect Gorman to do the shooting. Now, that was ridiculous. Gorman had never fired a gun in his life. He had hardly even *seen* a gun.

Still, somebody had to do it. There was no choice. Legitimate police action was out—no evidence. Sly diplomatic maneuvers such as deporting Liseau were out—he had too much prestige as a surgeon. There was only one thing left to do, and that was shoot him. Shoot the whole bunch.

The kid returned with the file, a slim gray packet with CORTEX stenciled on the cover. He handed it to Gorman, who broke the seal and signed the slip, which the kid took back to the file room.

He sighed as he thumbed through the pages detailing the entire history of the Norway–Israel arms shipment, which had been designated CORTEX. It was all there; Liseau and his group had been implicated for weeks as U.A.R. agents, but there was nothing you could do about it. Nothing but shoot them—or sit around and watch them shoot everybody else involved in the shipment. The telephone rang. "Gorman here."

"Harry." It was a statement, flat and colorless. That would be their man at the airport. Gorman was about to tell him to stop worrying, that Morgan wasn't on the flight, when Harry said, "Our man's here."

Gorman gripped the phone tightly, as if it were his salvation. "Are you sure?"

"Fits pretty well. He went through the doors a few minutes ago."

"Did you contact him?"

"No...I'm afraid some of the opposition is here, too."

"Oh?"

"Two dogs, one skinny dark, one blond."

Gorman swore to himself: Liseau and one of his trained apes. "Any action?"

"They just watched him go by."

"Recognition?"

"I'm afraid so."

"Hell," Gorman said, and hung up.

Some days, nothing went right, nothing at all. Morgan's life wasn't worth a plugged nickel if Liseau was on to him. Obviously everything was fouled up—the chief was wrong, there had been a massive leak somewhere, and now poor Morgan was going to get his head shot off. Gorman swore: always one step ahead of me, those people. Always one step.

He picked up his pen and doodled furiously.

CHAPTER V

Roger Carr awoke shortly before nine P.M. He had slept soundly for several hours, after spending time buying more clothes and picking up a rental car. Carr rarely slept in the afternoon, and he knew that this exception was his way of reacting to his experience that morning. It still disturbed him, and he decided he ought to plunge himself into activity and forget all about it. Specifically, he decided he needed a girl.

He shaved slowly, examining himself in the mirror. He didn't look bad—just a scrape on his cheekbone where he had fallen on the runway. Christ, it was just his luck, getting a booby-trapped plane. The world was full of maniacs, he thought cheerfully. With his face covered with lather, he tried to grin.

"Face it, Carr: you are an amusing bastard."

The phone rang, and he went out to the bedroom to answer it.

"Roger Carr speaking."

"Mr. Carr." The voice had a heavy French accent, and there was a peculiar background noise, a whirring mechanical sound.

"Yes?"

"I would like to meet with you."

"Yes?" Carr's voice was tentative.

"I believe I can be of great use to you."

"In what way?"

"I can help you. In your business."

Carr frowned. "What do you know about my business?"

There was a tense laugh from the voice at the other end. "I know all about your business, I'm afraid."

"I see. You have a villa to sell?"

Another laugh. "*Exactement.* Shall we meet?"

"All right." What harm could there be? "Who is this I am talking to?"

Still another laugh. Everything seemed hilarious to this man. Carr didn't understand.

"Your room, tomorrow at noon. Okay?"

"Of course."

The phone was dead in his hand.

Carr looked at it, feeling silly. He replaced it in the cradle, and it immediately began ringing once more.

"Hello?"

"Christ Almighty, why didn't you register as Morgan?" This was a new voice, which sounded greatly annoyed.

"Well, quite honestly, it never occurred to me." Who was this idiot, anyway?

"I see. Little games. Diversions. No wonder I'm paying half my salary to a psychiatrist. I have to worry about people like you all the time. Now why haven't you called? I suppose you have a good answer for that, too." The voice sounded gloomy, now.

"Sorry about that," Carr said, smiling. "I just haven't had a chance."

"You haven't had a chance. Sure. Why not? You haven't had a chance. I understand that. I also understand that you've been recognized. If I were you, I'd get over here right away."

"But I'm going out to dinner."

"Didn't you hear me? I said you've been recognized."

"So what?"

The voice at the other end swore lavishly. "What do you

think this is, Morgan, a vacation? You must be out of your mind. So what. Idiot, get over here right away!"

Growing bored with the game, Roger said, "Cheery-bye," and hung up. Then he left the room. On the way out, he would check with the concierge and make sure he wasn't getting somebody else's calls. That kind of thing happened so easily in these big hotels.

Holding the scalpel gently but firmly, Liseau made a long incision down the side of the face, just in front of the ear. Blood welled up; he dabbed it with a sponge and continued the cut around under the lobe of the ear, and back.

The only sound in the room was the hum of the air conditioner, and the rhythmic *whish-aaah* from the anesthetic equipment as the patient breathed. The patient lay on his side, and was completely covered by green cloth except for a small square around his ear and the side of his cheek.

"Don't be afraid to take your incision back as far as convenient," Liseau said to the resident. This was the resident's first parotid excision. "It never shows on the patient, anyway."

He began to dissect away the underlying tissue with careful, deft strokes. Soon he was able to pass a suture through the lobe of the ear and lift it up until the lobe touched the crown. This gave him clear access to the parotid gland, the major salivary gland of the mouth, lying in front of the ear where the jaw joined the head. Clinical tests had shown a large mass in this region, which upon biopsy had proved to be benign. The patient was a local banker of some influence.

Liseau continued to work until he had exposed the gland and cleared away the surrounding fatty tissue. To an untrained eye, it didn't look like much—just a bloody mass in the middle of other bloody tissue.

"From this point," he said, "you must proceed carefully. It cannot be rushed." With the incision held open by hemostats, he proceeded to dissect free the branches of the facial nerve, which ran through the substance of the gland. This was crucial: if these nerves were cut, the patient would lose control of his facial muscles, and one side of his face would droop.

The resident watched, tense and fascinated. But he didn't ask any questions, and Liseau was grateful. He did this slow work mechanically, without thinking much about it. His mind was on the American—the American who seemed not quite right, not quite the man they were after.

Liseau did not relish the prospect of involving an innocent man, particularly if he was American. These people always turned out to be friends or relatives of important politicians. Their disappearance or death would focus undesirable attention on the area, and too many of his group would be brought under surveillance. No, it was out of the question to risk it. They must be quite sure before they made their move.

He probed carefully through the tissues, clearing away the filamentous branches of the nerves, pushing them aside so he would be sure not to cut them.

The patient stirred. Liseau spoke sharply to the anesthetist before continuing his work.

Dinner, to Roger Carr's disappointment, was rather ordinary and overpriced, and he had gone from the restaurant to the casino, which he knew from past experience always revived his spirits. Carr was not a gambler, but he liked to watch others who were, and he enjoyed the clean green elegance of the gaming room. He also knew from experience that it was a good place to pick up girls. But the casino tonight was deserted—it was a Monday night, too early in the season—

except for two couples from the Midwest, who were playing the roulette wheel for ridiculously low stakes, and laughing loudly with each spin of the wheel. The men were wearing old dinner jackets with crooked clip-on bow ties; the women lounged, with careful boredom, in frumpy black dresses which were cut too low for their sagging bosoms.

Carr left almost immediately, feeling unaccountably annoyed, almost cheated. He caught a cab, and told the driver to take him to a nightclub. The driver, cigarette dangling from his lip, ash drooping perilously, looked back, trying to discern exactly what Carr had in mind. Carr gave him no satisfaction; he merely stipulated a good nightclub, *quelque chose amusante,* and sat back in silence, looking out the window.

He was taken to the Choo-Choo Club, a small place set down at the end of a dark alley, a block from the Place Massena. This was the red-light district of Nice, he knew, but he decided what the hell. He paid the taxi and got out.

The doorman was dressed in a heavy coat with brass buttons despite the mild evening; he resembled a solemn bear, and Carr thought he probably doubled as a bouncer.

He went through to the lobby, which was small, done in gilt and red velvet, with a large, leather-padded door leading to the inside of the club. The hatcheck girl, a sour-faced blonde with deep circles under her eyes, looked annoyed that Carr wasn't wearing a hat. He went inside.

He was surprised to find the club was large and comfortably appointed. There were round white tables scattered about the room, and the chairs were upholstered in the same red velvet as the lobby. The subdued lighting came from spherical ceiling fixtures. Taken as a whole, the room seemed rather like a French version of a Gay Nineties cathouse, but it was somehow soothing.

Carr took a corner table, ordered a Scotch and soda, and lit a cigarette. A half-dozen couples occupied—and filled—the tiny dance floor; they drifted hypnotically in each other's arms in time to the music. Carr watched for a while, then looked around. At other corner tables like his, men were leaning over to whisper into the ears of girls who gazed out at the room, bored, blowing cigarette smoke. A few blond effeminate men occupied tables by themselves in the center of the room, and gave Carr expectant looks. He ignored them.

The music stopped, and the dancers wandered back to their seats. Lights went on over the stage, and a fat man in a lumpy tuxedo appeared, spoke into a microphone that didn't work, rapped it irritably, and stomped off. He was replaced by a roll of drums and a woman wrapped in a floor-length fur coat. Music started up, and the woman strutted back and forth across the stage; her movements had a graceless, jerky quality. Carr knew she would be a lousy stripper. He was suddenly impatient for his drink.

It came, with a coaster and a paper napkin. The waiter set them on the table and left, and Carr looked at it hesitantly. A coaster *and* a napkin? Perhaps it was a hint to order food.

He sipped the drink, and found it as weak as he had predicted. Then he noticed a bit of paper sticking out from the edge of the napkin, drew it out, and saw writing. Squinting in the dim light, he was able to make out the words:

KV-7Ez YOU MUST BE AN IDIOT. G. WANTS TO SEE YOU IMMEDIATELY RAY CORTEX KV-2Et

The words were scrawled in pencil on a thin slip of paper, torn from the margin of a newspaper. They meant nothing to him. He read it again, to be sure, and looked around the room. He wasn't sure what he was looking for, but his first impulse was to check and see who was watching him.

At least six gay little blond lads were peering intently in his direction. Some were winking. Carr curled his lip, and all but the most blatant looked away. It was funny about them —some, you would never guess. One of those blond guys was damned powerfully built, and was to all appearances extremely masculine and virile. Of course, he was ugly as sin. That might have something to do with it.

Carr returned his attention to the paper. It simply didn't mean anything to him; that was all there was to it. Maybe it was a practical joke. Maybe it was delivered to him by mistake. But he wasn't going to worry about it.

He crumpled the message and dropped it on the floor; and allowed his attention to return to the stage. The girl in furs was now down to a fur bikini, and she was trying to make the removal of her bra interesting. It was hopeless. She was old, fat, and quivering, very unsteady on her spike heels. Most of the excitement she generated seemed to be speculation as to whether she would stumble and fall. It was a trip-tease, Carr thought, smiling. He was glad to see her leave the stage.

A new girl took her place, and immediately the background noise of conversation and clicking glasses died away. This girl was young, black-haired, and deeply tanned; she wore a tight dress of electric green which emphasized her full bust and hips. But it was the way she walked which was so arresting —fluid, slow, relaxed, and sensual. There wasn't a jerk or a bump in her movements. It was all gentle, sinuous, and very exciting.

Carr sipped his Scotch, and settled back to watch.

The girl glided back and forth across the stage, her thighs outlined inside the dress with each step. She had long legs, and smoothly muscular calves. She stopped to run her hands up and down her body, an expectant look on her face. She reached behind to undo her zipper—an action which thrust her breasts forward alarmingly—and shivered out of her dress. It fell to the floor, rustling, and she stepped out of it in a black lace slip.

The music changed, growing faster and more insistent, as she raised one corner of the slip and removed a stocking from her tanned leg; this was repeated a second time, and one of the men in the audience cheered. She breathed deeply, planted her legs wide, and drew the slip over her head while her torso kept up an unrelenting, twisting movement, almost a writhing.

Now, in half-bra and brief panties, she increased the speed of her movements. Her body glistened with sweat from her exertion. Carr could feel the entire club being caught in the controlled animal frenzy she radiated. The pace increased; she whipped around, still fluid but very fast, and flung aside her bra. Her firm breasts, large and pink-tipped, caught the light.

Her fingers ran down her flat belly to her panties, pulling them away, letting them snap back. The muscles in her thighs stood out. Her face was contorted, the eyes wide, the mouth open, the teeth bared. Slowly, inch by inch, the panties came down her long, tapering legs, and were kicked away. She made one final grinding movement with her hips, and then the lights were doused.

In the darkness, someone banged into a chair at his side. When the lights came on Carr saw a girl standing in front of him, looking down at her feet. She seemed to have stubbed her toe in the dark. Ignoring him, the girl leaned on the table, took off her shoe, and rubbed the injured foot. Her position allowed Carr a generous look at her legs and breasts. She seemed every bit as amply constructed as the girl on the stage. He offered her a drink.

She accepted, flashing a professionally shy smile as she sat down. Her name, she said, was Suzanne, and she spoke "sam Englesh." Carr introduced himself, and gave her a cigarette while they waited for drinks.

She was an attractive girl, small and pert, with enormous dark eyes and short red-blond hair. Her chest was enormous, exposed by her low-cut pink sheath. She was careful to lean across the table when she talked. Did Mr. Carr like Nice?

Oh yes, Carr said, he did. She gave him a coquettish smile. Where was he from? New York, Carr said, sipping his drink. He felt suddenly very tired—it was a strange feeling, a sort of lost, vague boredom, which struck him only rarely. He didn't want to continue the conversation, because he knew exactly how it would run. He would ask where she was from—and be told one of the provinces, though she had come to Nice some time ago. The conversation, polite and stereotyped in every country of the world, would ramble on for at least an hour, while he poured drinks into her. Then he would feel free to reach across the table and hold her hand, while he inquired solicitously after her foot. It would no doubt be much improved, and she would demonstrate by rubbing it playfully over Carr's sock.

He had a miserable headache.

They would have more drinks, but decide to leave before the next floor show, each professing boredom with it. Carr would suggest a nightcap somewhere else, and the girl would agree; as they left, he would have a sudden idea—why not a drink in his room? Oh, that would be fine, though Suzanne would protest that it mustn't be too late a night. Carr would agree, and off they'd go to spend the night. They both understood the rules.

Suddenly, almost surprised at himself, Carr found himself

wanting to leave. He wasn't interested in this girl, not tonight —that was all there was to it. Searching his mind for an explanation, he decided it was a combination of the time difference (which he had still not adjusted to), the business at the airport, and the crummy dinner. He wanted some aspirin, and a few drinks by himself, and then he wanted to go to sleep.

There was another girl stripping on stage now, to the clash of cymbals. It was a noisy act. The girl was attended by two musclebound men in leopard skins who caught her when she fell into their arms, which was often. The stripper had a nondescript body, a bland smile on her face, and a general expression of trancelike boredom.

Suzanne ignored the stage. She's probably seen it a hundred times, Carr thought. He tried to listen to her happy, cheerful conversation, tried to answer questions about himself. She wanted to visit the United States someday. Yes, marvelous. She must look him up if she was ever in New York…

After half an hour, when Suzanne excused herself, he gave her fifty francs for the "washroom attendant," paid the bill, and left before she returned.

He was deep in thought as he walked back along the dark streets of the town. He wondered if he were getting too old for this kind of thing, if his wild bachelor life had finally caught up with him. He was still wondering when he noticed that he was lost.

Carr had paid too little attention to the way he was going and now he was somewhere back from the water, in an area he did not know. Swearing softly, he looked around, and saw one of the blond men from the nightclub approaching. Christ, that was all he needed now—a fairy bothering him. He ducked down a dark alley, and walked quickly away.

That, he thought, should lose him.

But moments later, when he paused, he heard footsteps on the pavement behind. Almost immediately, the footsteps stopped, as if they had been caught in an illegal act. It made Carr shiver. Suddenly, he was no longer interested in merely avoiding an unpleasant encounter; suddenly, he was afraid. Something was wrong, something was very sinister and wrong. He began to run.

Behind him, running footsteps. Or was he imagining it? He didn't dare stop to check. Perhaps he was making it all up, perhaps he was being ridiculous. But somehow he didn't think so. He sprinted forward and came out on a brightly lighted main street, where he stood under a streetlamp, winded, gasping for breath.

He grabbed the first taxi he saw and jumped in quickly. As it pulled away from the curb, he saw the blond man emerging from the narrow street. The man had been running, too—his chest was heaving as he watched the cab draw away. It was the big man, the ugly muscular one. What was going on?

"*Où, monsieur?*"

"Negresco," Carr said, turning away from the window.

"Of course, sir." The accent was cultivated. It was a pleasant surprise, Carr thought, to find drivers who spoke English so well.

"In the future," the driver said, "you will obey instructions. Did you get the message?"

"Yes," Carr said slowly. He was startled. "But I—"

The cabby sighed. "You fail to recognize the seriousness of the situation. You are in extreme danger. Your cover is blown; do you understand?"

"No."

"No? It is as clear as day. Do you need pictures?"

"Yes," Carr said. This was incredible. It was beginning to be a kind of nightmare world in which nothing was agreed upon, and nobody played a fixed role, and the unexpected always happened. "Who are you, anyway?"

"*Who am I?*" The voice was shocked, disbelieving.

"Yes. Is that such a strange question?"

"That is an idiotic question." The cab drew up in front of the Negresco. The doorman opened it. Carr dug in his pocket for change.

"Make no calls from your room," the cabby said, counting his money in the roof light of his car. "Lock your door, and wedge it. And go to you-know-where in the morning. *Bon soir.*"

Carr watched the cab pull away. He felt paralyzed, totally ridiculous. The doorman was staring at him. Carr was staring at the taxi.

"You have left something in the car, monsieur?"

"No, no, nothing."

The doorman nodded, as if to say, "I knew it all along. You are just a crazy American who does things for no reason." But his only words were, "Very good, sir."

Carr went inside to the bar.

The bar of the Negresco was a large room with a high ceiling. It was paneled in dark polished wood, and the floor was wood of the same color. Persian rugs in red and blue were scattered about, and the chairs, arranged around low tables, were upholstered in red and blue leather. There was a balcony running around the room, above the bar, supported by large white pillars.

The bar itself was crowded as Carr sat down on one of the square stools to have a gimlet. For a while, he tried to concentrate on the conversation around him, but it was dull, and he gave up. He thought about himself, tried to figure out what was going on, and had three more drinks.

Feeling sleepy and rather drunk, he climbed off the stool and worked his way through the people toward the door, not paying much attention to anything. He stumbled into a girl at the door, knocking her purse out of her hands.

"Sorry," he said stupidly, and bent to pick up the purse. It was large, alligator, and expensive. The initials in gold lettering said *AC*. He handed the purse back, looking briefly at the girl, who was blond, rather beautiful, and sneering.

"Apologies," said the girl coldly, "are seldom of any use."

"That's not original," Carr replied, annoyed with her. He had said he was sorry, for Christ's sake. What did she want?

"Who said it was original?" she said, but her eyebrows had gone up.

"Garrick, maybe," Carr said. In a fog, he stumbled toward the elevator.

The lights were on in his room. That was a surprise. The covers had been turned back on the bed. That was another surprise. Somebody was lying on the bed. That was a third surprise, more than enough surprises for one night, as far as Roger Carr was concerned. He dropped into a chair and stared at Suzanne, lying fully clothed on his sheets.

"Comfortable?" he asked.

She giggled.

Carr rubbed his eyes with his thumb and forefinger. After a point, you just had to give up and admit you were insane. There was no earthly reason why she should be here, why she should know he was staying here, why she should be able to get into his room, why she should *want* to get into his room. After all, he had ditched her, quite firmly and rudely.

She giggled again.

"Are you all right? You keep making funny noises."

"Why deed you leave me?"

"I was tired," he said. The accent was getting him down. He wanted to go to sleep.

"How tired?"

"*Too* tired," he said, a little sharply.

"I do not beelieve you." She sat up in bed, and began undressing.

"No?"

"No."

"Why not?"

"Because…" She paused reflectively, a hand on her zipper. "Because I do not."

"Fine." He needed aspirin. His head was spinning. He staggered into the bathroom for a glass of water.

"Do not go," she said, pouting. She was half out of her dress, and she looked good. Any other time, he thought. Any other time.

He ran water in the basin, and waited for it to get cold. She came into the bathroom after him, stripped bare, her hands supporting her large breasts. Through her fingers, he could see the pointed nipples protruding.

"I see you have a living bra," he said weakly.

She leaned back, flexing the muscles in her legs. The stomach was flat, the waist firm; her thighs were slim for such a short girl. The outline of a brief bikini was imprinted in white.

"You don't like me?"

"I adore you," he said, hanging his head over the sink. Oh God, was he going to be sick?

"Good!" She ran to him and flung her arms around him, pressing up against him. He staggered backward, and fell into the bathtub. It took several minutes to get her off him, and himself out of the tub. When he was standing again, he gently pushed her into the bedroom. The water was still running in the sink.

She apparently interpreted his pushing her into the bedroom as capitulation, because she drew him down onto the bed and slid a hot tongue between his lips. She placed his hands over her nipples.

He pulled back, woozy. "Okay," he said. "Okay. Just let me get an aspirin first. I have a headache, you see."

She clung to him. "No."

"No?"

"No."

"Why not?" He had a feeling he had had this same conversation just a short time before. But he couldn't remember exactly. Everything was fuzzy.

"I do not want you to do that. I do not trust pills."

"Why not? It's only aspirin. You know, as-pee-reen. *Comprenez?*"

She sighed breathlessly, and ran her hands up his back.

"Stay here. Talk to me."

"Talk about what?"

"Many things."

"Suzanne," he said firmly, pushing her back. "The last thing I want to do is talk. First, I want an aspirin, then I want—"

Something appeared in her hand. He thought he recognized it.

"What's that?" he said.

"A gun."

He stared stupidly, wondering where it had come from. After all, she wasn't wearing anything. Christ, he thought, I must be drunk.

"Does it work?"

"Bien sûr."

He nodded. It figured: she didn't look like a girl who would fool with a rod that didn't work.

The water was still running in the sink. He could hear it.

"Talk to me," she said.

"What about?"

"You know what. Tell me."

"Tell you what?" He was practically shouting. And then he felt ridiculous. The whole thing was ridiculous. It had been an absurd day. This floozy wasn't going to shoot him. He got calmly out of bed and walked into the bathroom.

"I'm getting my aspirin. Be back in a minute."

She said nothing, but her hand was trembling. Feeling very cool, he took a glass off the shelf over the sink and filled it. The water was loud. He thought he heard a door open, but decided it was his imagination.

He swallowed the aspirin noisily, and turned off the tap. He walked back into the other room.

"Listen, Suzanne, you're a swell girl, but I really—"

He stopped. She was gone.

"Suzanne?"

He walked around the room, and looked in the closet.

"Suzanne? Don't play games."

He went out to the balcony, and stared for a minute down at the traffic coursing by on the Promenade des Anglais. The night was peaceful and quiet.

When he went back into his room, she still did not reappear. Had he imagined the whole incident? Was he dreaming?

No.

Her underwear was all over the floor. Not her dress—just her underwear. That was damned funny. He picked up her bra. It was an awfully big bra. Poor Suzanne. She must have remembered something very important to make her rush off without her bra.

His head was buzzing again. The day had been too much for him, and the gimlets had finished him off. There was only one thing to do, and that was sleep.

He hoped, as he lay down on the bed, that he would not dream.

Chapter VI

Things seemed better in the morning. Clear, bright sunlight poured into his room, and he awoke feeling normal, and almost happy. Of course, Suzanne's underwear and stockings were flung all over the floor, but if you could ignore that, you could manage to believe that all of yesterday, from the bomb in the airplane to the naked girl with the gun, had been one horrible mistake.

In fact, Carr decided, that was the only way to look at it. As he shaved and dressed, the only thought occupying his mind was whether he could get decent scrambled eggs and bacon for breakfast.

In Nice-Cimiez, the fashionable northern suburb of the city, Dr. Liseau sat behind his desk and buzzed his secretary on the intercom.

"When is my first appointment?"

"Madame Dallois, at ten-thirty."

He glanced at his watch. It would give him an hour. "Hold all calls until then."

"Yes, doctor."

He snapped off the intercom and turned to Brauer.

"You have the tape?"

The blond man shifted in his chair, and withdrew a five-inch spool from his jacket pocket. "I thought you should hear it for yourself."

Deftly, Liseau threaded the tape onto a portable recorder and clicked it on. He sat back in his chair to listen.

There were scratching noises for fifteen seconds, and then

the sound of a telephone ringing. A voice said, *"Dix-huit heures quinze minutes."*

The phone rang three times, and then was picked up with a metallic scrape.

"Roger Carr speaking."

"Mr. Carr."

"Yes?"

"I would like to meet with you."

"Yes?"

"I believe I can be of great use to you."

"In what way?"

"I can help you in your business."

"What do you know about my business?"

"I know all about your business, I'm afraid."

"I see. You have a villa to sell?"

"Exactement. Shall we meet?"

"All right. Who is this I am talking to?"

"Your room, tomorrow at noon. Okay?"

"Of course."

Another click. The reels spun silently. Liseau reached forward and shut off the machine. Then he lit a cigarette, a Sobranie Black Russian, dark with a gold tip. He drew on the rich tobacco for a moment, and stared moodily at the tape.

"I don't like it," he said at last.

"I thought you should hear."

"You know the other voice?"

Brauer shook his head.

"Neither do I." Liseau pursed his lips. This conversation spoke badly for Mr. Carr. But if his worst suspicions were correct, it also spoke badly for his own group.

"What is the other conversation?"

"The voice has been identified as the embassy man."

Liseau turned the recorder on, and heard Carr's second

conversation. When he was through, he was more confused than he was at the start.

"Has he gone to the consulate?"

"No."

"Has he met anybody?"

"Not yet."

Liseau stubbed out his cigarette in quick stabs. "It just doesn't make sense," he said, thinking aloud. Nobody talked to his boss that way—unless Carr had nothing to do with the consulate, and was genuinely confused. He certainly sounded that way.

"What happened last night, when you followed him?"

"He got away."

"I see." That was an interesting development. "And what about the girl, our darling Suzanne?"

Brauer looked uncomfortable. "She has disappeared."

"Disappeared?"

"Apparently. She was waiting for him in the room, and she tried to extract information from him. We have part of the conversation on tape. But then something happened—the water was turned on, and we could not hear. It is an old trick, masking with water. And she has not reported back yet."

"All right," Liseau said. His face was grim, his chin set. "Leave me now. I want to hear the rest of the tape, and make some calls."

Brauer nodded, and got out of his chair in a single, smooth motion. He moved well for a big man; his grace was swift, controlled, and his strength was deadly. Liseau watched him in satisfaction.

He clicked on the recorder and listened once more.

A door slammed.

A voice said, *"Une heure moins cinq."*

There was silence. Then Carr's slurred voice saying "Comfortable?" and Suzanne's answering giggle.

Liseau frowned as he listened.

Ralph Gorman sat outside the door and listened to the slapping sounds, and a female voice crying. He sweated as he listened. If there was anything he disliked, it was interrogating a woman. It ran against everything in his nature. Besides, it was perfectly obvious that this girl wouldn't talk. She might be the hottest thing going in bed, but she had nothing to say. Somebody had frightened the wits out of her.

Gorman puffed on his pipe. The sobbing continued. It was unbearable: he took out a pad and began doodling. Thank God he was seeing his psychiatrist that afternoon.

Agents, he thought, gloomily. Idiots, all of them. Think they can handle anything. Egotists. Why the hell hadn't Morgan called in? Who did he think he was, anyhow?

Liseau looked steadily at Brauer. "I think it is best," he said, "to arrange a personal interview with Mr. Carr."

The German nodded stiffly.

"As soon as possible. Do it neatly; I don't want little pieces or wagging tongues left around. Is that clear?"

"Clear." The German turned to go.

"Ernst."

The blond man stopped, his hand on the doorknob.

"Don't kill him."

"I won't."

"Ernst."

There was a pause.

"I will be very unhappy if he is dead. If he is dead, don't bring him back. And don't you come back."

Almost imperceptibly, Ernst Brauer nodded, then left, shutting the door softly behind him.

Liseau reached for another Sobranie cigarette, and contemplated the smooth surface of his desk. Perhaps it was unwise to trust Brauer with such a job. The man's every instinct was to kill—he did it as casually as another person might flick an ash.

Liseau hoped he wouldn't foul things up.

The girl stood up on the beach, yawned, and stretched her arms. Absently, she scratched her smooth dark stomach. Then, jiggling softly in her bikini, she went down to the water and gingerly stepped in. She sucked in her breath as the first roller washed across her knees; she could suck in her breath with great effect.

Roger Carr, standing above on the Promenade des Anglais, grinned as he watched her. She was bending over now, and her curved back glistened with suntan oil as she splashed water up on her body. She walked farther out until she was thigh-deep in the water, and shivered briefly, wiggling her bottom. She knew exactly what she was doing.

Still grinning, he turned away and continued strolling down the sidewalk. It was a beautiful day, clear and warm, and the drowsy afternoon silence was unbroken except for the laughter of people on the beach. Carr walked along and smoked a cigarette, noticing the other people on the promenade—the retired British dowagers, dressed in heavy shawls despite the heat, the navy sailors, strutting in groups of three and four, gawking at the girls, the young mothers, pouting and elaborately coifed, walking with their children.

He went down to the Quai des États-Unis, cut through the formal green lawns of the Jardin Albert I, and entered the crooked alleys of Old Nice. It was refreshingly cool in the old city; the yellow slanting buildings rose so high above the narrow streets that the sunlight did not reach the pavement. Carr passed along a street of fish shops, shuttered for the afternoon siesta, and deserted except for a pair of scruffy cats contesting a discarded scrap of fish tail. Their yowling and hissing died away as he approached, then resumed behind his back. He continued on, and came abruptly into a large square.

In the center of the square, shaded from the sun by a concrete canopy, was the flower market. Early afternoon was the busiest time for the market, and it was packed with buyers, wandering among the stalls and carts, haggling, arguing, gossiping. Carr joined the crowd, looking at the brightly colored blossoms wrapped in tissue-paper cones—scarlet and mauve carnations, orange chrysanthemums, white lilies and yellow daisies, blue hyacinths. The smells mingled to produce a sort of clean freshness. He finally settled on a dozen red roses, paid the toothless, taciturn old woman, and walked slowly back toward the water, whistling to himself.

He passed along a quiet street lined with produce and meat shops, and he stopped for a moment before the boxes of fresh strawberries, cherries, and oranges set out in the sun. It was at that moment that he noticed the man.

The man was walking down the street toward him, one hand in his pocket, an unlighted cigarette dangling from his lip. He approached Carr, and looked at him hesitantly. He was wearing a gray and black glen-plaid suit, cut in the current French fashion, with narrow trousers and a short double-vented jacket. His shoes were brightly polished. Above a florid face, his hair was thinning; he looked like any normal, middle-aged, prosperous businessman.

Still hesitant, almost doubtful, the man drew near and took the cigarette out of his mouth. *"Pardon, monsieur. Avez-vous de feu?"* He gestured, in an embarrassed way, with the cigarette.

"Huh? Sure." Carr laughed. *"Mais oui."* He shifted the flowers, tucking them under his left elbow, and fumbled in his pocket for his lighter.

The gun glinted in the sun. Carr saw it, and reacted instinctively, dropping his roses and catching the man's wrist. The gun swung high in the air, and the two men grappled silently for a moment, face to face. Then Carr began to shout for help.

Out of the corner of his eye, he saw the blue-and-white uniform of a policeman, directing traffic around the flower market. The policeman looked over, and moments later Carr heard a shrill whistle and running feet. The other man must have seen it, too; he dropped the gun, which clanked heavily on the pavement, and tried to run. Carr held on. He heard the man's suit rip.

Suddenly, a black Citroën came around the corner, moving very fast. Carr heard the rapid tatting of a machine gun and, releasing his attacker, threw himself to the ground. Above his head, windows shattered, and splinters of glass tinkled down around him. The car roared by, leaving a cloud of acrid blue smoke hanging in the air. Carr got up, dazed.

He leaned shakily against the wall, and looked down at the other man. The man lay beside the cigarette and the fallen flowers. Across his back, like a line of hot rivets, were three neat holes. The blood was already seeping into the sidewalk. Carr became aware that people were shouting, and a large crowd gathering around him.

The policeman arrived and took Carr away.

Chapter VII

The waiting room of the police station was long and gray, and very quiet. It had the immediately recognizable atmosphere of all institutional waiting rooms—the remnants of a halfhearted attempt, long since abandoned, to make things pleasant for people who were forced to sit and do nothing while they contemplated some future disagreeable event. This room was furnished with dusty leather chairs that slowly leaked white stuffing onto the wooden floor. A scarred coffee table displayed old magazines, copies of *L'Express* and *Paris Match* dating from the Algerian war, and one incongruous issue of *Elle*. On top of the magazines, like a battered crown, rested a triangular Cinzano ashtray. It had been broken once, and glued together.

Besides Carr, there were only two other men in the room, both policemen. One, a clerk, worked at a corner table, typing sporadically and occasionally making brief phone calls in a low voice. The sergeant, whose job it was to watch Carr, sat slumped in one of the leather chairs, patiently cleaning his fingers with a toothpick.

Carr waited, smoking one cigarette after another. His mind seemed incapable of organized thought. After a while, he ran out of cigarettes, and asked the sergeant if he could go buy some more. The sergeant said he couldn't. Carr began to make a scene, and the officer, with a disgusted look, finally sent someone out for them. They came—Disque Bleus—and Carr drew the rough smoke into his lungs with a sense of relief. He realized, then, that he was more nervous than he had thought—that for the first time in his life, he was really scared.

He looked often at his watch, only to discover each time that it had been smashed when he fell. The hands beneath the shattered crystal remained frozen at 2:46. There was no clock in the waiting room, and it irritated Carr. He kept asking the sergeant what time it was, partly to find out, and partly to express his annoyance. After an hour, the sergeant snapped that it didn't matter what time it was. Carr said nothing after that.

Finally, another officer came into the room, and the sergeant pulled himself into a semblance of attention. The new man walked briskly up to Carr.

"Suivez-moi, s'il vous plait."

Carr shrugged, got up, and followed him through dirty swinging doors, out of the waiting room. They went down a long gray corridor, turned left, and continued down another. The air here was stale, and the bare bulbs overhead cast a harshly utilitarian light.

The officer stopped at one door and opened it without knocking. Carr noticed that there was no nameplate on the door as he stepped inside.

The office he entered was the same institutional gray as the rest of the building, but the room was carefully dusted. Through a large window on the left, he could see the bright afternoon sunlight falling over plane trees. Heavy green filing cabinets, padlocked, lined the wall to the right

The room was dominated by an oversized oak desk, crowded with forms, two telephones, and an aging typewriter. A large desk lamp threw a blue-white light over the clutter of papers, and cast deep shadows under the eyes of the man who looked up.

"Asseyez-vous, monsieur." The man did not stand, or show any particular interest in Carr. He regarded him in a de-

tached way, as if he were a prospective buyer for a product of dubious usefulness.

Carr sat down.

"My name is Captain Vascard," the policeman said. "It is my job to investigate accidents of the kind your sort are involved in." He sounded disgusted.

While he spoke, the other officer went to the window and drew the shades, then left the room. The office was entirely dark, except for the desk lamp.

There was a silence.

"To whom," said Vascard, "are you responsible while you are in this country?"

"I don't know what you mean."

"Of course you do. But if you prefer to play it straight, I have time." Another silence. "Tell me, do you think we *like* it when you people come in and start murdering nationals right and left? Do *we* do that sort of thing when we're in the United States?"

Carr shrugged helplessly. What was this man talking about, anyway?

"Very inconsiderate of you," Vascard said. "Particularly since there are now so many forms to fill out." His beefy hand reached into the light and pushed at some of the papers. "It is a waste of my time."

Another long, rather tense silence.

"You look nervous, Mr....Carr."

"I'm not nervous," Carr said.

Vascard smiled. He had a pleasant smile, which spread across his wide, rugged face like a spring bubbling over. "A consummate actor, without question." He got up and walked around the desk—a big man, broad-shouldered and deep-chested, but light on his feet. He seemed entirely relaxed except for his eyes, which moved constantly, always alert.

"Cigarette? French, I'm afraid, but you may find they are an acquired taste." He smiled again innocently. "You will not reconsider, and be more helpful?"

"I will be as helpful as I can."

Vascard sighed, and resumed his place behind the desk. He leaned back in his chair, almost completely hidden be hind the bright glare of the lamp. "I have been reading your report of the incident. Is there anything you wish to add to your statement?"

"No. It was quite complete."

"Complete as only a lawyer could make it, Mr. Carr. That is what amazes me." He paused, as if something had occurred to him. Then he said, "You were attacked on the street in mid-afternoon by a man you did not know. You struggled with him, called for help. The man was then shot from a passing car. That seems to be the essence of it, am I right?"

"Yes," Carr said warily.

"A very strange business indeed. What do you make of it?" The voice came out, disembodied, from behind the bright pool of light.

"I don't know. I suppose he was going to rob me."

"I see." Vascard paused. "How long have you been in Nice, Mr. Carr?"

"I arrived yesterday."

"And how long do you intend to stay?"

"I'm not sure. Until my business is finished."

"Your business here is"—fingers reached into the light for Carr's statement— "to purchase a villa for a client?"

"That's right."

"Who is the client?"

"You know I can't tell you that."

"Mr. Carr, a man has been murdered, and you have been… involved."

"My client's name is immaterial."

"Perhaps. But that is my decision."

"I'm sorry. I can't tell you my client's name."

"I see." The voice was unperturbed. Carr watched the smoke from Vascard's cigarette snaking across the desk into the light. "They have shown you the body of the dead man?"

"Yes."

"And you do not recognize him?"

"No."

"You have no idea who he might be?"

"None."

Vascard's voice was soft, drifting across the room with the cigarette smoke. "Mr. Carr, are you quite sure?"

"Yes. Of course I am."

Another pause. "About the Citroën—had you ever seen it before?"

"No, I don't think so. But there are a lot of black Citroëns in France."

"Did you happen to notice the license number?"

"No."

"The color of the license plate?"

"No," Carr said. "Does it matter?"

"It might. Rented cars have different-color plates."

"Oh."

"When the car went by, did you see anyone inside clearly?"

Carr was annoyed. "They were shooting at me, remember?"

"At *you*, Mr. Carr?"

He hesitated. "Of course. Who else would they be shooting at?"

"The other man."

"That's very strange," Carr said slowly.

"This is all very strange. Try to see the situation from our viewpoint. An American arrives in Nice, on business he will not explain, and—"

"I have explained. I'm buying a villa."

"Buying a villa." For the first time, irritation crept into Vascard's voice. "That's the crudest cover I've ever heard." A puff of smoke, blown in exasperation, slid into the light. "Now then. You arrive here, and the next day a man pulls a gun on you. You fight him. We do not know what he intended, and now we will never know."

"I told you, I assumed he was robbing me."

"Very well. That seems logical, doesn't it? Tell me, do you attend horseraces?"

Carr frowned, puzzled by this new line of questioning. "No, not usually."

"Spend much time in casinos?"

"No. I'm not the gambling type."

"And yet, as a man untrained in this sort of thing, you took a great gamble in fighting with an armed robber. How do you explain it?"

"It was instinctive."

"Was there anything about his manner, his dress, or his actions which alerted you beforehand?"

"No, not really."

"Frankly, I would never have thought him a robber. He was very well dressed."

"For all I know, he was a very successful robber. This must be a good part of the world for robbers."

Vascard sighed. "His gun was not loaded."

"Well, hell," Carr said. "If I were a robber, I wouldn't load my gun either. You just want to frighten people into paying up, not kill them."

"Precisely."

Precisely what? Carr wondered. He couldn't see what Vascard was leading up to.

"How much money were you carrying with you at the time?"

"About forty, maybe fifty dollars."

"And yet you chose to fight."

"I tell you, it was instinctive. Reflexive. Automatic. I didn't stop to think about it."

"Why not?" Vascard asked, in a curious voice.

"I don't know, I just didn't, that's all." Carr angrily stubbed out his cigarette.

"If I had been in your place," Vascard said quietly, "I would have been much more willing to fight if I had known—or suspected—that the gun was not loaded."

There was a very long, dead silence.

"What are you getting at?" Carr said.

"I am merely trying to understand why a young American lawyer will risk his life rather than pay a robber fifty dollars. You underestimate your worth, perhaps."

Carr couldn't think of a good comeback, so he said nothing.

"You mentioned earlier," Vascard said, "that you believed the men in the Citroën were shooting at you. Why is that?"

"My natural sense of self-importance, I guess. Probably the machine gun was a birthday present, and they wanted to try it out."

Vascard's thick hand reached into the light and stubbed out his cigarette. He lit another, and Carr found himself straining to catch a glimpse of the man's face—some expression, some indication of emotion—in the match-light. "Sarcasm will get us nowhere. Do you want to spend all day here?"

Carr threw up his hands. "I don't know why I thought they were shooting at me. I just assumed it."

"You seem to be assuming a great deal today. You assumed you were being robbed, and you assumed you were being shot at. You're a man very much in demand, aren't you?"

"Look, if you're accusing me of something, why don't you come right out and say it?"

"All right," Vascard said. "You've fired a machine gun. I've fired a machine gun. We both know perfectly well that if they had wanted to, those people could have added half a pound of pure lead to your bodyweight."

"I've fired a machine gun?" Carr said. "Me?"

Vascard sucked on his cigarette and groaned inwardly. The man could obviously act, but he was so weak on his stories. He'd had more than an hour out there in the waiting room to come up with something good, and he hadn't managed a thing. In the war, he thought grimly, this poor bastard wouldn't have lasted ten minutes.

"All right," he said patiently. "Let's begin again: a man approaches you with a gun in broad daylight. You do not know him. Assume he is not going to rob you. What does he intend?"

"Maybe he was going to kill me."

"With an unloaded gun?"

"I didn't know that."

"But he knew it quite well. Or perhaps he didn't…" Vascard lapsed into a long silence. Carr shifted in his chair and lit a cigarette. Things were suddenly, hideously, impossibly complicated. Damn, he needed a drink badly.

"No." The policeman's voice broke the silence with its certainty. "No, murder was not intended here. Nor was robbery. The aftermath of this business is too bizarre for that. Mr. Carr, did you ever think that this man wished to abduct you?"

Carr laughed. It was ridiculous. He had a vision of himself, flung like a bag of potatoes, over the shoulder of a scarred brute and hustled off to a mountain retreat. "Why should anyone want to do that?" he asked.

"That is my question."

"I can't imagine why."

"Ransom perhaps? Something to do with your…client? Please consider carefully."

"No. Sorry. It's just impossible. My father has money, but he would like nothing better than for somebody to kidnap me. He'd pay *them* to keep me."

"What about Victor Jenning?" Vascard said suddenly.

"What about him? I've never heard of him."

"He's actually quite well known. Perhaps you've heard the name mentioned, at a party?"

"Never."

Vascard sighed. "All right." He stood up and opened the shades. Hot sunlight poured into the room; Carr squinted.

"I doubt," Vascard said, "that we will gain anything further from our conversation." He looked at Carr thoughtfully, a long, peculiar look. "But I would like to give you some advice, and I hope you'll take it."

"Yes?"

"Your position here is very difficult. You have been involved in an incident which you insist you know nothing about. The incident is serious. There may be repercussions, repetitions."

Carr nodded.

"I can do only one thing for you, and that is look the other way. You people make it very hard for me, but I can arrange it this one time. Next time..." He shrugged.

"What are you saying?"

"I think we understand each other, Mr. Carr."

"I don't think we understand each other at all. I need protection. There's been a murder, and the situation is pretty confused. You should be doing something for me. Otherwise I'm at the mercy of—"

"Mr. Carr. Your energy is a source of wonder to me. Please stop protesting. I am doing all I can for you, I swear it. Don't ask more."

"You're trying to frighten me."

"I doubt that you are easily frightened. Although I must

say you are an excellent actor. I mean that in all seriousness. Superb."

"Son-of-a-bitch," Carr said. What kind of a lousy joke was this, anyhow? He got up and stomped out of the office.

In his office, Dr. Liseau picked up the phone and listened for several minutes. Then he said, "I don't care to hear your explanations. You messed it up. There is nothing more to be said. How much time did he spend with the police? Really? I am surprised they kept him so long."

He listened again, and reached into his desk drawer for a scalpel. He held it up and tilted it so it caught the light. The blade gleamed, in contrast to the dull metal of the handle.

"All right," he said at last. "Try again. But I cannot wait forever."

Liseau replaced the receiver and looked closely at his knife. It was a Hamilton Bell and Company scalpel, with a number-twenty-two blade of German steel—a rather large and clumsy blade, in the opinion of many. But Liseau disagreed. He liked an instrument with plenty of cutting edge.

Chapter VIII

Roger Carr sat in a chair and looked at his hotel room. It was a large room, with a double bed and balcony looking out over the beach. It was decorated in the style of Louis XIV, with a large pink flower-print canopy over the bed, and the same fabric for drapes at the window. The chairs were covered in cloth of green and gold, and the gilded wooden arms were encrusted with leaves and curlicues. Altogether, it was a very feminine-looking room, he decided. He looked at the double bed as he lit a cigarette, and recalled how pleased he had been at the tactful way the hotel had given him a double bed without his asking. He was no longer pleased about anything. The police interview had unnerved him, and he badly needed a drink.

He picked up the white telephone beside the bed. "Room service, please." Clicking while he was put through. "I want a dry vodka gimlet, and a chicken-salad sandwich. Room Three-oh-four."

He got up and paced tensely across the thick pea-green carpet for several minutes. There was a knock at the door. Awfully quick service, he thought. He opened the door, and to his surprise, a man slipped furtively into the room, giving the hallway a last check as he stepped inside. He was a small man, swarthy, with short bristly hair and a lewd grin. He had a two-day growth of beard, and what looked like gravy on the breast of his dark sweater. His hands were filthy, covered with grease and grime. Carr noticed it as the man put his finger to his lips and shut the door.

"What—"

The man clamped one smelly hand over Carr's mouth, shook his head, and took his hand away. Carr stared wide-eyed as the fellow glanced intently around the room and began rummaging about. He squinted at the ceiling lamp, looked under the bed and behind pictures. Then he lifted up the telephone, and beamed. He showed Carr the flat object taped to the bottom. Then he took out a knife and cut it away.

"What—"

The man shook his head insistently, and Carr quickly shut his mouth. The little man continued searching, but now Carr understood, and joined in. A second microphone was discovered over the molding of the closet door. The man yanked it free and threw it out the window. Then he gave a long sigh.

"At last. We can talk, eh?"

"Sit down," Carr said, hesitantly. Who would want to bug his room?

"No. I will stand. You sit." The man smiled. "You are surprised at the microphones?"

"Yes, frankly."

The man shook his head wonderingly. "I agree. It is not like the old days. It used to take hours to find them. Now..." He snapped his fingers.

"What do you want?"

The man laughed. And then Carr remembered—the telephone conversation, and the appointment to meet at noon. He'd forgotten all about it, but obviously this man hadn't.

"What do *you* want, my friend?" the little man asked.

"Don't be silly. I don't want anything."

"There is no need," said the man, airily waving his hand and lighting a cigarette, "to be cautious. I can deliver, I assure you. I have exactly what you want."

"Why is that?"

"You might say that there is a weak link in the chain, eh?" He laughed, right in Carr's face. Garlic wafted toward him. "A link about to break—a link that *wants* to break, my friend. Now!" He stamped his foot down. "What do you say to that, eh? Are we in the business?"

"Listen, I think you're making a mistake. I'm here to buy a villa, nothing else. I don't know anything about—"

The man patted Carr's shoulder agreeably. "Sure, sure. You think I want your life history? I trust you, my friend."

Carr scratched his head and lit a cigarette.

"But let us waste no time, eh? I took a risk coming here. And it would be bad for both of us if I were found. Bad for all three of us."

"All three?"

"Mais oui: the link, too."

"Of course." Carr had the disturbing feeling that he was no longer surprised at meaningless conversations. They were becoming an accepted part of his life.

"Alors! Down to business. How much do you pay?"

Carr shrugged.

"America is a rich country, my friend. For such important information, you should pay well. I have been thinking of, perhaps, five percent of the value of the shipment. What do you say? Agreed?"

"Perhaps."

"It is cheap, at the price."

"Maybe."

"You want to think, and talk to your friends, eh? I understand. The information is not exactly free." He laughed and slapped Carr heartily on the back. "But just imagine! To know everything, from the inside, the entire plot. *Incroyable,* eh?"

He stepped back and smiled, as if he had just performed a magic trick.

"And you want some proof I can deliver, so I tell you a few things. *Bon.* But I cannot say much, or you will guess all. Only that there are five in it, and the plan is a master—they will get him, unless you act. There is no time, so we will meet tomorrow, eh? Here." He pulled a small gold ring off his little finger and handed it to Carr. "Tomorrow, at noon, in the *toilette publique* on the beach. You know it? Near the American Express. Wear this, and a man will contact you. Perhaps me, perhaps another, eh?"

Carr looked doubtfully at the ring.

"Remember the price," the man said, moving toward the door. "Five percent, no less. There can be no bargains over the price."

And with that, he was gone. Carr was left with a ring in the palm of his hand, a small gold circle, leading him nowhere.

Chapter IX

Pierre Morneau had but one dream, and that was to become a chef. True, at his present job, he did no cooking; but he was young, at sixteen, and even as a waiter he was learning.

He stepped into the elevator with the tray ordered by Room 304. That was the American, the one who usually ordered only drinks. This was little better: a chicken-salad sandwich and a gimlet. Pierre wrinkled his nose at the thought. It was hopeless, Americans had no taste.

Since he was alone in the elevator, he followed his usual custom, which was to sample a bit of the food going up-stairs. He did it out of curiosity, and a certain feeling of spite —the chef who handled room-service orders was old, and falling off the mark by a good bit. Pierre could tell, and he felt somehow renewed and hopeful whenever he tasted one of the old man's dishes that was not quite right—or down-right bad.

He lifted the heavy silver cover and looked at the sandwich. A barbaric invention, the sandwich. Carefully he drew out a bit of chicken on a small leaf of lettuce and popped it into his mouth. He replaced the silver cover while he chewed; you never knew when the elevator would stop and someone get on.

His opinion of the old man was confirmed once again. The chicken tasted very strange indeed. Salty, a little tart. No, it wasn't salt—something else, something similar. What could it be?

As he wondered, he felt a wave of dizziness, and his knees buckled. The platter clattered down, and the sandwich fell open onto his shirt. But Pierre did not notice; he was unconscious.

Twenty minutes after the little man had gone, there was a knock at the door. Carr, who had been debating whether to call the desk about his sandwich and drink, opened the door, saying, "Well, it's about time—"

He stopped. Instead of a waiter, two men in business suits were standing before him. They seemed as startled as he, and for a long moment nobody said anything.

"Can I help you?" Carr asked finally.

"I think," said one man hesitantly, "that we have the wrong room. You are not Monsieur Raymond?"

"No, sorry."

"Pardon us, monsieur."

The men left. Carr went directly to the phone, called room service, and bitched about the fact that he still hadn't received his chicken sandwich and, more to the point, his drink. The man at the other end made clucking, soothing noises. It seemed there had been an accident; one of the waiters had taken ill while delivering the order. In the confusion, there had been some delay...

While he was on the phone, there was another knock on the door. This time it was a liveried man with a silver tray on which lay a telegram. He took it back to the phone.

The man on the phone was upset at the delay, he wanted Mr. Carr to know. The order was on its way, and he hoped that Mr. Carr would accept the drink with the compliments of the hotel. Carr said he would, and hung up happy. He tore open the telegram. It was from New York.

*FRIENDS REPORT VILLA PERRANI FOR SALE
AGENT K D GRAFF STOP BUY IT UP TO HALF-
MILLION TRY FOR 400 STOP KISS ONE FOR ME
GOOD LUCK*

                          SONNY

So the governor had found a villa by himself. That was a development. He checked his watch, and discovered for the hundredth time that it read 2:46. He would have to get it fixed in the morning. Looking out the window, however, he saw that the sun was dropping; it was probably too late to call Graff and make inquiries. He would see the man tomorrow.

The sandwich and drink came, and he found he badly needed both. When he had finished, he went into the bathroom to shower before dinner.

Liseau tried to suppress his annoyance with Brauer. The German had fumbled again; obviously, he was not a trained kidnapper. But the idea of drugging the American and taking him from the Negresco was absurd—worse than daring, it was foolhardy. It was a stroke of purest luck that it hadn't worked; they would all surely have been caught.

But now there was more important, more pressing business at hand, business which concerned the unity of his own little group. "You say the microphones were found and destroyed?"

"Yes," Brauer said. "Shortly after he came into the room. So there is no record of the conversation."

"That," said Liseau slowly, "is damning enough. Where is he now?"

Brauer nodded toward the door. "We picked him up just as he left the hotel service entrance."

"Excellent." Liseau gripped his black doctor's bag. "I will

see him now. Have Josette prepare a beer and a tray of hors d'oeuvres."

He entered the room.

It was bare, except for two chairs and a table. Fading sunlight entered through broad windows, casting a reddish glow over the empty white walls. A short swarthy man, stripped to the waist, was bound securely to one chair. It was a strange chair, padded, like a dentist's chair, with solid armrests. The armrests ended in flat boards, to which the man's hands were firmly taped, fingers spread.

The man had short bristly hair and an unpleasant expression on his face. He swore as Liseau came in.

"I hope you are not too uncomfortable," Liseau said, setting down his bag. Whenever he ran an interrogation, he always began with a thorough physical. It was important, he felt—it would never do to overwork a man with a weak heart. Countless sessions had ended uselessly because the subject had been pushed to his limit too quickly. To do such a thing was to play right into the hands of your victim.

He removed his blood-pressure cuff from the bag and took a reading; checked the pulse; examined the pupils for signs of high intracranial pressure. He listened to the man's breathing—wincing as he smelled the garlic—and tapped the chest to make sure the heart was not enlarged.

"You seem quite healthy." He stepped back, smiled disarmingly, and filled a hypodermic with 100 mg of ephedrine, which he injected. That was a useful step; it made the subject more alert, tense, jumpy. It also enabled him to withstand more punishment without passing out.

"Now then," Liseau said, rubbing his long fingers together. "Shall we have a little talk?"

The swarthy man looked up, his face a pale mask.

Liseau reached into his bag and removed a bottle of sulfuric acid, a medicine dropper, and two scalpels. The man looked at the gleaming instruments set out on the table, and then at Liseau. He began to sweat, and his mouth was twitching.

"I have no wish to harm you, my friend. But I do need some information. When you have told me what I must know, you are free to leave. Do we understand each other?"

The little man smiled bleakly. He knew that he would never leave the room alive. *"Espèce de con,"* he snarled.

Liseau shrugged. "As you wish. Let me tell you what I propose to do if you remain unhelpful. I will cut away the skin of your finger, exposing the nerves and flesh beneath. Then I will apply this acid, ninety-five percent sulfuric, drop by drop. It is quite painful, even on the bare skin."

To demonstrate, he filled the dropper and let a single yellowish drop splash onto the back of the man's hand.

The response was immediate. His face twisted in pain, his eyes shutting in agony. The muscles of his jaw and neck stood out strongly. Liseau wiped away the drop.

"That is nothing," he said. "Can you imagine how it must feel when the acid enters a cut so deep the bone is exposed? Can you imagine it applied to the raw, exposed nerves of your finger? Do you know how it will bubble and sizzle as it eats through your flesh?"

The man's eyes were wide with terror, but he said nothing.

"Tell me. What is your name?"

The man shook his head.

"I see we shall be here a long time. I had best have some refreshments." He went to the door, and returned with the tray of beer and snacks. "I'm very hungry," Liseau said, picking up a cracker and spreading *pâté* over it with his scalpel. He took a sip of beer. "Are you hungry, my friend? No?"

Quite abruptly, the man was sick, retching and heaving all over his bare chest.

"Dear, dear," Liseau said, crossing his legs and making no move to clean up the mess. The smell was horrible, but as a surgeon he had become inured to smells. They did not bother him; he ate calmly.

"Tell me," he said. "What is your name?"

The man swore, and retched again. Liseau, with the glass of beer in one hand, picked up his scalpel delicately with the other.

"Who are you working for?"

No answer.

"Why did you see the American?"

Silence.

"These are questions that must be answered," Liseau said. "And unfortunately, only you can answer them." He set aside his food, and examined the hands thoughtfully. He noticed, then, a white band of skin on the small finger. "I see you normally wear a ring. Where is it?"

The man shook his head.

Liseau picked up the scalpel and drew it lightly down the length of the middle finger. The skin was cut, but not deeply enough to draw blood.

This was the moment the little man had been waiting for. Up to now, it had all been bluff, psychology, words. Now came the pain—the pain he must somehow withstand, and turn to his own advantage, so he would die quickly. Could one commit suicide by holding one's breath? He didn't think so.

"Where is the ring?"

The little man made a vulgar noise.

Liseau sighed again, and held the scalpel poised over the finger. Abruptly, he jabbed the point into the knuckle. Pain streaked up through the man's brain; he threw his head back and sucked in his breath.

"Did you perhaps give it to the American?"

No answer.

Liseau cut again, deeply, along the length of the finger. He felt the blade scrape against bone. Blood flowed quickly, and he made no attempt to stop it. "Where is the ring?"

The little man's eyes were wide, and he retched again, dryly. "I lost it," he gasped.

"That's better. I am glad to see you can still speak. Where did you lose it?"

"I don't know."

Holding the cut wide with his fingers, Liseau added a drop of acid. The man closed his eyes and screamed wildly, struggling in his bonds, dripping with sweat. He did not stop screaming until Liseau added a drop of sodium hydroxide, to neutralize the acid. The man's head fell down on his chest, limp, exhausted.

"You are hoping to faint," Liseau said. "It is quite impossible. I have given you an injection which will keep your heart beating fast. I am afraid you will remain awake for everything. Did you give the ring to the American?"

"I don't know any American."

Acid dripped again, sputtering inside the wound, blackening the flesh. Acrid smoke rose in a thin stream. The man gasped, and screamed. Liseau paused to insert a plug in one ear, then added more acid. He waited several minutes before applying the sodium hydroxide.

"Now then, shall we stop our little games? Just tell me your name."

"Go to hell," the man said weakly.

Liseau frowned, but actually, he was beginning to enjoy

himself. He was always slightly disappointed when a subject turned out to be easy, quickly caving in and giving answers. He preferred the tough ones, the ones who hung on to the end.

"Perhaps you find this pain a trifle. If so, we can arrange a greater challenge. We could dissolve the ear off your head. That is quite amusing. Or we could listen to the interesting hissing sound this acid makes as it burns into your eyeball. What do you say, my friend? Have I captured your curiosity?"

Liseau talked calmly, conversationally. He knew perfectly well that the worst pain was in anticipation. The psychological component was far more horrible than the physical affliction. It was like pleasure, like sex—all in the head.

The little man knew this, too, and he tried to ignore the quiet voice. He did not want to know what was coming, did not want to think of it, to imagine how it would be.

"The tongue?" Liseau said, as if thinking aloud. "Or perhaps the nose? I have seen a man's nose destroyed by acid, drop by drop, until there was nothing but a gaping hole in the skull. That is *quite* painful."

The man said nothing.

"What is your name?"

"I don't know."

Liseau chuckled. "Quite a brave man, aren't you? But as a man, I will make you talk. Do you know what I have in mind?"

The little man did not look up, but his skin crawled.

"There are many areas of the body more richly innervated than the finger. Can you think of any?"

Oh, God, thought the man. Oh, God, no.

Liseau gave a slow laugh. "I imagine you have the general idea. Instead of your finger, we will try somewhere else. The same technique, but in a much more…responsive area."

He reached forward.

"And you will talk, my friend. You will tell me everything."

❀

"Tell me everything," the psychiatrist said. "Anything that comes into your head." Ralph Gorman lay full-length on the couch. It was silent in the room, except for the faint scratching sound of the doctor taking notes.

"It was a bad day," Gorman said. "I don't really think I'm cut out for this sort of work. It was much better when I was in Amsterdam—bigger operation there, with more people to do the nasty jobs. Here, I have to be in on everything."

"Hmmm," the psychiatrist said, stroking his goatee.

"But mostly it's my agent." This was classified information, of course. Gorman knew it, but he had told his psychiatrist classified things before. It was all confidential, and besides, he had to talk to *somebody* about it, didn't he? He couldn't let it just sit inside him, building up his neuroses and aggressions. That was one of the first things he had learned from psychiatry.

"My agent won't contact me, and my ulcer has been acting up. He's cheeky, that's the problem. He thinks he can do without me. He doesn't think he *needs* me. But he does; he could get killed. They're on to him; I know it."

"Hmmm," the psychiatrist said. "You have contacted him?"

"Oh yes, I did that yesterday. He just pretended he didn't know who I was. And my ulcer kicked right up. Then we had the girl to question, and—"

"You did not mention any girl before."

"Well, we picked her up last night. Snatched her right out of my agent's bedroom. She was one of them, you see. And we questioned her. Beautiful girl. Very large breasts. Beautiful girls make me nervous."

"Of course," the psychiatrist said, taking notes. Gorman was reassured by the quiet, cultivated Viennese accent. When he was finished talking about the girl, they would look over his doodles together. That was the part Gorman liked best.

The doctor said he had some real artistic potential, though naturally it was the subconscious meanings, the sexual symbols, which were important. Gorman had learned a lot about himself since he had started analysis.

Roger Carr dined in the hotel and went directly to the bar after dinner. He did not feel much like going out on the town; just a quiet evening, and early to bed. That was unusual for him, but he was depressed by what had been happening to him.

He sat down at the bar and ordered a gimlet. Alongside him, two meticulously dressed men were arguing in vehement Italian. He understood none of it, but caught the French idioms sprinkled throughout their dialect. Probably Ligurians, he thought, from just across the border. Whatever they were, they were making a lot of noise.

His drink came, and shortly afterward the two men left. He sipped the cold, smooth liquor and lit a cigarette, and the next thing he knew, a soft voice was saying, "Do you have a match?"

He looked over to see a stunningly beautiful girl. She was Eurasian, her body slim and hard beneath a tight silk sheath which emphasized her firm, small breasts. Her face was gentle, friendly, sensual.

"Day or night," he said, lighting her cigarette. He looked around. She seemed to be alone—what tremendous luck. Or was it? Another trap? He squinted at her critically. If this was a trap, he could have a hell of a lot of fun falling into it. "Join me in a drink?"

Her smile was demure. "You are very kind."

He ordered for her, and they left the bar for a corner table, with high-backed leather chairs. Her silk dress rustled as she walked, and a slit up the side gave a glimpse of a dark smooth thigh.

When they were seated, she gave him a beautiful smile. She was a very feminine girl, but without the delicate, fragile look of so many mixed Orientals. Her sloe eyes were large, and very brown; her lips were large, her teeth even and brilliantly white. Her face was a perfect oval, framed by long, jet-black hair.

Roger Carr introduced himself, and told her he was a lawyer. She said she was an airline stewardess, with two days free. It seemed a very pointed announcement, and his heart thumped. He turned on his most boyish, engaging grin.

"I have a message for you," she said.

Oh, oh, he thought.

"We are pleased with what you did today," she said, "although G. still wants to see you. He wishes you to call tomorrow, or give me a message."

"This is the airline company?"

She laughed, very gently. *"Très drôle."* She seemed genuinely amused.

"It is strange," the girl said, as the drinks arrived. "I did not think you would be this way. So open, and friendly." Another smile. "I know what you did today. It was so daring. You must have very good nerves."

"Steel, pure steel," he said, puffing up his chest. With luck, he'd have this little thing in bed inside an hour. He grinned.

"Are you really a stewardess?"

"Of course. And you are a lawyer." She smiled back at him. "You're cute. I expected someone much more serious, with perhaps a scar on his cheek."

"Well, you know how it is," he said, hoping she did.

"Yes," she answered, in a small awed voice.

Oh, baby. Easily an hour.

"You must be very strong," she said, her hand still on his arm.

"Not really," Roger Carr said smoothly, but he flexed his bicep. "I believe in delicacy."

"I agree," the girl said. She hesitated. "Do you have a message for me?"

Oh, do I. "Well," he said, leaning back, "I think this place may be a little too public." He glanced around the room, as if to confirm his judgment.

"Shall we go to my room?" she asked.

"That's a very good idea," Carr said, his face solemn and businesslike.

As they left, Carr saw the big blond fellow standing at the bar. For a brief instant, their eyes met, and then the big man looked away. It was slightly unnerving, that exchange of glances, but the girl was on his arm, soft and warm, and his thoughts were elsewhere.

It was dark in the room, and warm under the covers. The girl rubbed up against him, and purred softly.

"You are wonderful," she said.

Carr smiled in the dark. It's true, he thought. What can I say?

"So strong, yet so gentle."

He put his arm around her and drew her closer.

"You must have many women, all over the world."

"Well—"

She put her finger to his lips and kissed his shoulder. "Don't tell me about them. Tonight, I have you all to myself. Is there more champagne?"

"A whole bottle."

"Ummm." She pushed back the covers and turned on the

tiny bed lamp. In bare feet she padded over to the silver ice bucket. A truly sleek body, Carr decided, watching her. They just didn't come in that model in America. All those firm, slender muscles, yet still soft and feminine.

She picked up the bottle and turned to him. Her long hair covered one breast. "Would you open it?"

"My pleasure," he said, in his most gallant voice. Roger Carr would never refuse to open a champagne bottle for a nude lady at two in the morning. It was one of the few things in the world which he regarded as unthinkable.

As the cork popped and bounced off the ceiling, she said, "You must tell me the message, in the morning."

"In the morning," he promised, and they went back to bed.

By nine-thirty the next morning, Roger Carr was in his own room, taking a shower, humming "I Want to Hold Your Hand." Things were cheerful again. He had left the girl in her room, blissfully asleep. That was convenient, since he had avoided any "message."

Obviously, she wanted to be told something, but he couldn't imagine what.

Chapter X

"I am not surprised," Liseau said to Brauer. "I did not really think he would last the night."

He concealed his frustration well. The little porcupine of a man had taken unbelievable punishment, and yet said nothing of any importance, nothing Liseau could not have discovered for himself. To fight the pain, the little man had bitten his tongue so often that finally, toward the end, it was a swollen, bloody pulp; he could not have talked then, even had he wanted. And he had not wanted.

It was a serious setback—particularly since Liseau was now convinced that one of his group was about to sell out. Perhaps the American could shed light on the question. He thought back to the taped conversation he had heard, and shook his head. If the American was genuinely uninvolved, he would be merely confused and confusing. There was no sense in complicating things still further. At the same time, he had to know which of the group was going to double up. It was absolutely vital to discover that.

"Has Carr gone to the consulate yet?"

"No," Brauer said.

"Let us see," said Liseau, "if we can put a little pressure on him. Let's see which way the cat jumps when the heat is on."

If he went to the consulate under stress, that would settle everything.

"What do you have in mind?" Brauer asked.

"It's rather gruesome," said Liseau cheerfully.

*

The real-estate offices of K. D. Graff et Fils were located along the Boulevard Victor Hugo. Monsieur Graff, a man with a neatly clipped moustache and a gold-plated cigarette holder, seemed surprised at Carr's inquiries—the villa had only recently been offered for sale, and had not been advertised. Carr remarked that he had his sources, and asked the price. He did not like Graff.

Monsieur Graff sighed. "Signor Perrani has not yet set a price," he said. "He is Italian, a businessman, and you know how the Italians are." Graff shrugged helplessly with his cigarette holder, a gesture which scattered ash over his silk shirt. He brushed it impatiently. "Everything with the Italians is hot air and hand motions. Not that I have anything against the Italians, of course. Italian culture is the second greatest in Europe." He finished brushing, and adjusted his tie with two delicate fingers. "But I would say, monsieur, that when the price is fixed, it will be about three million francs, *nouveau.* That is about…"

"Six hundred thousand dollars."

"More or less. Is that the price range you are considering?"

"It seems reasonable, for the moment."

"Because if it is, I have several other villas available in that range. If you are interested, perhaps I can—"

"Thanks," Carr said, "but I'd rather see the Villa Perrani first."

"Of course, of course. I will call Signor Perrani myself this morning. Allow me to take your name." Graff pulled out a gold-plated pen. "You wish the villa for yourself?"

"No, for a client."

"I will take the name of your client as well."

"I think my name will be sufficient." Carr handed Graff his card, which the other man studied for some time, running his finger across the engraved surface.

"You are a lawyer." He shook his head slowly. "You should know that Signor Perrani will be most particular about who buys his home. It is a lovely villa, in a lovely area. He will not simply sell it to *anyone.*"

"I don't expect a *trou* for three million francs," Carr snapped, "and I don't think Signor Perrani will object to my client when I tell him who it is."

Graff looked as if he had just stepped in a tub of scalding water. "Of course, as you wish, of course. I will call this morning. Shall I telephone your hotel later today?"

"Yes. The Negresco."

"Very good, monsieur. I shall see to it immediately." He bowed and led Carr to the door. "Good morning, monsieur."

"Good morning."

As he walked out, he wondered what he should do for the rest of the morning. Pass an hour at a café? Get out on the beach?

At that moment, he saw the advertisement for the Cannes Film Festival.

"He was very nice," said the girl, shaking her head so her long hair fell across her shoulders.

"I'm sure," Gorman said. "But what did he say?"

"So strong," she said, stretching her arms over her head. "So gentle."

"Did you tell him I wanted to see him?"

"Oh, yes. That was *before.*" She sighed, and stared wistfully out the window.

Christ, thought Gorman. Never send a girl on a man's job.

Cannes maintains a quiet, restful, and elegant atmosphere that is virtually indestructible. All the starlets in tight slacks, wiggling down from Saint-Tropez, all the sailors leering and hooting at the bodies on the beach, all the tour buses and all the Americans loudly discussing "Cans" are unable to spoil the relaxed and sophisticated tone of the town. After 130 years as a resort, it remains primarily a place where the very rich come to spend money, and to spend it with taste.

Carr had visited Cannes some years earlier. He had been prepared to find there all the gaudy, pubescent sensuality of Saint-Tropez, combined with the stifling onus of a dull and determined snobbism. To his surprise, he had found neither. His old sense of delight was renewed as he parked at the far end of the Boulevard de la Croisette and walked along the water toward the port.

He noticed changes since he had been there last, which he attributed to the film festival. Flags lined the street, representing the countries participating in the festival; shops displayed large photographs of film stars and scenes from movies in the competition. Posters for other films were set up between the palm trees which formed the center divider of La Croisette.

A silent crowd waited in front of the Carlton Hotel, watching as cars came up the elevated ramp and the drivers got out and went into the lobby. Several people in the crowd held binoculars, which they used to scan the upper windows of the hotel; others kept cameras poised. Cars stopped, thinking a celebrity was about to emerge, but nothing happened. He went on.

Across the street, on the sidewalk above the beach, people were clustered against the rail. Something seemed to be going on. He pushed his way through the bystanders and eventually managed a view down over the sand.

It was a photographic session for a fashion magazine. The model, a skinny girl with a dark tan and large, brilliant eyes, reclined on a striped beach mattress. She was wearing a kind of lace leotard. Draped over her toe was a string of gold beads, and she held an oversized cigarette holder archly in her skeleton fingers. Her hat was a vast wicker affair, which looked rather like a denuded lampshade.

"Who is it?" a navy sailor asked, as he elbowed his way to Carr's side.

"Don't know."

The sailor peered down. "It's nobody," he announced. "Some model. I saw her yesterday, when she was wearing blue satin long johns. Skinniest broad I ever saw—stab you to death." He wandered off.

Carr grew tired of watching, so he continued down the sidewalk. Coming toward him was a young, pouting girl with a dog on a leash. The girl wore dungarees and a very thin silk blouse. She was quite clearly without a bra. It was all part of the game, he told himself, part of the festival spirit.

Up ahead was another large group looking down at a knot of people clustered around someone lying on the sand. As he approached, he saw that the people were photographers, and they were bending over a girl in a red bikini. They were talking to her, encouraging her. One tickled her feet. It was too far to hear, but he could see the girl shake her head. One by one, the photographers straightened, looking disgusted.

The girl jumped up suddenly and took off the top of her bikini, waving the bra above her head like a banner. She posed briefly, putting one leg in front of the other, knee bent. Then she flashed a smile and scampered down the beach, still topless.

The crowd cheered. The photographers chased after her. She ran along the water's edge, occasionally pausing to turn around, squirm, and pose. When she stopped, the photographers stopped, dropping to one knee to shoot; when she ran, they ran after her, raising a great cloud of sandy dust.

Most of them were so encumbered with their webbing of cameras, lenses, film bags, and filters that they could barely move.

The girl stopped, throwing herself down on the sand. She lay on her stomach, and the panting photographers were outraged. They argued with her, pleaded with her, tried to tickle her. Carr, sensing that this was where he had come in, walked on.

He absorbed it all—the gray ships of the Sixth Fleet, anchored in the harbor; the private beaches, swept smooth until they resembled well-tended lawns; the groups of Germans, wearing shorts and sandals, burned a painful red and grunting with each step. And he looked at the girls.

He saw one who was really remarkable. She was wearing almost nothing, just a few strips of blue-checked material, and her body was breathtaking—long, firm, deeply tanned. He could not see her face; it was covered by a broad straw hat, and only a few strands of blond hair were visible at the edge. Alongside her was a half-finished drink, a pack of cigarettes, her sunglasses, a paperback book. And her purse, a large alligator handbag, with gold initials that gleamed in the sun: *AC*.

He decided to say hello.

Chapter XI

He paid the musclebound beach boy two francs, and dropped down on the striped mattress beside her. He felt faintly ridiculous, lying on the beach in a suit. She did not move, but a voice came out from beneath the hat.

"Vous obscurcissez le soleil."

"Try English," he said.

"You're blocking my sun, stupid."

Charming girl, he thought, reaching over and taking one of her cigarettes. Meanness tax. "I'm not. Besides, it isn't your sun."

"My apologies, Romeo. Now, clear off."

Carr struck a match, then said, "There are occasions when all apology is rudeness."

The hat came off, and the girl looked at him. She had a roundish English-looking face, with a clear, direct gaze.

"Oh," she said. "It's you. You should know better—it's 'occasions on which,' not 'occasions when.'"

"Hard to remember exactly."

"How did you know who I was?"

Carr looked at the firm body stretched out on the sand. "You underestimate yourself."

"Not a chance." She propped herself up on one elbow and put her hat back on. "How do you know Johnson?"

"Friend of the family."

"No, seriously."

"Well, when I was at Groton, I had a choice between doing a paper on Johnson or Franklin. Franklin was a pompous bore, and Johnson was pompous and interesting. Besides, Boswell was dirty. I liked that."

He turned on his best boyish grin. She smiled back, with no trace of her earlier irritability. It's probably just a necessary defense mechanism for a girl around here, he thought. Just as natural and essential as swatting flies.

"You know," said the girl, still smiling, "you look like an eleven-month baby."

"Thank you very much," Carr said, puffing on her cigarette. She didn't look like any sort of baby: green eyes, beneath long lashes, gazing steadily back at him. Her hair, which barely reached her shoulders, was shorter than he had remembered. It was dark blond, and lacked the dry frizzy quality of dyed hair. Her lips were large and well-shaped; she wore no makeup.

She was well-built, with broad shoulders and an easy grace to her smoothly muscled limbs. Her breasts swelled over the top of her bikini. She had a habit of pointing her toes forward, making a clean line from shin to toe. She did it so naturally, he guessed she must be a dancer.

"Are you a very amusing man?" she asked.

"Very."

"You look as if you are." She glanced at his clothes. "Are you rich, or a ne'er-do-well? I think it's a fair question, since you've pinched one of my bloody cigarettes."

"I'm a rich ne'er-do-well."

He tried to place her soft accent, which seemed American, though her vocabulary was more English. She guessed what he was thinking.

"Australian," she said. "I'm a dancer. An honest job, and a very dull one."

Carr introduced himself, and told her he was a lawyer who had come to buy a villa.

"Anne Crittenden," the girl said. "Have you found one?"

"Not yet."

"That must be why you're wearing a suit. You look terribly businesslike."

"I've noticed it's not exactly the fashion down here."

"I take it you saw the exhibition a few minutes ago."

Carr nodded. "You don't approve?"

She gave him a slow, appraising look. "If you know anything about art," she said, "you know that the best galleries arrange private showings, by invitation."

Carr suddenly became aware of the heat on the beach, and said, "I've always been a compulsive buyer, myself."

"I can imagine. Aren't you hot in that suit?"

"Yes, as a matter of fact."

"Then why don't you ask me to lunch?"

"Why, thank you. I'd be delighted to accept." A strange girl, he thought. He wondered if she was always this forward, or whether it was just her way of putting people off balance. He watched her stand, graceful and slim. She noticed his eyes.

"Hungry?" She was smiling, and yet not laughing at him.

"Getting there."

"You have a very evil look on your face."

"Congenital deformity. It runs in the family."

She laughed and shook her head; her hair swirled around her face. "I'll be right back." She disappeared into a cabana, and he picked up her book—*La Chartreuse de Parme*. Stendhal seemed an unusual choice for a lazy day on the beach. He glanced quickly through it, noticing that she had underlined phrases and marked page numbers on the inside cover.

Anne emerged, wearing a simple but expensive-looking dress of pale green linen. The color matched her eyes. As he stood, he realized that in sandals she was nearly as tall as he; she was a big girl, but not in the least masculine. Not with those breasts jutting forward under the dress. Not with that smile.

"You're very quick."

"It's one thing you learn, as a dancer," she said, slipping a white chiffon scarf over her head. "Quick changes. Where shall we go?"

"You've been here longer than I have. Why don't you pick the place?"

"All right. Are you interested in art?"

Carr looked at her quickly, searching for a double meaning. "Yes," he said hesitantly.

"Good. There's a marvelous place not far away, in Saint Paul. Shall we go?"

"Fine."

"You have a car?"

He nodded, and she took his arm as they walked back down the street, following the beach. "Eventually, this place gets to you," Anne said. "It's all right for a while, but sooner or later, you come to feel that the Riviera combines all the worst features of Miami Beach and Las Vegas."

"You've been to the United States?"

"Yes." They passed a line of deck chairs set out on the sidewalk. Old ladies were feeding pigeons; there were several young mothers, beautiful girls, sitting next to their baby carriages, faces turned up to the sun, eyes closed. "Just look at the people: the retired old ladies, and the retired young ones." She shook her head. Carr detected a note of bitterness in the voice, but said nothing. He noticed again how expensive her clothes were—too expensive, he thought, for a dancer's salary.

As they crossed La Croisette in front of the Miramar, Carr saw a young girl coming the other way. She was sexy, in a sort of hot-bitch way, with long auburn hair, tight slacks, and a very tight sleeveless pullover, but her walk was what caught his eye. She moved forward with her back arched, leading with her hips. He watched, slightly astonished.

"Sometimes I think I'll go nuts if I see another one," Anne said. "The pelvic trot. Jesus."

Carr laughed.

A car roared by down the street, silver and swift. It was a fastback coupé, with the clean, powerful lines of an Italian coachmaker. Anne waved as the car went by, and Carr had a glimpse of a neat face wearing aviator sunglasses.

"A friend?"

"Sort of."

"Nice car."

"Yes, it's a Ferrari. He's very proud of it."

They came to Carr's Alfa, and for once he was embarrassed to see it. It looked so small and puny after the Ferrari. But Anne didn't seem bothered; she nodded her approval and he helped her in, watching the way she swung her long brown legs under the dash.

He slipped behind the wheel, started the engine, and pulled into traffic. They left the town, following the road through Juan-les-Pins toward Cap d'Antibes. Traffic was light; it was noon, and everyone was off the road for lunch.

"Are you going to the race next weekend?" Anne asked.

"I hope so." The Grand Prix de Monaco would be held in five days, on Sunday. He had planned to see it. "It's just that I hate to go alone."

"You're faster than a speeding bullet," Anne said. "Won't you even wait until after lunch?"

"More powerful than a locomotive," he growled.

"Is that a proposition?"

"Yes."

"I'm insulted."

"Charming."

They came to the turnoff for Vence and took it, following the road as it snaked up in high, winding bends. The view was magnificent, looking out over the villas and flower-growing farms of the Alps foothills. Anne talked, not expecting him to answer, and Carr was pleased. She was the first girl he had ever met who instinctively realized that he did not like to talk when he drove.

He found out that her father had been a diplomat, that she was an only child, and that she had traveled extensively with her father. He also discovered that she knew a good deal, in a sort of offhand way, about astronomy, automobiles, art, and French, German, and English literature. He liked to listen to her talk, and enjoyed the way she put things.

He was happy: it was turning out to be one of those rare meetings which just seemed to go well from the start, for no reason at all. Carr liked her, and felt she liked him.

Off to the left, sitting on a nearby hill, was a walled town, bright in the sunlight. Carr pulled off the road, and they got out to look. The town of Saint Paul was yellow-brown, quite large; the buildings, jumbled inside the wall, were dominated by a cathedral and belltower. The ramparts seemed to be entirely intact, and the green valley dropped off steeply on both sides.

"I wouldn't like to scale that," Carr said. "It looks almost impregnable."

Anne smiled slowly. "Don't you know? There are no impregnable fortresses, only those badly attacked."

Carr gave her a quick glance, which she returned with startling directness.

"I thought you were insulted."

"I am, but I can't help it Do you know you look like a satyr?"

"Tell me more."

"Not all at once," she said. They got back in the car and continued down the road.

"In the Michelin guide, Saint Paul gets two stars," Anne said. "That means it's worth a detour. Three stars means it's worth a journey. They think Cannes is worth a journey." She laughed.

"You really don't like Cannes, do you?"

"No," she said. "I really don't."

"Why not leave?"

She bit her lip. "I can't."

"You Cannes, but you can't," he said.

"Stop it," Anne said, laughing. "That was terrible."

"A specialty, I'm afraid."

"Oh, dear."

They continued along the road, which curved slowly toward the town, and parked just outside the ramparts. They looked much grayer close up. The restaurant was actually a country inn—the Colombe d'Or, the Golden Dove. It was a large yellow-stucco building built outside the walls, on the lip of the hill. A blue sign hanging over the entrance showed a golden dove flying over the walled city. They passed under an old arch and came onto a sunny terrace. The white tables, set out with a view over the verdant valley, were decorated with bright flowers.

Anne took him inside the inn to a small, rather dark room, with crude wooden chairs and heavy, rough-hewn tables. "The owner of this restaurant used to give struggling young artists free meals in exchange for paintings. Look what he was left with."

Carr walked around the room, examining the pictures on the walls. He read off the names: "Modigliani, Matisse, Picasso, Leger…" He looked back at Anne, who was smiling happily.

"Bright man, wasn't he?" she said.

"I'll say."

"They're all early, and some aren't so good. My favorite is the Matisse in the corner." Carr looked at it, a face drawn with the unmistakable lyrical line of Matisse. "Have you seen the chapel at Vence? Well, we'll have to go sometime." She caught herself. He was grinning at her.

"You haven't succeeded yet, you know," she said. "What's so funny?"

"Nothing. I just like you." He took her hand, and they went out onto the terrace to eat.

They chose a side table, with a good view over the valley. It was a green, damp valley, with neat terraced fields surrounding red-roofed farmhouses. Just below their table was a dovecote, from which the restaurant derived its name.

While they were waiting for hors d'oeuvres, Carr said, "This place is worth more than a detour, and so are you."

"Is that a line?"

"Of course."

She smiled. "Am I worth a journey?" Her green eyes flashed in the sun.

"Oh well," Carr said, "that's hard to say. How can I compare you to Chartres, or Notre-Dame?"

"Well," Anne said, "it would be interesting to compare you to Mont Saint Michel."

Carr squirmed. This was a very upsetting girl. He said, "The results would depend on who had inspired me."

"*Touché,*" she said, and laughed.

"If I get the chance," he promised, and they were both silent.

The food came. Beautifully laid out in small dishes, there were at least twenty hors d'oeuvres, and a large bowl of raw vegetables.

"Is there actually another course?" he asked.

"Oh, yes." A waiter came with a bottle of rosé wine in an ice bucket. "I can't do this very often," she said. "Have to watch my weight."

"You're joking," Carr said, remembering the slim body on the sand. "I would have thought you're the type that never has to diet."

"Not a chance," she said, chewing on a crayfish. Her blond hair fell over her face, catching the sun. "I normally live on fruit, lettuce, and diluted water—plus three hours of hard exercise a day. Have to. The competition around here is fierce. I was lucky to get a job as a dancer in the first place."

"Where do you work?"

"At the Cannes casino, in the floor show. We're between seasons now—the winter show has closed, and the summer one doesn't open for ten days. We're practicing, twice a day, at the Palm Beach. Once in the morning, and then after dinner. Keeps you from stuffing yourself at dinner."

Carr nodded. "You live in Cannes?"

"Menton." She picked up a radish, examined it thoughtfully, and popped it into her mouth. "Actually, though, I can't complain about the work. Not only do I have the chance to exhibit my fair body every night before the drooling masses, but I can discuss philosophy with the other girls. It's very stimulating, I can tell you. The radishes are sour."

"Why don't you leave?" Carr asked again.

"You know," the girl said, "the art in this *auberge* is nothing compared to what's around here. Have you seen any of the museums? The Picasso museum in Antibes?"

"No, not this time. I was here a few years ago, and I saw it then. Picasso lives near here, doesn't he?"

"Ummm." She discarded the rest of the radish and tried the cucumbers. "He has a villa called La Californie, north of here. And a new wife, who barricades him in and won't let him see anybody. It's quite a local scandal."

"I can imagine."

She pushed her hair back from her face with one hand. Her fingers were slender and delicate. "You're not really very interested in art, are you?"

"No," Carr said, "that's not it." He paused, wondering how he could explain it. It wasn't that art didn't interest him; it was just that he had never given it much thought. He had never had the time: Carr's girls, like his life, were relaxed, pleasant, full of fun and good times. They weren't bright, they weren't interesting, but they had been good sports and that had been enough.

Slightly irritated, he corrected himself mentally—that *was* enough. Wasn't it?

Outside, in the parking lot, Brauer sat behind the wheel of the Citroën, playing poker with the two pugs in the back seat. His eyes moved constantly—from his cards, to the entrance of the restaurant, back to the cards again. He did not resent having to divide his attention. He was winning handsomely.

"You look young," Anne said. "How old are you?"

"Thirty-seven."

"Married?" She asked the question with complete casualness.

"No."

"Ever been?" Carr shook his head. "That's interesting," she said. "That makes you an idealist, a misogamist, an inveterate playboy, or a liar."

"Do I get my pick?"

"You look like a playboy to me," she said. "Let me guess what kind of line you use. Are you really rich?"

"Not particularly."

"But you have an Alfa. Rented, I suppose. What kind of car do you have in the States? A Porsche?"

"Austin-Healey."

"Okay. You must have a private home—a little retreat of some kind?"

"Yes," Carr said reluctantly. This girl was coming rather close to the knuckle. He did not mention that he had sold his Porsche to buy the Healey.

"And your clothes are carefully cut. Do you have a little tailor tucked away in Rome or London?"

"No," he said, glad she had missed.

"Brooks Brothers," she announced. "American all the way. I should have known. All right." She leaned back and looked at him critically. "I think you probably rely on the good-humored-elf approach. Tone down the money, play up the funny-guy personality. All spontaneous good times. Joke them into bed, one big laugh all the way. Either that," she said, "or the brilliant, dashing-young-man approach: sweep them off their feet, into the sportscar, into the sheets. Fly away with me to my cozy little retreat, I am an up-and-coming, handsome, gregarious—"

"Lawyer."

"Yes. And if that fails, there is always the sincere treatment. Deep stares into her eyes. Mumblings. Doubts about yourself. An honest fellow, intelligent but bored with his exciting life, hoping to find meaning and true values, and possibly to settle down—if he finds the right girl. That always works with the difficult cases."

Carr shifted in his chair. "How old are you?"

"Twenty-nine." She seemed delighted to have forced him to change the subject.

"You don't look older than twenty-two."

"I know. It's a great disadvantage. The old ones think I'm pure and unspoiled and won't know what tired lovers they are. They're always pestering me."

"Ever been married?"

"I think I've heard this conversation before."

"Witness is directed to answer the question."

"Yes," she said, "I was married. I'm basically the type. I got married when I was nineteen—over my father's dead body, quite literally. The guy was a writer, or thought he was. He was a very self-important bugger and he made a grand impression on a girl of nineteen, and I'd rather talk about something else."

"All right. Why don't you leave the Riviera?"

"Say, you are curious, aren't you, counselor?"

"Can't help it."

"Your grin is absolutely devilish. You must be an unbelievably successful seducer."

"Well, I like to think—"

"Never mind. I'm not sure I can bear it. Why don't you pour some more wine? Here comes the main course."

Chapter XII

Lunch was a delight. They finished two bottles of wine, and even after coffee, Carr felt a little high, and very happy. They had discussed everything, and he had become increasingly astonished at her. At one point, he had playfully accused her of being too literal, and she had responded by quoting the gravedigger scene from *Hamlet*—not just one speech, but the whole scene, taking on all three roles, twisting her face and changing her voice.

Later, he found himself listening to her explain with equal facility about the security measures in the casino, the air-oil suspension of the Citroën, and the way Mann wrote—ten sentences a day, never more. She preferred that to Balzac, who wrote his novels from the middle, expanding one central incident until he had reached both the beginning and end of the book, or to Wolfe, who wrote standing up, dropping finished pages into a wastebasket.

She had gone on to talk about Poe, who was underrated; Larry Rivers, who was "a nothing"; De Gaulle, whom Americans couldn't understand; sex, which nobody could understand; and the problems of the rich, which she envied.

"I would like," she had said, "to be rich enough to be unhappy, but not rich enough to be miserable."

She was quick, she was witty, she was gorgeous, and Carr found himself entranced. She refused to be snowed by him, fending off his gambits with amusement and good humor. He was intrigued by the lighthearted challenge she presented, but his interest went further. Just how much further, he couldn't be sure; it was not the sort of thing he normally worried about.

After lunch, she grabbed his hand impulsively and dragged him back to the car, saying there was a place he simply must see. They drove for only a few minutes before they came to an incredible building perched in the woods overlooking Saint Paul and the sea.

"This is the Fondation Maeght," Anne said, as they parked. "It was built a couple of years ago, and it's the greatest museum on the whole Riviera."

Carr looked at it—starkly modern, with huge wings of poured concrete rising above the roof. In front, a giant spider-like contraption stood on the lawn.

"It's a Calder stabile," Anne said as they walked toward the entrance. "Isn't it incredible?"

"Incredible," he agreed.

Through the entrance doors, they could see a central court-yard, where several skinny, elongated Giacometti statues stood. There was very little furniture in the museum; the floors were dun tile, the walls white.

"Maeght is a dealer who built this place especially to hold the work of five artists. There is a room of each. This is all Chagall," she said as they entered one room.

Carr didn't care if it was Grandma Moses. He held her hand, and was happy. They wandered from Chagall to Kandinsky, then to a room of Giacometti. Then they went outside, to a garden where a giant egg stood in a pool of water. "Miró," Anne said. "All the artists contributed original work to the museum. Right around the corner there's a mosaic by—"

Carr had stopped listening. In a far corner of the garden, he had just seen the blond man, standing with two huge brutes. The three were glancing at Carr, and talking together in low tones. There was something disturbingly sinister about them, and he felt tension grip him. Unaccountably, the words of Vascard came back to him: "Did you ever think that these men wished to abduct you?"

The men talked, huddled together, superficially interested in a Giacometti nude.

He remembered the two men who had mistakenly knocked on his door the day before, in the hotel. He recalled the surprised look on their faces.

It was the same two men. He was sure of it, And the waiter who had suddenly "taken ill" while delivering Carr's food?

It all fitted together. He shivered.

The three men began walking toward him.

"I want some postcards," Carr said to Anne.

"What?"

"Postcards. I want some."

"But we haven't seen all the sculpture." She was giving him a very puzzled look.

"We can come back."

"Do you feel all right? You look a little pale."

"Never better."

The three men were drawing closer. They all had their hands in their pockets. They were all staring at Carr.

"Well, frankly," Anne said, frowning, "if it's all the same to you—"

"It's not."

He grabbed her arm and pulled her back into the museum, walking briskly toward the room where books and postcards were sold.

"Hey, what's got into you?"

"Nothing."

He paused at the desk and picked up a book of lithographs. "There are people here I don't want to meet is all."

"Really? Where?"

"Don't look around. Pick up a postcard."

Something in his tone must have frightened her, because she immediately took a card and examined it critically.

"Are you in trouble?" she asked, looking at the cards.

"I might be. I don't know."

"It sounds exciting."

Oh, for Christ's sake, he thought. Out of the corner of his eye, he saw the three men enter the room and examine a stack of reproductions for sale.

"I'll take this," he said to the salesgirl, handing her the book he was holding. It was a collection of Miro paintings.

"That's the most expensive thing here," Anne said.

"It's for you."

"Oh, you shouldn't—"

"I should. And when I give it to you, you will repay me with a great big kiss, and then you will put your arm around me very tightly, and we will walk out of here."

Her eyes were wide. She said nothing. The salesgirl wrapped the book, and Carr paid her two hundred francs, then gave it to Anne. She let out a little squeal and flung her arms around his neck. They kissed for several moments.

As they walked out, arms around each other, Anne said, "Was that all right?"

"That was just perfect."

"Pretty sneaky way to get a kiss. Was it the three over in the corner?"

Carr did not dare look back. They came to the door, and he opened it, saying, "Yes. Now, let's get back to the car. Fast."

He felt a tap on the shoulder.

Oh, Christ, he thought, bolting through the door.

The tap became a firm grip. Carr was almost hauled off his feet. He turned to face the blond man.

Ugly as sin, he thought, Like a greasy, smooth pig.

"You had an appointment today?" the man said.

"Me? An appointment? I don't think so." He tried to pull free of the blond man, but no luck. He might as well be gripped by a clam.

"Yes, an appointment. At noon, near American Express." He spoke English slowly, with a thick German accent.

"Wrong fella," Carr said. "Really. I don't know what you're talking about."

"Your friend," the blond man replied. "He said to give you this."

A small box was thrust into Carr's hand. It was not large, no bigger than a cigarette packet, and quite expensively wrapped.

The blond man released Carr, bowed slightly, and turned back into the museum. Carr stood there, dumbfounded, holding the box in his hand.

"I don't think I understood all that," Anne said.

Carr shivered, thrust the box into his pocket, and tried a smile. "Neither did I."

They went to the parking lot, and he started the Alfa, throwing it noisily into gear but not caring. They roared off down the road.

"Did you really have an appointment?" she asked.

"Yes," he said. "I forgot all about it."

Carr's mind was working furiously, churning with his stomach. He was very confused, and very upset. He had never panicked before in his life, and now he was a little ashamed.

Warm sunlight, not yet fading, poured onto his face as they drove toward the coast. The sky was crisp and blue. Somehow it all seemed unreal, absurd.

"You still look pale," Anne said. "Is there anything I can do to help?"

"No," he said.

She lit a cigarette and stuck it between his lips. He was grateful.

"If you're in trouble, why don't you go to the police? Or the consulate?"

The consulate, he thought. Now, there was something he hadn't even considered. He could go to them, and dump the whole business in their laps.

Dump what? He had nothing, really. A series of strange incidents, made sinister by his overactive imagination, embroidered childishly. No, there was nothing they could do for him, any more than the police.

He felt the sun on his face and the wind tugging at his hair. Once again he was struck by the absurdity of it all. Kidnappings just didn't *happen*, for no reason at all. He had merely been involved in a series of freakish incidents. If he ignored them, they would all go away. In a week, he'd look back and laugh.

Still, he would rather not be alone tonight.

"As a matter of fact, there is something you can do."

"What?"

He looked over at her. Her face was so serious, he laughed. "Come to dinner with me."

"Am I going to have to kiss my way out of the restaurant?"

"No, I promise."

"All right," she said.

"Eight o'clock? The casino?"

"Sold."

At her request, he dropped her off in Cagnes-sur-Mer, and returned to Nice.

❋

It was five-thirty when he arrived at his hotel room, ordered a drink, and remembered the package. As he reached in his pocket for it, he felt the ring as well, and brought them both out together. He placed them side by side on the table and looked at them.

He had examined the ring before. It was nondescript, battered, real gold. The package was wrapped in glazed white paper, and tied with a white ribbon bow. It was elegantly, expensively simple. A card was tucked under the ribbon: "With our regrets. The Associates."

He shook the box, holding it next to his ear, and heard nothing. He supposed it could be something terrible, like a bomb—but so small and light?

"With our regrets. The Associates."

He had never heard of the Associates.

His drink came, and he sipped it, walking around the table and looking at the ring and package. He realized that he was afraid to open it. Why? No reason, really. Just afraid.

The drink relaxed him, and finally he got up the nerve. He tore away the ribbon and ripped off the paper. The box was simple white cardboard.

He opened the lid and saw nothing but cotton padding. Beneath this, he found a human finger.

Chapter XIII

Hastily Carr sat down in a chair and gulped back the rest of his drink.

He leaned forward and looked again. Gingerly he picked it up: there was no doubt—it was a finger. Tanned, grimy, severed cleanly at the knuckle. Clearly visible was the circle of pale flesh where the ring had once been.

"With our regrets. The Associates."

"God almighty," Carr said aloud, dropping the finger back into the box. It was stiff, and fell with a thump, like a stale cigar. "God almighty."

This was too much. He had to do something.

In a sudden burst of clarity, he picked up the phone. "American consulate, please."

A few minutes later a girl answered.

"I need to see somebody right away," Carr said.

"I'm afraid the consulate is just closing. It will open to-morrow at eight—"

"This is important. It can't wait."

"I see. What exactly is your business, sir?"

"It concerns a finger."

"Yes, sir," the girl said. Her voice had an abstracted quality; he guessed she was writing it down.

"I just received it in a package."

"I see, sir. Is it yours?"

"What?"

"The finger."

"God, no!"

"I see, sir. I think we can arrange an appointment for you tomorrow morning. If you will just hold the line, I'll—"

"It can't be tomorrow! Don't you understand? This is serious: I'm not accustomed to getting fingers in packages."

"I see, sir." There was a pause. "What is your name, please?"

"Roger Carr. C-a-r-r."

"Carr...Carr...Roger...Carr, Roger." Obviously she was checking his name against some sort of list. But he was startled to hear her say briskly, "I'm sorry, sir. You can see someone here immediately. Do you wish to meet at the consulate, or elsewhere?"

"At the consulate, of course. Why the hell would I want to meet anywhere else?"

This seemed to confuse her. She made little flustered noises at the other end of the line. Then: "Yes, sir. We will be expecting you."

"Fine," Carr said, and hung up.

The American consulate, 3 Rue Dr. Barety, had the clean, rather friendly look of a place that had no function more unpleasant or difficult than extending an occasional visa or renewing an expired passport. Carr went through the swinging glass doors and stopped in front of a pert, uplifted receptionist.

"Ah, Mr. Morgan," the girl said. "Everyone here will be very glad to see you." She pointed down the hall, flashed a clean little smile, and pressed a button on her desk console. "Third door on the right."

"My name isn't Morgan," Carr said. "It's Roger Carr."

The receptionist blushed. "I'm sorry, sir. Of course. I'm new at the job, you see, and these things are so complicated."

Carr stood dumbfounded.

"I promise it won't happen again," the girl said. "You can count on me." She watched him patiently, expecting him to leave. "It *is* the third door on the right."

Feeling strange, Carr walked down the hall, which was narrow, painted white, and spotlessly clean. Solid pine doors opened off both sides. The third door on the right had a shiny brass nameplate that said "Mr. Gorman." Carr knocked.

"Come in."

He opened the door, to see a compact man with a crew-cut rising from his desk. "Well, isn't this a jolly surprise? Coming back in from the cold, eh? After raising hell with my ulcers, you decide to pop up. High time, Morgan, high time. I must say frankly that you've given me more bad moments—"

Carr said nothing. The little man peered intently at him, screwing up his eyes.

"You're not Morgan, are you?" He paused, then seemed to think better of his statement. "I mean," he said hurriedly, "I don't want to be insulting, for all I know you've had a little PS, or been in a scrape of some kind and gotten bashed up. I hope you haven't been bashed up."

"No," Carr said.

The two men stood looking across the room at each other. Gorman was wearing a dark blue, chalk-stripe suit, with a gray tie. On another man it would have looked solidly diplomatic; on Gorman, it gave the impression he was trying to play Little Caesar. There was an uncomfortable silence.

"You never were much of a talker, were you?" Gorman said.

"What's PS?"

"Plastic surgery.... Say, you're *not* Morgan, are you?"

"I never said I was."

Gorman scratched his head. "That's strange," he said. He

seemed suddenly embarrassed and looked down at his desk. He poked among the papers strewn across it, and finally unearthed his pipe. "How do you like that?" He continued to scratch his head while he examined the pipe minutely. Then he seemed to remember Carr, and looked up.

"Well," he said. "That changes things, doesn't it? If you're not Morgan, you must be somebody else. I don't know who you are. Who are you? Do come in, and shut the door behind you. Thanks. Nasty draft, that's the reason—for the door, I mean. My name is Ralph Gorman. Good to meet you. Have a seat."

Carr shook hands and dropped into a tan leather chair. The other man sat down and carefully filled his pipe. "What can I do for you?"

"I have a problem," Carr began.

"Oh well, I would have expected that. Nearly everybody who comes here has a problem." He chuckled nervously. "After all, when do you turn to your consulate? When you have a problem. That's what we're here for." Gorman hesitated. "You do look a hell of a lot like Morgan," he said. "You're not kidding me, are you? I mean, it's not very funny. Really it's not." He looked at Carr, pleading.

"No, I'm not Morgan," Carr said. "Who's Morgan?"

"An attaché who is coming to the office. We expected him two days ago, and now—but that's not important. You have a problem."

"Yes," Carr said. "There was a shooting near the flower market yesterday. I was involved."

All right, Gorman thought to himself. Here we go. Now you have to decide how to play it. Now you have to decide whether you're going to let this guy off the hook.

"Oh, you're the one," he said. "I'm surprised. I thought you would have come straight here afterward."

You might have done that, he thought. It would have saved all sorts of problems.

"Well, it was very confusing," Carr said.

"I'm sure. I read about it in the papers," Gorman said, lighting his pipe. "Terrible thing. Awful."

"There's more."

Gorman's eyebrows went up over the pipe.

Carr told him about the interview with the swarthy man, and then about the package. "This is it," he said, tossing it onto the desk.

"What's this? A finger?"

"Yes," Carr said.

"I'll be damned," Gorman said, holding it under the desk lamp. "It *is* a finger."

Carr waited.

"Isn't that amazing!"

"Yes," Carr said.

"Is that all?"

"Isn't that enough?"

"I meant, was there anything else—any further incidents?"

"No. I came straight here after I received the package. There was this note with it."

Gorman took the note. Then there was a buzz from the intercom.

"Yes?" Gorman said.

"Amory on line one," the secretary said. "Eggs."

"All right." Gorman picked up the phone. Eggs meant that he would have to use the scrambler. Gorman enjoyed talking over the scrambler; it gave him an important feeling. He pressed the button and said, "Hello?"

The Paris chief wasted no time. He demanded to know why the hell Gorman had been sitting on his ass for two days, doing nothing.

"A small confusion," Gorman said. "We thought Morgan was here."

The chief pointed out that Gorman had been told he wasn't. Morgan was, in fact, still in London.

"I know," Gorman said. "Things have just been cleared up at this end." He did not look at Carr.

The chief wanted to know what the trouble had been.

"Double-take. Overhang."

The chief interpreted this correctly to mean that it was mistaken identity, and that Gorman had somebody in the room, so he couldn't be specific. Amory asked how close the similarity was.

"Very."

Too bad, the chief said.

"What should I do?"

What did Gorman think he should do? There wasn't much choice, was there?

"No, I guess not."

Had anybody attempted to murder the poor bastard?

"No. It looks like intact recovery."

Well, that was all right. They'd kidnap him, and find out he wasn't the real thing. Or maybe they wouldn't bother, if he kept his nose clean. If the guy wasn't dead already, the chief said, it probably meant there was some confusion in their minds.

"I suppose so," Gorman said doubtfully.

Well, it was just too damned bad, the chief said. But it was also convenient as hell. Paris would get a new killer down right away for Gorman. This lookalike would be a perfect decoy to divert them while they slipped a new man onto the scene. Was that all right?

"Fine," Gorman said. He still didn't look at Carr.

Try to cheer the bastard up, the chief said. Give him confidence. Have him go about his business and be normal. As long as he stays away from the Associates, he ought to be just fine.

"All right," Gorman said.

The chief hung up.

Carr had been listening with absolute attention. He had a feeling this conversation was somehow involved with him, but he couldn't figure it out.

"Now then, Mr. Carr, about your own problem." Gorman bent forward over his desk and doodled on a pad. He was frowning. "As I understand it, you have received a great deal of annoyance since your arrival in Nice, and you want to know what to do about it, and what it all means."

Carr nodded, and lit a cigarette.

"I've given those up," Gorman said.

"What?"

"Cigarettes. Given them up. Bad for you. You know the surgeon general's report, all that—it's been very influential within the government. None of the top diplomatic or military people smoke cigarettes anymore. Not if they want to get ahead. You just have to cut them out. Why, at parties, the aides don't carry lighters anymore. Makes it a little hard on the wives who haven't quit, I can tell you."

"Look," Carr said, "I don't want to change the subject—"

"Of course, of course. Your problem. I assume you've seen the police?"

"Yes."

"Do you remember the name of the officer who interviewed you?"

"He was a big brute named Vascard."

"Hmmm. I don't think I know him. I'm still rather new to

the office, you see. Recently in from Amsterdam. You have to give a man time to adjust, learn the ropes, the office routine. I keep telling the staff here—" He broke off and looked curiously at Carr. "What explanation did they give you?"

"Who?"

"The police, of course."

"None. None at all, as a matter of fact. There were no explanations offered."

"Well, now, you know, this is one of those ticklish situations we often encounter in diplomatic work. Tact, patience, sensitivity—that's what it takes." He drummed his fingers on the table, apparently in a demonstration of his sensitivity. "Reading between the lines, that sort of thing." He looked at Carr and cocked his head. "Surely they told you something."

"Nothing at all."

Gorman was reassured. "Well, then, perhaps I should explain the situation as I see it."

"You're very kind," Carr said, a little annoyed.

"Yes. Well. I'm still feeling my way in this part of the world, bear that in mind. But the situation is something like this: the Riviera is a very rich area, and a gambling area. That is a rare and unbeatable combination. It draws unsavory characters like flies. Gangsters, con men, second-story men, card sharps. The whole range. In Nice, the police like to think these people have their headquarters in Marseilles, with the smugglers. In Marseilles, they like to think the headquarters is in Nice, with the Corsicans. The fact is, both towns have grave problems. Feuds are common. I think you have somehow managed to get involved, and that you have therefore suffered these…indignities. Now, I remember a somewhat similar case we had in Amsterdam. Not really similar, of course. Say analogous. But we handled that one quite well, and I think the same solution may apply here. Frankly, if I were you, I would ignore the whole thing. Go about your business. Act naturally."

"You're kidding," Carr said. "Act naturally?"

"That's right," Gorman said, puffing at his pipe. "It strikes me as the only sensible thing to do. This will all blow over in a day or so, I'm sure. In the meantime, just pretend nothing has happened. Just act naturally."

When Carr had gone, Gorman sat forward in his chair and doodled furiously. He knew, just as Amory knew, that Carr's chances of remaining alive were less than even. He was convenient, no doubt about that. But it was very, very ugly.

He sighed again. Scratch one nice, confused American, he thought. He picked up the finger and looked at it again, noticing the clean way it had been severed. The work of a scalpel, for sure.

"Act naturally," he said aloud, to himself.

What a laugh.

Carr was laughing. The music blasted through the small, darkened room, amplified by several hundred watts of stereo equipment. Across from him on the dance floor, Anne was doing the monkey with a vengeance, whipping her pelvis in a precise, exciting way. She, too, was laughing, because he amused her.

They were in a Saint-Tropez discothèque called, inevitably, Whiskey à Go-Go. There were hundreds of places all along the coast with the same name, and he had never found anyone who knew what the name meant.

The crowd here was typical—men in tuxedos and women in floor-length gowns, dancing hip to hip with young boys in jeans and child-women in tight striped sweaters and unbelievably tight stretch pants. Half the dancers were barefooted.

Many of the girls wore the clinging jerseys with the embroidered white ship's steering wheel right between their breasts; in recent years, this had become a Saint-Trop symbol.

The record changed, and Carr recognized it as "Carol," a Chuck Berry tune sung by Johnny Hallyday in French. It was loud, and the place swung. He was feeling good.

They had had a pleasant dinner at Mouscardins, after a rapid drive from Cannes along Route 98. It had been a beautiful drive, twisting first along the rocky, rugged coastline known as the Esterel, then to the flatland from Saint Raphael and Fréjus to Saint-Tropez. They could have taken the high-speed auto route, of course, but that was inland, and Anne wanted to go along the coast.

Now, with a good meal and several drinks inside him, Carr was feeling very good indeed. Anne's face was flushed with exertion. Anne was a good dancer—as he might have expected—moving expertly on high heels, her movements perfectly controlled. He knew that girls who danced well were good in bed.

It was funny, he thought, as the record switched to the Rolling Stones, doing "Route 66." He didn't think about getting her into the sack anymore. He felt no urgency; partly because a sort of unspoken agreement had grown up between them that they would eventually go to bed, and partly because, quite simply, he liked her. He enjoyed being with her, doing almost anything with her. Nothing else seemed to matter.

Victor Jenning, accompanied by two blank-faced bodyguards, stepped into the garage on the outskirts of Monaco. It was a large place, smelling of grease and gasoline, paint and oil. Yet despite its size, the little car dominated the room.

It was low, cigar-shaped, with huge wheels that nonetheless left it a bare three feet off the ground. The snout was oval, the body running sleekly back to the cramped cockpit, set in front of the engine. In the rear, the car ended abruptly, squarely, with two exhaust pipes protruding rather oddly.

This was Jenning's car, and he had come to love and hate it. He turned to the single mechanic who was standing by the tool bench.

"What's the problem?"

"It's Gerard. He hasn't come in since yesterday morning."

Jenning thought back. Gerard was an assistant mechanic, a new man, one he did not remember well. He was a short fellow, swarthy, cocky. "You've called his home?"

"Yes. His wife hasn't seen him. She's upset."

Jenning frowned. The Monaco race was less than a week away. "Can you get somebody else?"

The mechanic shrugged. "I think so."

"Good?"

"Good enough."

"All right. I'll try to look into this business." Damned hired help. Always running out on you. It was so difficult to get a good, steady man. Jenning nodded toward the car. "How is it?"

"Okay. I think we've licked the timing. And third has been beefed up."

Jenning nodded. The transmission was crucial in the Monaco G.P.; it took a tremendous beating over the short, twisting course.

He gave the mechanic a few words of encouragement and left the garage.

Jenning was a Formula I race driver, and reasonably good. Not first rank—that took more than he had, both in ability and dedication. He was unusual, in that racing was not his life; he made his money in guns, and raced only for his own amusement. At least, that was how he preferred to look at it; he did not like to think of himself as hooked, though he knew he was.

Sooner or later, that car—or another like it—would kill him. At thirty-nine he was getting old, and the lap times were faster with each succeeding year. He knew, in an isolated corner of his mind, that more than 180 drivers had been killed racing since the war. He knew it, and he did not think about it, any more than he thought about the necessity for the two men walking with him in the cool night air of Monte Carlo. One was to his left, a little in front. The other, to his right, a little behind. Both were armed, and he needed them.

It was all a matter of risks—what interested you, and what you were prepared to put up with. Victor Jenning had chosen his life many years ago, and he was satisfied with it.

Preparation for the shipment was going smoothly. Sunday evening, after the Monaco race, he would sign the final papers, and his job would be finished. He dismissed the possibility that he would not be there to pick up his pen.

Liseau scanned the faces of his five associates and sipped a *lait grenadine* to settle his stomach.

"He will sign the papers after the race," he said. "That has been confirmed by our most charming and close source."

There was mild laughter in the room. He allowed himself a smile.

"Thus we can proceed with the final planning."

He looked again at these men, carefully. His mind was not on the plans. He was almost certain that, in the next twenty-four hours, the plans would have to be changed radically. He had considered carefully the stubborn little man who had not talked, and he was quite sure what was going on.

Someone in their midst, one of the five faces before him, was going to go over. At first, it had seemed impossible to him, but now he had grown accustomed to the idea. The shipment was worth over thirty million dollars American, and its significance was still greater. Betrayal, he thought grimly, would be very good business.

His hope now lay in the American—the man who was so unpredictable, so strange. Only the American knew what had been discussed at that meeting in the hotel, when the microphones had been torn out. Only the American could provide a clue.

And he had indeed rushed to the consulate that evening. Perhaps, after all, he was an agent. Well, they would soon know. Liseau had two plans for this man—one of them was certain to work.

Chapter XIV

Roger Carr awoke feeling strange. He got out of bed, walked to the balcony, and walked back into the room, trying to understand. Something was bothering him, something not quite right.

Then it hit him: no hangover. None at all, not the slightest trace.

Well, he thought. What do you know? It wasn't such a bad feeling after all.

He had dropped Anne off at a café in Cannes the night before, after twenty minutes of heavy necking in the car. Normally, he would have considered that a very poor conclusion to the evening, but somehow it seemed to him just wonderful.

He went into the bathroom and smiled at himself in the mirror. He looked disgracefully cheerful and awake.

"Thank God none of the boys in the office can see me now," he said. And he winked at the reflected face.

After an enormous breakfast, he set out toward Graff's office, but decided to stop for a cup of coffee first. It was a perfect day, and he was feeling lazy and relaxed. He turned toward the Avenue de la Victoire, one of the main streets of Nice—a broad avenue lined with a double row of plane trees which cast a speckled shadow over the street and sidewalk. It was a touch of rural France in the bustling city, a typically Provençal street which might have been anywhere—Avignon, Arles, Aix. He paused at a newsstand to buy an international edition of the *Times*, and walked along toward the nearest sidewalk café. As he crossed the Rue Biscarrat, it occurred to him that he should stop by and see an old friend of his, the proprietor of the restaurant L'Estragon. It was an unpretentious little place, where he had often gone on his first visit to the city—the food was superb, and the proprietor, a tall hawk-nosed man who looked rather like De Gaulle, had a very entertaining philosophy about women.

But it was too early, he decided. There would be time to renew old acquaintances later. He went on to the first café, which was crowded with a midmorning throng, and was able to find a small table toward the rear. He ordered a *café noir*. Two men squeezed into a table next to his, crowding him; he almost said something, but decided not to bother. He turned his attention to the people walking by, noting that *le style Américain* was the current fashion rage: the French teenagers paraded past in sneakers, faded dungarees, and button-down madras shirts.

He opened the newspaper and read for several minutes. His coffee did not come, and he looked around for his waiter. The man was nowhere in sight. It was, he thought, the indolence bred from having the tip automatically added to the bill. Finally, Carr spotted him coming forward, with the coffee and a glass of water on a tray. One of the men at the next table hurriedly got up, nearly knocking Carr over; it was irritating, but before Carr could say anything, the man had pushed past and walked over to the waiter, talking to him. For a moment, Carr could not see the waiter—the other man blocked his view.

Carr felt a tap on the shoulder, and looked over to see the second of the two men at the table next to him. *"Le service,"* said the man, "is very slow here. It is necessary to be patient."

Carr nodded, thinking that this man showed a very unFrench lack of reserve. He looked back at the waiter, now

coming toward him with the coffee; the first man was gone
—he had probably asked directions to the men's room. The
waiter served the coffee and turned his attention to the next
table. Carr resumed reading his newspaper.

"Un *café express*," he heard the man say. That was odd,
Carr thought. Perhaps the first man had gone for good. He
continued reading and sipped at the coffee, which was strong
and good. The Parisians were having trouble with parking
regulations again, and there was a mysterious flu epidemic
in Bristol. He found an article on the latest Supreme Court
ruling on reapportionment, and read with interest for about
two minutes.

Then he began to feel strange.

He dropped his paper on the table, knocking over his
drink. A wave of nausea hit him. His stomach churned, and
he felt cold and very woozy. The man at the next table
peered over; Carr scarcely saw him. His vision was getting
blurry. Things swam in and out of focus.

"Are you all right, monsieur?" It was the man next to him.

"Yes, yes," Carr said. He was looking at the street before
him, at the crowd; things drifted into fuzziness, then back to
clarity, then fuzzy once again. He could see the first man—
the one who had talked to the waiter—standing at the curb,
looking back at Carr.

"Pardon, my friend, but you do not look well. May I get
you a doctor?" He felt a hand grip him firmly—tightly, ex-
cruciatingly—just above the elbow.

Sluggishly, as if in slow motion, he shook it off. He said
nothing. He tried to stand, tripped, and fell back into his chair
again.

There was no sound anywhere; the world around him was
strangely, deathly silent. His head seemed to be rolling on
his neck.

He saw the black Citroën pull up in front of the café, and the man at the curb open the door.

"Come, my friend." It was a voice, very loud, from nowhere. Carr felt himself lifted up, floating away toward the street. He was very light; his body weighed nothing.

Then he passed out completely.

Silence, painful and hot. Someone was kicking his head, repeatedly, snapping it back and forth. He opened his eyes to bright, hot light, and shut them again. Silence. He was sweating, and his clothes stuck to him. He heard a ticking, smelled an awful smell.

"Coward," a voice said. "Open your eyes. I can't wait here all day."

He turned toward the voice, shaded his eyes, and tried again. For a moment he couldn't see anything except a bright blur, and then he began to make things out. Gray things, black things, a white face.

"You are a stubborn man, Mr. Carr. Don't you know when you are well off?"

"Hello, Vascard," Carr said. "What are you doing here?" He winced at the sudden pain that streaked across his forehead. "Where *is* here?"

"The police station. You are on a cot in a room we occasionally use for interrogation of suspects."

Carr groaned. "What kind of suspects? Cripples?"

Vascard sighed and blew a stream of cigarette smoke toward Carr. "Interrogation," he said, "is sometimes strenuous."

"What's that horrible smell?"

"You were sick."

"Oh."

"You no doubt want to know how you got here. It was purest luck, I can tell you. Some of your friends were in the process of hustling you into a black Citroën when a young sergeant stopped them. You were apparently drunk, and this sergeant, who is new to the job and eager to assert himself, had you arrested for disorderly conduct. It was, after all, shameful to be drunk at ten in the morning. Your friends protested, but to no avail. A police car brought you here, and you were recognized by somebody at the desk. You've been here ever since."

"How long is that?"

"About an hour. We had a doctor in to look at you, and he said it was scopolamine. How do you feel?"

"Terrible."

Vascard smiled bleakly. "I worry about you, my friend. Why don't you take a little vacation?"

"I *am* taking a little vacation."

"I know. But the Riviera does not seem to agree with you."

"Funny you should mention that."

"Surely your business is not so pressing that you must stay here?"

"Why are you suddenly so solicitous?" Carr asked, frowning.

"Let's say I have changed my mind about you." He looked down at Carr's face, pale and tired. Nobody is that good an actor, he thought. I should have known from the first. The consulate must be fiendish to allow him to stay in France. "I really think a little trip is the best thing. Seriously, what keeps you here?"

"A girl."

"Ah." His eyes lit up. "That is a reason any Frenchman understands, though I confess I would not have expected it from you. The world is full of girls."

"I like this one."

Vascard shrugged. "It could happen to anyone." He paused. "You received a telegram yesterday. What was in it?"

"You get around, Vascard."

"You are discussing my business, and if you are surprised I do it well, I am insulted."

"It was from my client, advising me to buy a particular villa."

"Ah. And you are making the arrangements?"

"Yes."

"Good. You should be able to finish in a day or so, I think. Then, you ought to do yourself a favor and leave Nice. As for the girl, take her with you somewhere—Morocco, perhaps, or Madrid. I don't care. Do we understand each other?"

"Yes," Carr said, and groaned again.

"Stay here as long as you like. I will have them send coffee to you in a few minutes." He laughed. "It is a *spécialité de la maison.* And after, you can take a cab back to the hotel. Just be careful"—he poked his cigarette at Carr—"and remember that a man should not expect to be lucky more than twice."

The door shut, and Carr was alone.

"Don't worry about it," Liseau said easily.

Brauer looked doubtful.

"I have a second solution. It cannot possibly fail," Liseau said.

If he had felt any better, Roger Carr would have been acutely embarrassed as he walked into the Negresco. His hair was matted, and his suit looked like a crumpled paper bag; his shirt had somehow been torn, and there was a dark stain on his trouser leg. He smelled quite distinctly of dried coffee grounds.

But Carr just didn't care. His meager reserves of energy and concentration were focused on the problem of getting from the cab all the way across the lobby, and over to the elevator. When he finally stumbled into his room, he leaned against the door to shut it. He felt terribly weak.

He went into the bathroom, turned on the water, and began slapping it against his face. The water was icy cold, and it helped clear his head a little.

"Aren't you even going to say hello?"

Anne was standing in the bathroom doorway. She wore a yellow cotton dress, very simple, and she looked wonderful.

"I don't feel so good."

She glanced down at his rumpled clothes, then back up to his bloodshot eyes and pale face. "You don't look so good."

Carr nodded sluggishly. Water dripped off his chin into the sink. "How did you get up here?"

"Well, I waited for you in the lobby, and then decided you'd overslept. We were supposed to meet at noon, remember? So I went to the desk—"

"I've got to have a shower," Carr said, rubbing his head. "Take my clothes, will you? Keep talking, I'm listening."

"The man at the desk said you'd gone out at ten." She helped him out of his suit jacket. "So I decided to wait for you here."

"How does that work?" Carr asked, peeling off his shirt.

"No problem. They're very nice about it—it's a discreet hotel, you know. Do you want your suit cleaned?"

"Thanks. They'll pick it up if you call down." He turned on the shower. "Oh, and have them send up some drinks. Whatever you want, and a large orange juice for me. I won't be long."

The stinging spray was a blessing. He could feel much of his weariness washing away with the dried and salty sweat; when he came out, he decided he was as close to human as he could hope to be for the rest of the day. Anne was at the balcony, gazing out at the sea. "I've laid some clothes out for you," she said. "On the chair."

Carr dressed quickly. That girl has taste, he thought, as he put on gray worsted slacks, a white oxford shirt, a wine-red ascot and a navy blazer. She came back as he was slipping on his shoes.

"Better?"

"Much. Where's my orange juice?"

"In the corner."

He went over, sat down, and took a slow, cool drink. Anne gave him a lighted cigarette and a soft kiss on the cheek. She sat down on the bed opposite him, holding her drink in her lap, waiting patiently.

"I suppose," Carr said, "I should explain."

"My father taught me never to pry," Anne said, "but you did look pretty funny when you walked in. Were you in a fight?"

"Not exactly," Carr said, and before he knew it he found himself telling the whole story to her, beginning with the first day—the plane, the phone calls, the girl with the gun, the shooting at the flower market. He finished with the finger, and what had happened to him that morning. It felt good to talk, to tell it all to another person.

No, he thought. It felt good to tell it to her.

She listened in silence, looking down at her drink, twisting the glass in her hands. She was about to speak when the telephone rang. It was Graff.

"I have talked with Signor Perrani. He is most anxious to meet you. Could we say this afternoon, at three?"

"Fine."

"Excellent. If you will meet me first at my office, I will drive you—"

"I'd rather meet you at the villa," Carr said, looking at Anne. "At three. Is that all right?"

"Perfectly all right," Graff said, but he sounded displeased.

Carr rang off and turned back to Anne. "You look very nice," he said, "there on the bed."

"You really must be feeling better."

"Not that much better," he admitted, as a sudden throbbing pain pounded his head. "I think I need lunch. Shall we send some up?"

"Well," Anne said, looking suddenly shy, "I was hoping… I have food for a picnic. Very simple. Do you feel up to it?"

It sounded wonderful to him, and he said so. "Where shall we go?"

"I know just the place," Anne said.

When they got to the car, Carr suggested she drive. His head still ached without warning, and he had found even the short walk from the hotel exhausting. Anne drove smoothly, sitting very straight in the bucket seat and letting her hair blow in the wind. Watching her, Carr realized he was happy.

"Where are you taking me?"

"It's a surprise."

They drove north out of Nice, up the Rue de la République, and he thought she must be heading for the Moyenne Corniche. But she passed the turnoff, continuing straight north through the industrial region of La Trinitie. This was a poor area; the land was arid and barren, and the little farmhouses were no better than shacks. They passed sand and gravel pits, the cement and gas works in the region of Drap, and then began to climb into the hills to the east. The Alfa went into a series of true hairpin turns, cutting back and forth up the rock face of a broad valley. Anne handled the car deftly; she seemed to know the road well. But Carr couldn't help feeling twinges of concern as the rock wall loomed up, slid by, then loomed up again. The tires squealed. She was driving very fast.

"Look right," she said. "There's a beautiful perched village called Peillon coming up." Carr saw it, stuck high on a rock crag.

"You seem to have a thing about peaks," he said.

"Wait till you see where we're going."

They continued north, Carr watching the signs curiously as they flashed by.

"I don't think I've ever been here before," he said.

"Most people haven't. That's why I like it. Only a few German tourists, intent on seeing *everything,* bother with Peillon, and even they don't go farther."

"Are we getting near?"

"Soon."

They shot over a rise, and down into a town called Peille. Carr had never heard of it. It was a peaceful little village, with a large shaded square.

"Looks nice," Carr said.

"Dull." She sped through the center of town, ignoring a startled policeman who blew his whistle at them as they went by. "It won't be long now."

The road began to descend, and the signs of industry—the trucks, the dust, the markers reading "Sortie de Camions"— disappeared. They came around the side of a broad hill, and suddenly they were plunged deep in a narrow green gorge.

Carr sucked in his breath, and Anne seemed pleased by his reaction. "It's unexpected, isn't it? It's not very deep— only about five hundred feet or so—but I like it. It's so green and restful. This is the gorge of the Peillon River, actually. There are several better ones around, like Verdon and Cians, but I've always preferred this."

"You come here often?"

Anne didn't answer. She had slowed the car and was looking intently at the side of the road. The road was cut into the rock wall, partway up the canyon; the drop over the pavement was so sheer, Carr could not tell how far below the water was, though he could hear it rushing and boiling.

"There's one particular place," Anne said, still watching the side of the road. She pulled over. "Here. Come on."

They got out, and Carr walked to the low stone wall lining the lip of the road. The water was at least forty feet below them, a narrow fast stream barely a yard wide. It continued to cut an ever-narrowing slit into the stone; the lowest section of the gorge was so narrow it didn't seem a man could get through if he waded down the stream.

"Come on," Anne said. "Grab the lunch basket and let's go." She was smiling, impatient. She held out her hand.

"You're going down there?" Carr looked at the drop—it was not sheer, but it was very steep, and the rocks were worn smooth as a woman's backside, and covered with fine sand. It was insane, he thought.

"Follow me," she said. They walked a few yards down the road. "Now," Anne said, "just watch me, and do exactly as I do. Put your hands and feet where I do, and hold onto the bushes the way I do. It's very simple if you go slowly." She slipped off her sling-back high heels. "And take off your shoes—it's easier that way."

"I don't feel very good," Carr protested. He was telling the truth. His headache had returned, and his legs felt undependably rubbery.

"It's worth it." She started down the slope. Carr could see there was a path, of sorts, but it was overgrown with brambles, and made dangerous by pockets of sand and dried leaves. There wasn't a firm foothold in sight.

He watched her go, noticing how she first held onto the slim trees near the road, then stretched her arms out for balance, and stepped carefully across the smooth, almost polished rock. She slipped once, momentarily, but regained her balance. The sound of the water below was a roar in his ears.

I'll never make it, he thought.

She turned and called to him, but she was now almost halfway down, and her voice was lost in the rushing water. She looked at him, shading her eyes from the sun with her hand. Then she waved him on, impatiently.

I'm a fool, he thought.

He started down. The first few yards were not so bad. He could hold onto the trees, and the lunch basket did not get in his way. But soon he had left the trees, and faced a smooth hump of rock which he had to work his way across—it was impossible to go straight down. He began cautiously, and became immediately nervous and tense.

It was the worst thing he could have done.

Carr slipped, fell, and slid several yards down the rock before his flailing hands clutched one of the clumps of heavy grass which grew out of the rock wherever there was a bit of dirt and moisture.

He did not move, but tried to decide what to do next. He was lying on his stomach on a gently bulging rock surface, and he could feel his legs sticking out over the bump. The water below was very loud. He began to sweat.

All he could see in front of him was the lunch basket, which rested farther up on the rock, where he had dropped it when he fell. Now, as he watched, it began to slide—just as he had, and right toward him. It gathered speed as it went.

Oh, Christ, he thought. It's going to hit me right in the face.

A second later, it slammed into his nose. But he hung on to the rock, and didn't slide farther.

Crazy broad, he thought.

"Give me your hand."

Anne crouched over him, and he allowed her to help him to his knees. "I'd better take the food," she said briskly. He stood slowly, trying to keep his legs from shaking.

"Take off your shoes, and stay relaxed. It's the only way."

"I really don't feel so good."

Anne made a face and continued down. He slipped off his shoes and socks and followed after her.

As it turned out, the rest of the descent was simpler. They came to a place where the rocks were less sandy, and he was able to get a firmer hold. And although he refused to admit it, his balance was much improved in bare feet. As they approached the level of the river, they found more young trees and sturdy foliage, and Carr managed the last part without difficulty.

The sound of the water, reverberating off the rocks, was astonishingly loud. He looked at the churning stream—at this point only two feet wide and a foot deep—in wonder.

"From here," Anne said, "we go through there." She pointed along the stream, past a place where it cut a particularly narrow cleft. Sunlight played on the water, throwing a flickering fishnet of light on the rock walls. To the right, upstream, was a small noisy waterfall. Carr looked up—up to the road above, and farther up to the high crest of the canyon, hazy in the bright sunlight.

They set off, stepping from one stone to the next. Anne was agile; her long body moved quickly, surely. Carr followed along behind, carefully estimating the distance between the slippery stones, feeling retarded. They passed through the cleft, and came out into a small pool of calm, deep water. Anne pointed to a small crescent of sand, tucked back behind two large boulders, completely hidden from the road above.

"Like it?"

"It's gorgeous," Carr said, dropping onto the sand.

"I will have to reform you," Anne said. "Your puns are quite miserable." She opened the lunch basket and passed him the bottle of wine. "Stick that in the water, would you?" When Carr looked at the label, she said, "It's good wine, I think. Côtes de Provence. Not very good, but good. I don't claim to know anything about wine, and besides, it would be a waste of time. I smoke too much. Anybody who smokes and starts reeling off vineyards and years is kidding himself—or you. He's just a vintage mumbler."

Carr, a vintage mumbler himself, nodded silently. He slipped the bottle into the water, propping it between two small rocks. The water was clear and cold; his fingers were numb when he took them out.

Coming back, he found she had spread a white tablecloth. "What style," he said.

"That's all right. You'll be drinking wine from the bottle."

He laughed. She poked among the contents of the basket. "I've got a quarter of a chicken, grilled with herbs, some good *pâté*, and lots of onions and red cabbage and pimento and things. What would you like?"

"I'll have whatever you're having."

"I doubt it. I'm having this." She withdrew from the basket an orange, some lettuce, and a bit of cheese.

"The chicken," Carr decided, looking doubtfully at her.

They ate in silence, passing the wine bottle back and forth, hearing the water gently swirl at their feet before it bubbled over the next waterfall downstream. Carr finished the chicken, and Anne made him a sandwich, flavoring the mild *pâté* with onions and pimentos and fiery green peppers.

"Quite a domestic, aren't you?" he said, watching her work.

"Not really." She shook her hair, and looked up at the sun. It struck Carr as an embarrassed reaction. She had a strange look on her face, as if she were puzzled at herself, or at him.

Later, when they had finished the wine and were leaning back, smoking cigarettes, she said, "What are you going to do now?"

"About my problem? The finger and everything?"

She nodded.

"I don't know. There doesn't seem to be much I can do. Buy the villa and clear out, I guess—and hope nothing happens to me in the next day or so."

"Maybe it would be better to move out of Nice, to Cannes or Menton, or across the Italian border."

"I thought of that," Carr said, "but it might look suspicious, and I don't want to give that impression to these people, whoever they are. Besides, the hotel would be furious—I've been trouble enough already."

"That's your business," she said, "and it's theirs to put up with the whims of the customer. If anyone makes a face, chew them out."

"Tough girl."

"Yeah." She curled her lip. "You should have seen me when I smoked cigars."

"When was that?"

"A few years ago. I started it as a kind of joke, smoking cigarillos, and you should have seen the jowls quiver on the old blokes. They couldn't believe it. It worked fine."

"Why'd you give it up?"

"They tasted awful, that's why. I used to go to bed green." She flicked the cigarette into the water, and watched it carried off by the current. "How are you feeling?"

"Much better, but a little wary of the climb up."

"It's easy, going up," she said, "and we'd better start if you intend to make that three-o'clock appointment. You can drop me off in Menton."

"No I can't. You're coming with me."

"You assume a lot," she said, but he could see she was pleased.

"It's a trick I learned from some girl," Carr said, and he kissed her.

Chapter XV

The Villa Perrani lay in the wooded hills between Villefranche and Monaco, looking out over Cap Ferrat, which
stretched like a vast verdant hand into the blue Mediterranean.
The house itself, an enormous, rambling structure, was built
at the turn of the century in imitation Second Empire style,
with an elaborate facade of turrets, curlicues, and balconies.
Despite the ornamentations, the villa somehow managed a
drab appearance, Carr thought.

Anne was more direct. As they drove up the tree-lined
gravel drive she said, "It's bloody vulgar. Who told you to
buy this place?"

"The boss," Carr said.

"Well, at least the flowers are nice." Blossoms were everywhere, neatly maintained, providing brilliant patches of red,
purple, and orange around the grounds.

They were met at the door by Graff, who looked his
unctuous best. He reminded Carr of an otter just emerged
from a stream.

"My friend, Miss Crittenden," Carr said.

With a theatrical flourish, Graff kissed her hand. *"En-
chanté."* He smirked slightly, just to show Carr that he thought
Miss Crittenden was far too pretty to be merely a friend.
Anne saw it, and blushed angrily. They walked up the marble
steps to the broad mahogany doors.

"I have just been talking with Signor Perrani," Graff said.
From his gravely self-important tone, it might as well have
been the Pope. "Signor Perrani is in a foul mood, I am afraid.

I suspect it is mistress trouble. The Italians cannot handle women, they are always in difficulty. But I hope you will not allow yourself to be prejudiced by his rudeness."

Carr said his interest was purely business. They passed through the doors into an oversized hall, dominated by a gilt and crystal chandelier—a giant cascade of glass beads, replete with cherubs and swans. To the left, a stately marble staircase led to the upper floor.

A butler approached from one corner and announced that Signor Perrani awaited them in the library. They were led through a pair of double doors into a long rectangular room.

Books were everywhere. The ceiling must have been twenty feet high, and the bookshelves went all the way up. In the center of the room was a large fireplace, and facing it were three comfortable sofas in black leather. Signor Perrani was seated on one, reading. He looked up, surveyed the three, and fixed his eyes on Carr.

"Monsieur Carr?"

"*Oui.*"

"*Bon.*" He turned to the butler. "Serve Monsieur Graff and the lady tea in the living room," he said. "Something stronger if they prefer."

The butler bowed. Carr and the man were alone.

"*Parlate italiano?*"

"*Non. Seulement français. Beaucoup de mauvais français,*" he added.

Perrani laughed, rose, and shook Carr's hand. "I am about to have my afternoon brandy. Will you join me?"

"*Avec plaisir.*"

"Good." Perrani poured two glasses from a crystal decanter with a silver top. Carr studied him. He was tall, dressed casually in a blue silk shirt and dark blue slacks. He wore espadrilles without socks. His hair was white, made even whiter by his tan, and he had the easy manner of a comfortably and elegantly rich man.

"To good business," Perrani said. They both drank. "Please sit down. I am sorry you had to put up with that pig, Graff. He has contacts among the kind of purchasers I am after, though how they tolerate him is beyond me. A filthy fellow. Do I insult a friend?"

"No, indeed."

"I had hoped not." Perrani appraised Carr. "You are the first prospective buyer, and I must say you have moved quickly. I spoke to Graff only three days ago. May I ask how you discovered the villa was for sale?"

Carr explained about the telegram.

"Your client and I must have mutual friends," Perrani mused. "That is good. Who is your client, Mr. Carr?"

Carr told him about the governor, and began to relate something of the politician's past record when Perrani held up his hand,

"You need not praise him in my presence. I am not interested in the buyer because—as the pig would have you believe—I am concerned for my neighbors, or the maintenance of this house which I love. Money settles all such problems. Money buys the maintenance of the villa, and money will buy the respect of the people living around. They may choose to whisper among themselves about taste, but even that is trivial. What difference does it make if he owns a Maserati or a Bentley? None, really. And even if he were a gangster—well, some of my best friends are gangsters."

Carr nodded politely.

"It is to be expected," Perrani said, "There are more rich people here than can be reasonably accounted for by inheritance, keen business sense, or luck. Many of them must be crooks." He sipped his brandy. "By and large, I prefer the crooks. Dishonesty is their profession, and they are so good at it."

Carr laughed. "May I smoke?"

"By all means. As I was saying. I do not care about your client because of what he may be. I care because when I sell my house, I sell this as well." He gestured toward the room. "The library remains with the villa, it is a part of it. More, it is the very heart of this sprawling and ugly place. Without the library, this becomes just another Riviera villa."

"Is this your personal library?"

"No, not really. A few books, here and there—a few first editions. Particularly the volumes of Dickens. I have always been partial to the Cruikshank illustrations. But mostly, no, Each successive owner has added to the library, and stipulated that it remain with the villa, intact.

"When you have lived with this library for a time, you come to understand."

"I'm sure," Carr said. He stood and walked around the room, pretending to examine the titles; he felt this was expected of him, though it had little to do with what was to come. Carr could recognize a phony sales pitch when he heard it.

"One of the greatest luxuries of the rich is time," Perrani continued. "Time to yourself, time to kill, time to spend chasing women or gambling—or, if you are inclined, time to read."

"I'm afraid the governor is very busy," Carr said.

"I know little of American politics, but you are undoubtedly right. Yet he is still a young man, and he will eventually settle. It is the same with rich men everywhere. Business, politics—always the same. You feel tired, your health is not what it was, as you retire while you are still in the lead, still at the top. Any man who does not do it," he said, "is a fool."

He finished his drink and set the glass down gently. "But enough, I am sure your governor will appreciate the library, or at least respect it. I have great regard for his mind, despite his propensity for, shall we say, saltiness."

"You are well informed," Carr said.

"Not really. I met the man two years ago. Charming. What is his price?"

"What is yours?"

Perrani shrugged. "You seem a cultivated man, Mr. Carr. How would you estimate the value of this room?"

"It's priceless," Carr said dutifully. He was disappointed in Perrani. The buildup of the library as the bargaining point had been so obvious from the start that he had almost begun to think the Italian had a more subtle motive, perhaps even sincerity.

"Exactly. Priceless. And quite literally so. It could be donated, in entirety, to a library—and then it would have no price. It could be sold, volume by volume—and then it would have a value, though nothing like its real value. You cannot get your money out of books, you know. Forty percent, perhaps sixty. They are a poor investment, taken singly. But a collection such as this is different, since its value lies in the collection itself, the total sum. Split up, it is just so many books, but together...I am asking half a million dollars for the villa, paid in Swiss francs or Venezuelan bolivars into a Geneva account. Is that satisfactory?"

"The governor was thinking more in terms of half that amount."

"The governor has not seen the villa. You have, and I am sure you realize it is worth more."

"It is not a question of that. The governor wants a villa, and he has advised me to investigate several specific offerings. If this is too expensive, I will simply inform him, and go see some others."

Perrani frowned now. "How much money are you talking about, Mr. Carr?"

"Three hundred thousand dollars."

"Impossible." He laughed. "That is barely an hour of prime television time in America. Your client must know it."

"He also knows that he has an election coming up. His image as a leader in urban reform, as a man dedicated to cleaning out the slums, might suffer if it were discovered that he had just purchased a half-million-dollar Riviera villa. He is rich, but there is no need to flaunt his wealth before the voters."

"Four hundred seventy-five. I can go no lower."

Carr stubbed out his cigarette. "I'm sorry," he said. "I am not authorized to pay that much."

Perrani hesitated. This was the crucial point, Carr knew. If the Italian balked now, the negotiations would end, and Carr would be forced to wait a day while he pretended to telegraph the governor for extra funds. And he would, in the end, pay the price Perrani asked. There was nothing wrong with that, of course—it was a perfectly fair price, and they both knew it. An honest man would hold out for a fair price, but then an honest man would not ask for his money in stable currency, paid into a numbered Swiss account. It might be nothing more than a tax dodge—but it might be a great deal more.

"May I ask," Perrani said, "how high you are willing to go?"

"Four hundred thousand." On an impulse, Carr decided to press his advantage, to put on the pressure. "It is possible," he said casually, "that when I tell the governor of the villa, he will agree to pay more—that is, if he really wants the Villa Perrani badly enough. He may, of course, decide against it, and tell me to look elsewhere. But the problem in either case is time."

Carr noted with satisfaction that Perrani's eyes had narrowed. That was *his* problem, too.

"The governor is about to tour the country, inspecting metropolitan planning techniques across the nation. He will be caught up with many problems, and he may not wish to be bothered. I could cable him, and meantime look at other villas. I might get a reply tomorrow."

"And if not?"

Carr shrugged. "A week, two weeks, two months. It is hard to say."

There was a long silence. Perrani played with his empty brandy glass. Now was the time for the final maneuver.

"On the other hand, I am authorized to pay immediately any sum up to four hundred thousand dollars. You could have the check now, to cash tomorrow morning when the banks open."

"You catch me at a difficult time, Mr. Carr."

"I am sorry to hear that."

Perrani continued to toy with his glass. Finally he said, "The villa is yours. I will call my lawyer and have the final papers here within the hour. Is that satisfactory?"

"Perfectly." Christ, he really *did* need the money.

Perrani was glum. He did not offer to shake hands, but immediately excused himself, and left the room to call. Anne came in to tell him that Graff had left; he'd made a pass at her and she'd slapped him.

When Perrani returned, he seemed in better spirits. "My lawyer will arrive shortly. Another brandy? I don't believe I've been introduced to the young lady. And perhaps you'd like to see the rest of the villa. You will, I think, find it most charming."

❖

The papers were signed by five, when Anne and Carr left the house. As they got into the car and drove down the shaded drive, she said, "I don't like him."

"Graff?"

"No, Perrani. I don't trust men like that—all smiles and cultivated talk. He's as cultivated as an eggplant."

"I thought he was nice enough," Carr said, still feeling the warm glow of victory.

"Just call it a woman's intuition," Anne said. "Where are you going now?"

"That depends. What time do you have to be at the casino? I thought we might have dinner first."

"I'm sorry," Anne said, "I can't."

Carr must have shown his disappointment, because she said quickly, "You're not the only man in the world, you know."

"I know." Dammit, he thought, what's the matter with me? A girl like this must have an army of begging escorts. But he noticed that she seemed pleased by his dejection, and it irritated him.

"Why don't you pick me up at the casino about twelve-thirty?"

"Do you want me to?"

"You're acting like a child, Roger." She dug into her purse for cigarettes.

"You're right. I apologize." She had used his first name, and it made him feel better.

"Besides, you have things to do. You'll want to wire your client, won't you?"

"Yes," he admitted.

"All right, then. Let me off at the Place Massena, and I'll see you at twelve-thirty in front of the Palm Beach. Right?"

"Right."

She squeezed his hand, smiled, and said, "And take care of yourself."

"Don't worry," he said, smiling back.

He returned to the hotel, feeling lighthearted and faintly foolish. It was quite a girl, he thought, that could make you feel good when she turned you down. He stopped at the desk to write out a cable to the governor, who would be pleased that the villa had come in at four hundred thousand. Then he went to his room, sat down in one of the Louis XIV chairs, and lit a cigarette.

He had finished what he had come to do. He could leave now and return home—or, as Vascard had suggested, he could stop off in Morocco or Madrid, taking the girl with him. It was a good idea; anything was better than playing a weird game which he didn't understand, and didn't particularly want to understand.

Would she be insulted if he asked her to take a trip with him? He stopped himself; she could only say no. What difference did it make? He realized that he had been treating her with caution, with a care and delicacy that was not usual to him. Perhaps he was being too careful. Carr had learned the difficult lesson that, though every woman wishes to be put on a pedestal, sooner or later she wants to be hauled down. He probably could have made love to her after lunch, he reflected. Perhaps that was why she had taken him to such a secluded spot. Was she annoyed with him now, insulted? She didn't act it, but he remembered what the French men always said of American men—too busy with business, too caught up with money, to have time for *l'amour.*

He felt suddenly irritated with himself. This girl wasn't a ticking bomb, about to explode at any moment. Either things would work out or they wouldn't. He wasn't about to worry.

❖

Brauer sat in the Citroën in the parking lot in front of the
Nice Gare, off the Avenue Thiers. The 5:03 from Paris was
just arriving. He watched the people get off. He was not
particularly worried about missing his man—he had seen a
consulate official drive up in a little gray Deux Cheveux, the
most inconspicuous car in France, park, and walk away.

Brauer marveled at the extent of Liseau's network. Their
contacts within the consulate knew that morning that a new
man was coming from Paris, and they knew what train he
was coming on. Such efficiency, Brauer thought. It made
work a pleasure.

A man with a small suitcase stepped off the platform and
scanned the cars parked around the station. Brauer's eyes
narrowed. He was a tough-looking customer, all right, with
dark, faintly cruel good looks, with a scar visible on his left
cheek. He had a muscular build, deep blue eyes, and a short,
firm mouth. His hair was jet black, and rather unruly; a hook
curled down over his forehead. He was dressed in a blue suit
and a black knit tie.

The man saw the 2CV and went directly to it. He got in
and looked around.

He's hunting the keys, Brauer thought. Now, where would
they be? Under the seat? In the back seat?

The man searched, then bent forward, his chest touching
the steering wheel.

Of course, Brauer thought. Under the dash.

A moment later the 2CV started up and pulled out into
traffic. Brauer followed closely in the Citroën.

The car turned right on the Avenue de la Victoire, and
went right to the Place Massena. The man behind the wheel
drove purposefully, never hesitating at turns. He knew exactly
where he was going.

Left at the Place Massena, past the casino, around the

fountain of Neptune, and up toward the Place Garibaldi. From here, following the river on the Rue de la République, and right on the Avenue des Diables Bleus.

Going right to Menton, Brauer thought. He allowed a car to cut between himself and the 2CV, just to be safe.

Just outside Menton, the little car made an abrupt left and went up into the hills. Brauer followed, a short distance behind. When the car parked about a mile past Liseau's villa —on a curve overlooking the house—he continued past, for another mile or so, until he found a spot where he had a view down over the other car. Then he stopped and got out.

It was a quiet stretch of road, with villas all around; no traffic, really. He took out his binoculars and observed the man.

A handsome devil, he thought, if you liked them mean.

He would be a great success with ladies who preferred their sex swift and brutal. And he dressed well, in a sort of English way.

The man took out a cigarette from a black morocco case and lit it. He was watching Liseau's villa through binoculars.

Brauer sighed. Better get it over with. He went back to his car and got the .22. He loaded it with a handful of shells, all of which had a deep cross filed into the nose. These bullets would go in cleanly, but would come out leaving a hole big enough for a cat to walk through. Dumdum bullets were strictly against Geneva Conventions, of course, but then technicalities were waived in this business. There was only one way to fight, and that was dirty.

He put the man's back in the crosshairs of the telescopic sight. The man wasn't moving; he was peering intently through his binoculars. It was the simplest shot in the world.

He moved the sights down, and slightly to the left. Hit

the heart squarely, that was the point. It wouldn't really matter, but he might as well carry it off with finesse.

He squeezed the trigger.

Through his sights, he saw the man shudder and collapse. He fell forward onto the road and did not move. The blood must be gushing from his chest, Brauer thought. It was clearly visible, even from here.

He got back into the Citroën and drove calmly off.

She got into the car. "Been waiting long?"

"No. About ten minutes."

"It's a beautiful night." She brushed her hair back from her face and looked up at the sky. "Where shall we go?"

"Wherever you say."

"Let's drive back to Nice, then, while we think of some-place special."

They started off, and she said, "You're quiet tonight. Is anything wrong?"

"No."

There was little traffic at this hour, and they made good time passing through Juan-les-Pins and Antibes. Soon they could see Nice lighted before them, and the white apartments curving around the four-mile stretch of beach.

"Did you send your telegram?"

"Yes."

"Have you decided when you're leaving?"

"Not yet."

She bit her lip and watched the road intently.

"What's the matter?"

"Nothing." She shook her head, as if to lose a bad day-dream. "Shall we go along the Grande Corniche? The view is superb at night."

"All right."

He reached over and squeezed her hand. He had felt unaccountably depressed earlier in the evening, mostly because
he had been reviewing his life, and found it dull, monotonous,
and empty—all the things he had most emphatically believed
it was not. But now, with her at his side, he was more cheerful.

They drove for nearly an hour, feeling the cool night air
against their faces. Carr followed the Basse Corniche through
Nice and Villefranche, then cut up to link with the Grande
Corniche.

"Napoleon's road," he said as they pulled out.

"That's right," Anne said. "How did you know?"

"I read the guidebooks. Napoleon the First built it to re-
place the old Aurelian Way." They gathered speed, and Anne
slipped on her sweater against the chill of the wind. "How
about a drink at Le Visiteur?"

"Fine."

It was a favorite of Carr's. The hotel and restaurant, new
and modern, was almost one thousand feet up, with a view
over Cap Mortola, Monte Carlo, and Monaco. They parked
and went onto the terrace, feeling their skin tingle from the
wind.

The terrace was nearly deserted, with only a few couples
sitting out on the neat white chairs. They ordered drinks
and took them to the rail.

"It's almost like the Milky Way, all those lights," Anne
said.

Carr looked from the Monte Carlo beach, directly below,
across to the casino, then over to the Oceanographic Museum,
standing gray and upright, and finally to the palace. Monaco,
he thought—that was all there was to it. A little U-shaped
piece of land, with the old town, Monaco, on one arm, the new
town, Monte Carlo, on the other, and the port in between.

Brightly lighted, it looked much larger than it really was. Carr had trouble believing that the little country was actually half the size of Central Park, one-eighty-sixth the size of London. It was rather like a fairy kingdom, fabulously rich, bypassed by the rest of the world.

Anne shivered at his side.

"Cold?"

"No. I want to go home."

"You sure?"

She nodded and gulped down the rest of her drink. Then she ran from the terrace to the parking lot. Carr watched her go, too astonished to protest. Then he put his drink down, left a few francs with the check, and hurried after her.

She was standing beside the car, looking out at the road, smoking. Her cigarette flared in the dark as she drew on it. For a long moment he watched her, saying nothing, not knowing what to say. Then finally he asked, "Ready?"

"Yes." Mechanically, she got into the car.

"Where to?" He tried to keep his voice light, but did not succeed.

"Menton. I'll direct you." Her voice was flat, expressionless, and she did not look once at him as they went down into the city itself, then up into the hills, following a steep path through a fashionable residential area. It was dark, and he wondered absently if he would be able to find his way back.

"Stop here."

He halted in front of a high wrought-iron fence. Through open gates, a long drive led inside to a villa he could not see.

"You can leave me here." She looked at him. "I'm sorry," she said.

Carr thought once again of her expensive clothes. He felt sad and helpless. Anne started to get out.

"It's all right," he said, "I'll drive you in."

"No!" But he was already turning in the drive.

"For a no-nonsense girl," he said, "you certainly pull some funny maneuvers. What does this act mean? Listen, I don't care if somebody is keeping—"

"Please stop," she pleaded. "Please turn around."

"When will I see you again?" The drive ended in a stone wall, perhaps six feet high. A door opened through it. It was a modern stone wall, and he wondered if the villa might be modern as well. Four cars were parked in front of the wall—two Citroëns, a Renault Dauphine, and a sleek silver Ferrari.

Anne said nothing.

"When will I see you again?"

"Oh, you're a fool," she cried, and tears began to slip down her cheeks. She jumped out of the car and disappeared through the door in the wall. Carr was left alone in the night, hearing his motor tick over, staring into the patch illuminated by his headlights.

He did not know what to think. Slowly, as if in a trance, he backed the car around and drove down the path back to the road. The evening had been strange from the start, he thought. Something was bothering her—yet she had been all right at lunch.

His attention was caught by the road ahead. He slowed the car. For a moment, he couldn't believe it, and then he braked to a stop. The gates were shut.

Perhaps the wind, Carr thought. Leaving the motor on, he got out to open them again. But long before he reached the iron bars, he could see the heavy padlock, bright in the light of his headlamps. The bars cast long shadows on the road outside. Carr bent to examine the lock.

Two men grabbed him, one from each side. He struggled

free of the first, and gave the second a hard kick in the groin. The man moaned and rolled over onto his back, knees pulled up to his chest. Carr turned to face the other man, and took a heavy blow to the stomach, and then felt a sharp pain between his eyes, and heard bone break. He began to fall, slowly, sickeningly, and he kept falling for a very long time.

Chapter XVI

Lights went on.

Carr opened his eyes to find himself slumped in a chair, with blood all over his jacket and shirt. Something white and fuzzy was stuck in his nose, which was numb. He looked up.

The gently floating fragments of a red and green mobile bounced before his eyes. He watched, fascinated, as the colored pieces drifted and caught the light. Slowly he looked around the rest of the room, which was spacious. The decor was modern, and all the walls were glass.

"Curtains," a voice said. Someone pressed a button, and gold drapes began to move around the walls until the entire room was enclosed. It was very quiet in the room, which was furnished in the most simple and expensive taste—Barcelona chairs, Picasso ceramics, Italian lighting fixtures, and Danish furniture. The floor was slate, giving contrasting texture to the harsh smooth lines of the sofas and chairs.

"Mr. Carr."

A face moved before him. It was a neat, cleanly elegant face, with a fine, thin mouth, high cheekbones, and short dark hair. Carr could not see the eyes; they were hidden behind dark sunglasses. The lips were turned up in a smile, showing very white teeth.

"We are sorry about your misfortune, but the guards had orders not to fail. You are acquiring a reputation as a difficult man to detain."

The face moved back, and Carr could see the whole man clearly. He wore a black suit with a dark tie, and stood slim and perfectly straight, hands at his sides. He gave the impression of being tall, over six feet.

"You will be pleased to know it is not serious," the man said, nodding toward the blood on Carr's shirt. "One's nose has many fine capillaries, and you have ruptured a few, that is all. A simple nosebleed. We have seen that you received an injection of benzedrine and dextrose. Shortly you will be given a sedative—of some sort."

"I want to see a doctor," Carr said. He reached up to touch his nose, and discovered that his elbows were bound to the arms of the chair.

"Then your wish is fulfilled. You are looking at one." The man watched Carr intently for a moment, then pressed an intercom button on a small console set next to the fireplace in the center of the room. "Call the meeting." He turned to Carr. "I am sorry about your arms; I know it must be an inconvenience. Let us hope that you can answer our few questions briefly, since we are extremely busy men, and you are undoubtedly tired."

That bitch, Carr thought, in a burst of hot anger. She knew from the start, she led me along every step of the way. He had been a fool—he should have known, should have suspected.

Four men came into the room and stood next to the man in sunglasses. Carr looked at each man in turn. They were unremarkable, all neatly dressed and blank-faced. One had a beard. No one smoked, and no one spoke, yet there was no tension in the room. They all seemed perfectly relaxed.

Sunglasses, who seemed to be the leader, turned to the other men. "We are missing someone, as usual," he said. "Always late, but no matter. We shall proceed without him. Are we ready?"

No one replied. The silence in the room was complete.

"Very well. Mr. Carr, let us get down to business. You have caused us a good deal of trouble in the past few days. We dislike trouble."

"You've been pretty annoying yourselves," Carr said. His voice sounded strange to him, and he realized it was because his nose was blocked with cotton.

"We would like to know something about you. That is why you are here. Antoine, will you begin?" One of the men, younger-looking than the rest, stepped forward. "Mr. Carr, we understand you are a lawyer. You should know that Antoine is also a lawyer, with considerable experience in American legal procedure. Reply with care."

He stepped back. Antoine said, "What is the name of your law firm?"

"None of your goddamn business." Carr expected to be struck, but he was not. The group watched him with steady, unwavering stares. Their faces showed nothing.

Antoine spoke slowly. "If you are a lawyer, Mr. Carr, then we must conclude that we have made a mistake. It will be an embarrassing mistake, but not serious—and you will live. If you are not a lawyer, then there has been no mistake. Please answer the question, and spare us your truculence."

Carr hesitated, looking at the faces. They were waiting, judging him with deadly seriousness.

"Harrison, Bentley, and Reed."

"Address?"

Carr gave it.

"Which floor?"

"Seventeenth."

"How long have you been with this firm?"

"Twelve years."

"That is a long time. What is your position?"

"Junior partner."

"Your field?"

"Tax and corporate law, broadly speaking, but—"

"It sounds like an excellent job," Antoine observed dryly. "Where did you receive your legal training?"

"Harvard."

"The years?"

"1951 to 1953."

"Did you enjoy Harvard?"

"Nobody enjoys the Harvard Law School."

"Why is that? Tell us something about it."

Carr paused. "Are you trying to establish that I was there?"

"You're very astute."

Carr shrugged, and felt the straps cut into his arms. "There isn't a lot to tell. I spent less time with the books than I should have, and—"

"Which library did you use?"

"The Ames Library."

"Where is that?"

"Just off Mass Ave, where it curves around—"

Antoine held up a hand. "Why are you in Nice, Mr. Carr?"

"I was sent to buy a villa."

"That is what we have heard. It is a common thing, a lawyer sent to buy a villa. It could be an excuse for any kind of activity. Who is your client?"

"I can't tell you. As a lawyer, you should know that."

Antoine considered this for a moment, pacing back and forth across the room. He would occasionally stop to glance at Carr, and the glance seemed to show amusement—Carr couldn't be sure.

"You know," Antoine said, "you are either a flawless liar or the genuine article."

"You're very astute."

"Tell me, is an airplane a motor vehicle?"

The question took him by complete surprise, and it was several moments before the shock set in. Oh, God, he thought, why didn't I pay more attention in class? He hesitated, then said, "It might be. It would depend—you'd have to give me a particular circumstance before I could decide the legal principle involved."

"You give me the circumstance."

The group watched, their faces showing no emotion and almost no interest. Only their eyes were alive, watching his hands, his face, his lips. Carr said, "A pilot is forced to make an emergency landing, and he chooses a highway, or a public beach. In landing, he kills some people."

"Would the airplane necessarily be considered a motor vehicle in this situation?" Antoine seemed to be probing now with a sort of professional interest, almost curiosity.

"No, of course not. A number of factors might or might not be significant: whether the airplane was military or government-owned, whether, if commercial, it was making an interstate flight; whether it landed in a state that had an ordinance that might apply."

Without hesitation Antoine said, "Tell me about *Baker versus Carr.*"

"Read the newspapers," Carr said. "Or shall we go on to *Marbury versus Madison*?"

"That won't be necessary. Tell me, is that Carr any relation to you?"

"No."

"What about the Henderson–Carr Transportation Bill?"

"My father."

"Your father is a senator?"

"Yes."

Carr saw it. The man in sunglasses twitched, quite visibly. So the mention of his father drew a reaction. That was interesting. But was it good?

"You say you have come to Nice to buy a villa. What steps have you taken toward that goal?"

"I've bought one."

Now everybody in the room reacted. The faces all showed interest.

"You move quickly," Antoine said. "You must have made the purchase this afternoon. Which villa?"

"I'm afraid I can't tell you that. It is part of my client's business." Carr was not about to implicate the governor in any of this.

"The situation calls for a stretching of ethics," Antoine said. "We have no interest in your client, or his business— only in establishing the truth of your story."

"The Villa Perrani, near Villefranche."

It was absolutely silent in the room.

The faces of the men grew grim. Carr sensed that something was wrong, and that his situation had become instantly more dangerous.

"We can tell when you are lying, Mr. Carr."

Keep calm, he told himself. Don't shift in your chair, don't play with your hands, keep your voice even. He said, "Ask the girl. She was with me."

"The girl does not concern us now. Give us the truth."

There was a soft knock at the door behind Carr. A man stepped into the room. Carr did not look around; he kept his gaze fixed on the other men.

"Welcome," Sunglasses said, speaking for the first time in several minutes. "You are just in time to help us question Mr. Carr."

Signor Perrani stepped into Carr's field of vision. His face, like the others, was blank—no emotion, not the slightest flicker of recognition.

"Perrani!"

Sunglasses remained calm. He turned to Perrani and said, "This man claims to have bought your villa, signor."

"I have never seen him before in my life," Perrani said.

Chapter XVII

There was a long, expectant silence. Carr looked from Perrani to Sunglasses, and then to the other members of the group. He was trying, very quickly, to decide how to play this new game. Perrani was lying, but the Italian had a disturbing confidence, an unshakable calm that Carr couldn't understand. Perrani was obviously a member of this group, but not an important one—they had started without him—and perhaps Carr could take advantage of the fact. He turned to Sunglasses and said, "He's lying."

"Try again, Mr. Carr," Sunglasses said. His voice sounded bored, slightly disappointed.

"I can prove he's lying. I can describe the Villa Perrani in detail: I was there this afternoon. I can tell you about the library, the butler, the upstairs bedrooms—"

"We have always been impressed with the depth of your cover. We have no doubt you can describe the villa with absolute accuracy."

"What about Graff, the agent? I was with him, he can tell you. Why don't you ask him?"

Sunglasses was unmoved. "We might ask the consulate as well. They would probably give an even more convincing corroboration."

"And the girl? Why not talk with her—she was with me, the whole time."

"The girl," said Sunglasses patiently, "is hopelessly in love with you. We do not need to bring her in to discover that."

Perrani smiled faintly and shook his head pityingly at Carr.

"Look, I *paid* for that villa. A check for four hundred thousand dollars, made out to Enzio Perrani, payable at the Société Général, Nice. I gave it to him. You can check at the bank in the morning."

"And if there has been no check deposited?" Sunglasses shrugged. "We will have wasted still more time, time which we cannot afford to waste."

Carr felt a cold chill. They were right, of course—if the pressure was on, Perrani would not dare cash the check. But he said, "What Perrani does with his money is none of my business. He originally wanted me to deposit the sum in a numbered Geneva account, but I refused. I prefer more straightforward dealings."

Sunglasses sighed. "Such an honest man." He looked around the group, apparently reading the faces where Carr had failed.

"Have we heard enough?"

The men nodded, and Perrani allowed himself a slight smirk.

Sunglasses said, "Mr. Carr, it seems you remain troublesome to us. We must now decide how most simply to be rid of you. Ernst, take care of him."

From behind, the blond German stepped forward. A long knife was in his hand.

"Wait a minute," Carr said. "You're making a big mistake. I think you ought to—"

What happened next came so swiftly Carr could scarcely believe it. The German leaped across the room and gripped Perrani's arms, holding them behind his back. The knife was at the Italian's throat.

"Stop!" Sunglasses ordered.

The German stopped. The blade had just nicked the throat, leaving a thin red line.

Perrani's eyes were wide.

There was dead silence in the room. Sunglasses walked forward and pulled a pistol out of Perrani's belt. He sighed. "Enzio, you poor fool. Did you really think you could succeed?" He smiled. "And did you think I would let your death be so painless as a quick stroke of the knife?" Sunglasses laughed bitterly. "It will take you *hours* to die, I promise you."

He went to a corner for his black bag and brought it back to the center of the room. "Observe, gentlemen, a traitor's fate. Roll up his sleeve."

Perrani's jacket was stripped off, and his sleeve roughly torn. Sunglasses filled a hypodermic. "Ether, my friend. Injected intravenously, it is quite amusing."

Perrani was sweating. His lips worked soundlessly. The German straightened the Italian's arm, and Sunglasses delicately inserted the needle into the hollow of the elbow. He squeezed out the contents.

The response was immediate.

Perrani collapsed on the ground and went into the most violent spasms Carr had ever seen. He rolled, twitched, and jerked, his body frantically in motion. He said nothing, but emitted quick wheezing noises, as if perpetually about to sneeze. Every limb shook violently, uncontrollably; his head hammered against the floor like a pneumatic drill. His face was a bright blue.

"Take him outside," Sunglasses said. "Let him roll on the grass and die."

It took three men to carry the quivering, shuddering body out of the room.

When he was gone, Sunglasses turned calmly to Carr. "We are most grateful to you, Mr. Carr. Allow me to introduce myself. I am Georges Liseau." He did not shake hands or offer to introduce the other men. "You have prevented a possible misfortune to our organization by telling us about Signor Perrani, and we would like to repay you in whatever way we can."

Carr looked at Liseau as if he were insane. He was completely confused. "How about a drink and a ride back to my hotel?"

Liseau nodded amiably as he untied Carr's bonds. "As a doctor, I would suggest vodka. It produces the least hangover, and has the fewest impurities. Will that be all right? Good. On the rocks?" He moved to a silver ice bucket and filled a tall glass with cubes, then began pouring vodka. "Say when."

Carr waited until the glass was one third full. "When."

"As for your hotel," Liseau said, handing him the glass, "allow us to show our gratitude more fully. As the distinguished son of an American senator, we would be pleased if you would remain here, as our guest, for a few days."

"Do I have a choice?"

"We will send a car to collect your clothes from the Negresco. I think you will find your stay here pleasant, and we will certainly do our best to make it enjoyable. Besides, you will need time to recover from your injured nose. It's broken, you know." He seemed to reflect a moment. "I think, in fact, that I had better attend to it right now. Bring your drink, and if you will follow me, I will show you to your room."

Once in the room, which was modern, with white walls and a glass wall looking out over the sea, Carr was told to lie on the bed. Liseau stripped off his jacket and examined the nose in the light of the bed lamp. Carr, remembering Perrani, shuddered at the touch.

Liseau sat back and said, "I think you will be happier if I

work while you are sleeping. Please roll up your sleeve."
Carr hesitated, and Liseau laughed. "There is nothing to be
afraid of, I assure you."

Carr finally decided he just didn't care, he was so damned
tired. He lay back, felt the cotton rubbing his arm, the cool
sensation of the alcohol, and then a sharp prick. "Shut your
eyes, Mr. Carr." The voice was confident and soothing. "Relax.
Breathe deeply."

He looked at Liseau, who seemed to be drifting back,
farther and farther away.

"Relax. There is nothing to fear."

Carr shut his eyes. He was asleep.

He awoke to the sound of birds chittering outside his window.
Sunlight, clear and bright, streamed into the room, nearly
blinding him as he groped for his watch. It was nine. He got
up and walked to the mirror to examine his face. The eyes
were a little bloodshot, and there was a cut on his chin that
would make shaving unpleasant, but otherwise he seemed
fine. A white triangle of cardboard was taped across the bridge
of his nose, which did not hurt as much as he had expected.
On the dresser beneath the mirror was a small box of yellow
pills, resting on top of a slip of paper which said, "One every
four hours as needed for pain."

He looked around the room and saw his suitcase standing
in one corner. It must have been brought in during the night.
He went over and opened it, and was momentarily confused
to find it empty. Then he checked the closet and found his
clothes neatly hung out.

There were two other doors in the room. He tried one,
and discovered that it opened onto the corridor. So he wasn't
locked in—that was a surprise. The other door led into a
spanking white tiled bathroom. His shaving kit had been

placed on a shelf above the sink, along with his toothbrush and a new tube of toothpaste. He remembered he had run out of toothpaste, and had forgotten to buy some in Nice the day before.

Someone was knocking on the door.

It was a maid, a very pretty one, who managed to look both apologetic and interested when she saw Carr in his pajamas. "I'm sorry I disturbed you," she said.

"No, no," Carr said, running his eyes over the girl. Very pretty indeed, he thought. Her uniform was not starched, but softly hugged the curves of her body.

"Dr. Liseau would like you to join him for breakfast, on the terrace, if that is convenient."

"Fine. Fifteen minutes?"

"I will tell the doctor."

He showered and shaved, then followed the corridor to a staircase, went down and out through what seemed to be the living room—the room he had been questioned in the night before—and onto the terrace. Liseau was there, hidden behind an opened copy of *Le Monde*. There was a copy of the *Times* International neatly folded alongside Carr's plate. He sat down.

"Good morning."

Liseau put his paper aside. "Good morning, Mr. Carr. I trust you slept well?"

"Fine, thank you."

"I have ordered fried eggs, ham, and orange juice; I thought you might be hungry. Does it suit you?"

"Perfectly."

"Bon." Without looking back, Liseau motioned to the maid, who immediately brought Carr his breakfast. It was hot and good, and he ate with relish in spite of himself. Liseau continued reading for several minutes, then said, "Your nose

presented no problem. It was a clean break along the fronto-nasal suture, which should heal quickly. You found the codeine pills?"

"Yes."

"Good." Liseau paused. "I must leave you soon," he said, checking his watch. "I have appointments in Nice. But before I go, I want to clarify your position here. You are my guest. You are welcome to use the house or the grounds in what-ever way amuses you, and it is my wish that you should do so. It is also my wish that you forget last night; it was an unfortunate business from beginning to end, and need not concern us further. I can assure you that you are in no danger here. But," he said, standing, "at the same time, it would be unwise to leave. The fence around the property, you will find, can be climbed with determination. That is why it is electrified. There are also guards, who have orders not to bother you unless you try to leave. Do we understand each other?"

"How long will I be kept here?"

"You had best let me decide that," Liseau said, "as your doctor. I have only your best interests at heart. And now, if you will excuse me, I must meet my appointments." He nodded politely and left.

The maid came up and said, "Coffee or tea?"

"Coffee."

She gave him a wicked, slow smile. "I hope you will enjoy your stay at Le Scalpel."

"What?"

"Le Scalpel. It is the name of the villa. Dr. Liseau has a strange sense of humor."

"I've noticed."

"The guests usually call it *L'estomac,* because the cuisine is so good. Dr. Liseau has hired a chef from Le Baumainère

to cook for him in the evenings. Oh, he pays him a fortune,
I can tell you."

She brought him his coffee.

"Does Dr. Liseau have many guests?"

"You mean staying here? No, not now. A month ago, we
had many—and six months ago, the same. But not now. Only
you and Miss Crittenden."

So the others don't live here, Carr thought. They probably had villas of their own, like Perrani. He said. "Where is
Miss Crittenden now?"

The maid seemed piqued by his question. "Out there," she
said, pointing off across the landscaped lawns. "You know
Miss Crittenden?"

Carr was about to answer when they heard the deep roar
of an automobile starting up. "Dr. Liseau's Ferrari," the maid
said.

"The silver one? That's his?"

"Yes. *C'est jolie, hein?*"

Carr nodded, remembering Cannes. He got up and set off
across the lawn. He wanted first to walk around the house,
to get some idea of how it was laid out. He stepped back to
get a better view of Le Scalpel.

It was immense: two stories high, and shaped like an L,
with the short arm cantilevered out over a sloping landscaped hill overlooking Menton and the sea. The short arm
was only single-story, and comprised the living room, with
the terrace right alongside; at right angles was the long arm,
two floors of bedrooms, a dining room, and probably a study
as well. Carr's room was on the second floor, near the bend
in the L.

The whole building was constructed from glass and metal,
and he could see why it was called Le Scalpel—inside and
out, it was sharp, clean, bare, and smooth. The unsparing,

almost harsh quality of the lines was broken by the occasional use of bricks to add texture, and the low stone walls which ran around the house, screening it from the view of anyone on the drive.

Carr thought it was the perfect house for Liseau, a direct statement of his personality. He wondered if the doctor had designed it himself.

Still curious, he wandered down the drive. He didn't get far before he saw the guard at the gate, sitting on the grass just inside the fence, playing idly with his gun. Carr's gaze shifted to the fence. It was heavy iron, seven feet high, and laced with barbed wire. It took a careful eye to detect the small insulators, painted dull black like the rest of the fence. Probably they did not carry a large charge—just enough to stun a man...

But why bother? He was safe, for the moment, and reasonably comfortable. Roll with the punches, he told himself, and play it cool. He walked back to explore the grounds.

The villa seemed to be surrounded by at least twenty or thirty acres, most of it wooded. For about a hundred yards around the house in each direction the trees had been thinned, and lawns, shrubs, and flowers planted. It was a pleasing arrangement—and one which made it impossible for an intruder to approach the house without detection.

Abruptly he came upon a swimming pool. There was nobody about; the still water looked cool and inviting. He was about to strip down and go in when he remembered his nose and decided against it. Instead, he sat down on a wooden chair which stood beside an umbrella-shaded table at the edge of the pool. He lit a cigarette, and his glance fell on a telephone resting on the pool deck. The cord led off into the woods. Intrigued, he picked up the receiver.

"Yes, sir?"

"Hello?"

"May I be of service?" It was the maid; he recognized her voice now.

"No, I was just curious about the phone. Sorry."

"Would you like something to drink?" Now, that was an idea, he thought. "As a matter of fact, yes. Vodka and lime will be fine."

"Immediately, sir."

Carr sighed. This might not be so bad, after all. He sat back in his chair and smoked. Roll with the punches—that was the answer to everything.

The maid came, bringing, to his amazement, a bottle of vodka, four limes, ice, a pitcher, and two glasses. "Dr. Liseau prefers his guests to mix their own," she said. She had an interesting way of standing that was both stiffly formal and lasciviously inviting at the same time. "That way," she said, "the guests are most satisfied."

"I'm sure," Carr said, "but why two glasses?"

"I thought you might be with Miss Crittenden," the maid said. She seemed pleased that he was not. "Shall I take it back?"

"No, leave it, thanks." The maid left, giving him a view of her mobile behind. He mixed up a stiff batch of drinks, telling himself it would dull the pain in his nose, which had begun to ache. He had forgotten the pills in his room. He poured himself a glass and sipped it experimentally. Sweet. He added more vodka, upending the bottle and listening to it glug-glug out. No point in being delicate.

"That's it, bottom's up," a woman's voice said.

Startled, he looked across the pool.

It was Anne.

Chapter XVIII

She wore tight white slacks and a loose-fitting purple print blouse. Her hair was piled carelessly on her head; in one hand she held a large beach towel.

"Well, if it isn't Delilah."

"Do you always flatter yourself when you insult other people?"

Carr said nothing, but poured her a drink and gestured to a chair.

"Not speaking to me?"

"Oh, yes, I'm speaking to you," Carr said. "And you're going to speak to me. There are a few things you're going to explain."

She took the drink. "You won't like it."

"I couldn't like it any less than I do already."

She bit her lip, then said, "All right. I've known Liseau for two years."

"Good friends, I'll bet."

"No—not for almost a year. I met him about eighteen months after my marriage broke up. It was a bad time for me until he came along, and I liked him. I thought he was cultivated and interesting, and I was attracted by his strength. My husband was a terrible weakling. Anyway, we started living together shortly after he built this house. It was months before I began to realize he was more than just a prosperous doctor." She paused and looked at Carr, as if for approval.

"Go on."

"Well, every few weeks, strange men would visit him. I'd notice lots of cars in the drive when I came back from the casino. On those nights, I was always told to stay in my room. The first few times, it just seemed odd to me. Later, it became different—sinister, and frightening. About that time, he and I stopped getting along."

"Why didn't you leave him?"

"I planned to. Then, one night I heard a noise outside my bedroom, which is on the first floor. I got up and looked out the window, and saw him with two other men, dragging something. At first I thought it must be a sack, or a trunk. Then I saw it wasn't."

She picked up her glass, and put it down again without drinking, and rushed on. "I was wearing a white nightgown, and I guess he must have looked back and seen me standing at the window. The next day I told him I wanted to call it off and move out, but he just said in that calm voice of his that I had better stay awhile. I was afraid, and I've been afraid ever since."

"That's ridiculous. Why don't you just buy a plane ticket and leave? He gives you freedom during the day, doesn't he?"

Her lower lip quivered. "Don't shout at me."

"I'm not shouting."

"You don't understand anything. You don't know what kind of man he is. He has me followed, all the time. Sometimes I know it, sometimes I only suspect it. Some days, I suppose, he doesn't even bother—he doesn't have to. When he calls me in and asks me what I've been doing, I always tell him."

"Did you tell him you'd met me? Or did he send you off especially to get me?"

Her voice was low and sad. "No. He knew I had met you on the beach that day. Until then it was an accident. Then he told me yesterday to spend the day with you. And last night, I got a note at the casino." Her voice was so low he could barely hear. "Saying to bring you here."

"So you did."

"I didn't want to," she said. "I had to, I was afraid. I was sure they were going to kill you, like that man they dragged out. I tried to warn you at the gate—then I could have told him you were mad at me, and had refused to drive me in. But you were so damned stubborn. You fell right into it." A tear rolled softly down her face, and his heart went out to her.

"I cried all night," she said, wiping her eyes on her sleeve. "Anyway, now you know." She sniffed and looked up at him. "What's that cardboard for?"

"They broke my nose." Somehow, it sounded very undignified.

"It's all right," she said, gulping her drink and rubbing her eyes again. "You were too handsome, anyway." She put the glass down sharply. "My God! What's in this, anyway?" She began to cough.

"I'm taking it as a painkiller," Carr explained. He was no longer mad at her. He just couldn't be mad at her, somehow.

"It must be a severe pain." She tried a smile.

He went over to her and kissed her salty cheek.

"I'm sorry," he said. "I didn't mean to give you a hard time."

"I'm sorry, too."

"How long do you think he'll keep me here?"

"Don't you ever think of anybody but yourself?" She seemed once again on the verge of tears.

"Keep *us* here," he amended quickly.

"I don't know, but not long. He's getting ready to move out."

"What makes you think so?"

"Just little things. He gets letters from real-estate agents in Hong Kong—he has, for the last several weeks. He sold a Modigliani sketch a few days ago; it was one of his favorites. And there just seems to be a general air of preparation— I don't know. Maybe I'm wrong, but I do know he's planning something very soon. Those men come here almost every night; they never used to come so often. They stay in the living room and talk until late, sometimes two or three in the morning. And he's become edgy as a cat—always hopping around, always tense, speaking abruptly. He wasn't like that before."

Carr recalled Liseau's suave and collected manner, and wondered just how different the man had been two years before.

"Did you know they killed Perrani last night?"

Her eyes went wide. "Was he one of them?"

"Yes, didn't you know?"

"I've never seen any of them, and I'm sure Perrani had never seen me. Why did they kill him?"

"I don't know, but it had something to do with selling the villa to me."

"I don't understand it."

"Neither do I." Carr poured her another drink. "Do you know anybody named Morgan?"

She shook her head.

"How about Victor Jenning?"

She gave him an astonished look.

"You know who he is?"

"Of course," she said. "Everybody around here has heard of him. He lives in Monaco, and has become a kind of legend: he's handsome but getting old, and he likes race cars and women. He's had six or seven wives, and they all come to watch when he races each year in the Grand Prix of Monaco.

They all hope he'll get killed. At least," she said, "that's what I've heard."

Carr frowned. "Is he a professional driver?"

"I don't think so. Nobody really knows, but he seems to have a big source of income from guns. I've heard he sells them legitimately—but then, I've heard he makes them, and I've heard he runs them. You know how stories go. Why?"

"They asked me about him in the police station, out of the blue. And when I was at the consulate, people kept thinking I was Morgan."

He struggled to put together the pieces, to make sense out of things. He had one brilliant flash of insight—that little man, the one with short hair and dirty hands, might have been a mechanic. Jenning's mechanic? It was possible. But what did that mean?

He hit a dead end. Every way he tried it, a dead end.

"It's all terribly complicated," Anne said. "What are you thinking?"

"Nothing much. Just that we'll be safe right here, at least for the time being." This was all none of his business, he told himself, and in the long run he'd be better off not worrying about it. "If what you say is true, he will finish what he's doing and release us both in a few days. After all, we can't do him much damage if he's in Hong Kong." He smiled. "Until then, we're trapped here, so there's no sense fighting it. Another drink?"

"Please." She watched him pour. "I hope you're right."

"So do I."

Any alternatives were depressing. Carr changed the subject. "Are you going swimming?" he asked, pointing so her towel.

"Yes," Anne said. "Am I going alone?"

"Afraid so. I'd better keep my nose dry for a few days."

"You may drown right there, if you drink any more." She stood up. The white slacks were bright in the midday sun, but Carr was more interested in the blouse, which was loose yet clinging. He couldn't help staring. She laughed. "Acrilan. It always does that."

He took a quick swallow of vodka.

Anne undressed, slipping out of her clothes with her usual effortless grace. He watched as the slacks came off, revealing her long brown legs; then the blouse went. He sighed. She was wearing a very brief bikini. Above the halter, her breasts swelled magnificently. Her stomach was flat and hard, and her hipbones were clearly visible, running down to disappear beneath the fabric.

"Sure you don't want to come in? It's pretty hot here."

"Yes," Carr said, "very warm."

"When I was a little girl, I was taught not to stare."

"You're no longer a little girl, and I'm not staring. I'm just fascinated by your talent for understatement."

She patted her flat stomach. "Do you think I'm getting fat?"

"I can't really tell, you have so many clothes on."

"You're a hard man to please."

"Oh, I'm pleased."

"Good." With scarcely a ripple, she slipped into the water, and came up smiling. "It's marvelous, you really should try it."

She floated on her back, kicking lazily; then she submerged, raising one firm leg, toes pointed, the smooth muscles in her thigh and calf outlined. With her body under water, she turned full circles, so the leg rotated above the surface. Carr stared at the leg, which glistened wetly in the hot sun.

When she surfaced, her hair glossy behind her head, he said, "What's that called? 'Periscope'?"

"I used to do underwater ballet. It's harder than you think."

"I'll take your word for it."

"It's the control, that's what's hard."

"Control, yes. Very hard."

"Here, watch this." She lay on her back, paddling rapidly with her hands, then brought both legs straight up. Dropping her head back, she allowed the weight of her legs to push her down in a slow, controlled dive; her ankles went into the water without a ripple. Somehow, it struck Carr as one of the sexiest things he had ever seen.

She surfaced with a grin.

"Your legs are your best feature," he said, thinking: something must be done about this girl.

"You'd be surprised," she said, "about my best feature." She ducked underwater again, before he could reply.

Yes, he thought, something must definitely be done.

Later, she went to lie in the sun and dry. Carr joined her, drink in hand, watching her body move. His throat felt sticky and he had trouble swallowing, but he attributed it to the vodka. Anne stretched out on her stomach on the warm green grass and looked up at him.

"Would you undo me?"

"What?"

"My strap. I'm trying to get rid of the white mark on my back."

"Oh." He had trouble with the catch, since the bikini was wet. That was the trouble: the bikini was wet. He finally worked it free, and straps fell away, revealing a thin white line across her back.

"Awful, isn't it?" she said.

"Very unsightly."

He leaned over and kissed her between the shoulders. She rolled over on her back, her top falling away and her arms coming up around his neck, drawing him closer.

"Hey," he said, feeling her cold against his chest. "You're all wet."

"The breaks," she said, biting his lip.

"My nose," he said. "Be careful."

"I'll try," she promised, and she kept her word. He didn't notice his nose for the rest of the morning.

Chapter XIX

That day and the next were like a dream to Carr. He wandered around the villa grounds, hand in hand with Anne. Sometimes they talked, but often they spent hours without passing a word; it was as if they had no need to speak to understand what the other was thinking. The sun was hot, the days gloriously clear, and they spent every waking minute together. Liseau was at the villa only rarely, and he never intruded; he seemed, in fact, pleased that they were preoccupied with each other.

At night, Anne went off to the casino, and returned very tired—the summer show was scheduled to open in two weeks, and the pace of rehearsals had picked up. But she never showed her exhaustion, and it didn't seem to matter. Carr was blissfully, peacefully happy with her. He felt as if he had found something he had needed for a very long time.

The confinement did not bother him. They walked, listened to Liseau's excellent record collection, or read, or swam— Carr decided on the second day to stop worrying about his nose. In fact, he no longer worried about anything. He cut down on his smoking, slept well, and felt better than he had in years.

Anne seemed to him continuously and radiantly beautiful. He was constantly surprised at the naturalness of her beauty; he could do nothing to lessen it, to disarrange it. He once tried—he rumpled her hair, scrubbed off her makeup, and made her put on some of his clothes. She took his breath away, sitting there with disheveled hair in an oversized man's shirt.

"You're beautiful," he said.

"You're handsome," she replied. "So what?"

He gave her a cigarette for that. "You must have been a lovely child."

"I was fat. Horrible, ugly fat. Rolls of fat all around my hips. Quadruple chins. Puffy knees. You wouldn't have liked me."

"You've made a remarkable recovery in your old age."

"Considering."

She honestly didn't seem impressed with her looks, and Carr was unable to get even a flicker of vanity or conceit out of her. He kept trying, out of a sort of perverse curiosity, and finally she said, "Listen, you're infatuated."

"True," he said, "but it's not your fault. It's your thighs."

She pouted. "You just like me for my body."

"I admit it."

"It's not so good. Every night, I get dressed with fifty girls, and they're all better-looking and better built than I am. Some of them are smarter, too."

"Introduce me."

"Not on your life." She rubbed her nose in his ear. "I know a good thing when I see it."

"It strikes me as an unfair monopoly."

"Yes," she said, "you definitely are a lawyer."

"It's not so bad. There are compensations."

"I know," she said, nibbling his ear.

"You'd better watch that. I'll get distraught."

"Is that an offer?"

"Try me," Carr said. "Just try me."

Ralph Gorman thumbed irritably through the CORTEX file. Everything was simply shot to hell: the Associates were far in the lead, and looked like favorites to win the race. Carr had disappeared without a trace—checked out of his hotel room—and the specially imported Paris killer had been summarily dispatched within an hour of his arrival.

They moved so damned fast, Gorman thought unhappily.

Now there was this Perrani business. Perrani was an Associate; they'd known that for a long time. He had contacts in the racing business. Last night they had found his body at the bottom of a sheer cliff west of Cannes, on the Esterel coast. It looked natural, but it couldn't be.

Jenning had reported the disappearance of one of his mechanics, vanished without a trace. Putting two and two together, Gorman came up with the idea that the Associates had planned to sabotage Jenning's car in the Monaco race, killing him before he could sign the papers. The mechanic was Perrani's man. But now both were removed from the scene, for reasons unknown.

It sounded good. Or was it adding two and two, and getting three? It might be something else entirely.

The real question, the important question, was: What would the Associates do next? They had to stop Jenning— he was crucial to the whole shipment, until the papers were signed. They would try to kill him again, as they had tried before.

But when? How?

It would be soon. The race was only two days away.

Roger Carr was awakened on the morning of the third day by the smell of hot coffee and something tickling his chin. Anne was leaning over him, swinging her hair back and forth across his face. The sun streamed, into the room, and she looked bright, fresh, and very excited.

"I have a problem," she said, pouring him coffee. She was

dressed in a pair of brief shorts, a white sleeveless jersey, and sandals.

"You don't look like you have a problem."

"I do: What are you going to name the first child?"

"That's a hell of a question to ask a man first thing in the morning." He hesitated. "You don't mean—"

"No, no. I was just wondering."

"I don't have any idea." He got up and stumbled off to the bathroom.

"Grouchy in the morning," she said, watching him go. He looked back, saw her folded in a chair, holding her coffee cup. He felt suddenly happy.

"How were rehearsals last night?"

"All right. Are you always so mean when you get up?"

"I can't think until I brush my teeth," he explained.

"I had no idea."

"Shave, too."

"How extraordinary."

"Alone," he said, and shut the bathroom door.

She opened it later, as he was shaving, and he smelled the coffee in the bedroom outside. She leaned against the door, folded her arms across her chest, and watched him draw the razor down his face. Immediately, he cut himself on the chin —always the toughest part—and stuck his jaw forward toward the mirror, trying to see the extent of the damage.

"You're responsible," he said.

"Why?"

"Driving me out of bed at this ungodly hour. No wonder I'm not awake." He finished shaving, washed the lather off his face, and came out into the bedroom. She sat on the bed as he picked up his coffee.

"Nell," he said.

"What?"

"The first child. Nell. We could call her Death Nell for short."

"Death Nell Carr. I don't like that one."

"How about Hubert?"

"No. If it was a girl, we could call her Coma. Coma Carr? Not bad at all."

"I prefer Carcinoma."

"Now, there's a name." She repeated it to herself. "Perfect."

"And for a boy, Hubert Tort Carr."

"Too abrupt. Lyndon Tort Carr, maybe—but even that isn't very good."

"Everett Corrugated Carr."

"Better."

"Horace Porous Carr."

"Definitely."

They stopped and sipped the coffee.

"Am I going to marry you?" Carr asked.

"I don't know. Am I going to accept?"

"Ever since I was a kid," Carr said, "I've had a great fear of being rejected for anything. Jobs, the Groton football team, the winter cotillion—anything at all." He watched her carefully, but she was concentrating on her coffee cup. "I just thought I'd tell you," he said.

Finally Anne said, "Marriage is something you have to take a chance with."

"I suppose." He suddenly wished he hadn't brought it up.

A car pulled up in the drive. Carr recognized the deep growl of the Ferrari. Anne got up and went to the window.

"Liseau," she said. "He's motioning to me. I'd better go see what he wants. Back in a minute."

Carr sat stirring his coffee. He knew that when this was all over, he would take Anne back with him—and not just as far as Morocco. She wasn't the only one who knew a good thing when she saw it. He felt happy, and strangely impatient. But there was nothing to do except wait until Liseau released them.

She came back, slamming the door behind her, and sat down on the bed. Her face was tired, drawn.

"What's the matter?"

"Liseau. He just gave me my plane ticket. He's taking me with him to Hong Kong."

Chapter XX

Carr was stunned. he continued to stir his coffee mechanically, staring straight ahead.

"When?"

"Tomorrow night."

"Tomorrow night!"

Her voice was flat and dead. "He told me to quit my job at the casino, and get ready to leave, I suppose he meant you."

Carr took out a cigarette and began to play with it, tapping one end against the night table, turning it, and tapping the other end.

"I won't let him do it," he said at last.

She hugged him, and let her head fall on his shoulder. "It's no good. He's got us just where he wants us. There's no sense or hope in fighting him—he'll let you go, at least."

"I wonder," Carr said. Anne began to cry softly on his shoulder. "Easy," he said. "We'll find a way out of this. I have friends. Perhaps, if I can escape—"

"If you try, he will kill me. I know it." She stood up. "I have to go." She gave him one long, final kiss, salty with tears. "Goodbye," she said.

"Wait—"

The door slammed shut, and he heard her running down the hall. He sat thinking, trying to believe what was happening. He could not quite comprehend that Anne was being taken from him; the realization came slowly, and very painfully. He did not want it to happen.

He could not allow it to happen.

Carr had a sudden image of Vascard, the policeman, shaking his head in sadness and amusement at Carr's thoughts. It was a stubborn, foolish idea to try to escape—Carr knew that. The odds were against him, all down the line. But he could try, and he would try. He had no choice.

In all his life, Roger Carr had never escaped from anything more difficult than a blind date. He had no idea of how to begin, or what approach to use. He was weaponless, and defenseless—or was he?

He grinned as he dressed.

One weapon, honed and polished from long experience. One weapon, and one possibility.

He would take his chances.

As he walked out onto the terrace, Liseau called to him. Carr stopped, and looked at Liseau in what he hoped was a friendly way. He had few advantages in this game, but one would be surprise. "Yes?"

Liseau put an arm around Carr's shoulder and walked with him away from the house. "I trust you have been enjoying your visit."

"Yes, I have. It's been marvelous from beginning to end. Frankly, I did not expect it to be so pleasant."

"I'm glad to hear that." Liseau did, indeed, seem genuinely pleased. "I can tell you in turn that you will be free to go shortly."

"In a way, that's sad news—I'm afraid you've spoiled me for New York life. But I suppose I will be better off at work. Shall I make a plane reservation?" He kept his voice casual.

"There will be time for that very soon, my friend. But meantime I must ask you a favor. Tonight I am entertaining some guests, and we would prefer not to be disturbed. Will it be too much of an imposition for you to remain in your room for the evening?"

"Not at all. But tell me, may I have a guest of my own in my room?"

"I fear," Liseau said apologetically, "that Miss Crittenden will—"

"I wasn't thinking of Miss Crittenden." He gave Liseau a slow wink, man-to-man.

"Eh?" The doctor was caught off guard, momentarily puzzled, and he frowned. This man does not like surprises, Carr thought.

"You don't mean…"

"Yes."

Liseau shrugged, covering his relief. "But of course. My house and everything in it are at your disposal, please."

"You are very kind."

"Not at all. Good luck, my friend." He paused. "I think you will find she is excellent."

Carr smiled and nodded, then walked idly across the lawn, the picture of nonchalance. He stood with his back to the house, apparently admiring the view. His mind worked furiously—this was a long shot, and the chances of success were slim, but he had managed the first hurdle already. That was something.

He strolled around to the drive and surveyed the parked cars. One was his little Alfa two-seater, standing with the top up; Liseau, no doubt, had the keys to that. The second was Liseau's silver Ferrari, looking lithe and powerful. The third was a yellow Renault Dauphine. That, he thought, would be the maid's car.

He did not think anyone was watching him, but he moved carefully. Hands in his pockets, he wandered over to the

Alfa, which he regarded with proprietary interest. He kicked one of the tires. Then he moved to the Ferrari, and spent several minutes admiring it from all sides, and peering in to look at the dash. This was his first opportunity to see the car close up, and his admiration was genuine: it was a beautiful machine, swift and businesslike, with the muscular grace of a mountain lion. Pininfarina styling, he decided, and probably Scaglietti coachwork. The car would do 150 miles an hour without straining, and it looked it. Inside, the black horse pranced on a yellow background in the center of the wheel; the dashboard was straightforward, cleanly designed; the twin bucket seats were black leather. There was a briefcase on the shelf behind the seats, and a pair of tan hand-tooled driving gloves on the passenger seat.

He straightened up and, out of what seemed curiosity, went to the maid's car. He glanced at it briefly, showing little interest, but he managed to examine the inside thoroughly. The seats and steering wheel had been covered in tasteless imitation leopard skin, and there was an empty packet of cigarettes, crushed, stuffed in the ashtray.

But there was no throw-rug in the back seat, as he had hoped.

It was still possible, he told himself, as he walked back around the house. More difficult, but still possible—and the most difficult part was coming now.

The kitchen was a clean large room with a broad central table, white cupboards all around, and a waist-high shelf of stainless steel which ran around the room. Off to one side were three glass-walled ovens. Liseau must do a great deal of entertaining, he thought.

The maid worked at one of the sinks, shelling peas. Carr

tiptoed up and kissed her lightly on the nape of the neck, just below her short-cropped hair.

"Oh!" She dropped a handful of peas in surprise. "Monsieur Carr! It's you."

"Josette," he said. "You must call me Roger. I'd like to know you better."

"*Avec plaisir*—Roger." She rolled the *r* charmingly, and looked at her feet in a reasonable imitation of modesty. This girl hasn't got a drop of it, he thought.

"Don't let me disturb your work."

She seemed to come out of a daze, and snatched up her peas once again.

All right, he thought. Now, careful—this girl can't be as foolish as she looks.

"How do you like working here?"

"Oh, it's good. Very good." She shrugged, apparently deciding she had showed too much enthusiasm. "It pays well."

"You certainly have a fine place to work. This kitchen must be one of the best equipped in the region."

"Oh! You have no idea. *Le docteur* entertains often, with many guests, and he has all the conveniences. Look here," she said, pulling a heavy door. "Even a dishwasher! *C'est magnifique, hein?*"

"Amazing."

"But that is not all. We have a mixer, a blender, and *voici,* an electric can-opener." She tapped a small white box resting on a shelf. "We do not use it to open cans, of course," she said quickly. "We have no canned food in this household. But it also has an electric knife-sharpener, right inside."

"Really?" Now he was getting somewhere.

"*Oui.* I will show you."

She went to a drawer and fished in it for a moment. Carr

heard metal clicking against metal. Probably the whole drawer was full of knives. Finally she selected one, slim and glinting, and took it to the box.

"*Alors.*" She put her left hand on a small bar and set the knife into a slot. There was a high-pitched grinding noise, and the knife slowly slid out of the box and dropped into her hand.

"Amazing," Carr said, examining the knife. "Very practical."

"*Vraiment.*"

"Shall I put the knife back?"

"If you please." Josette resumed her pea-shucking, and Carr went over to the knife drawer. He opened it and ran his fingers noisily across the knives. At the same time, he dropped the newly sharpened knife into his pocket. He shut the drawer and returned.

"Tell me, Josette, do you have any time to yourself?"

"Of course. Tonight, for instance—I must serve drinks to Dr. Liseau's guests at nine, and then I am free."

"And what do you plan to do?"

A sly look crept across Josette's features. "Usually, on my nights off, I drive into Nice—"

"You have a car?"

"Of course. A Dauphine." She smiled. "But tonight, perhaps I shall not go."

"I certainly wouldn't want to interrupt your plans, but…"

"Yes?"

He grinned engagingly. "I would appreciate it if you would bring some drinks to my room about ten o'clock."

"For you and Miss Crittenden?" Her voice was suddenly harsh.

"Oh no. I will be alone."

"Ah."

"Can that be arranged?"

"With pleasure, yes."

"With great pleasure, I hope." He smiled. "Until then, Josette." He had a last glimpse of her, eyes devilish, her hands busy with the peas.

He sat in his room, thinking of the three cars parked in the drive. The evening would be tricky, he knew, and a lot depended on luck. There would be more cars in the drive—would they block Josette's Dauphine? Probably not, if she were in the habit of leaving shortly after the guests arrived. So there was no problem there.

That left two major difficulties—getting from his room to the car, and making his way past the gate guard. The first should be difficult enough, but the second might prove impossible. Certainly if the gates were locked...

He wondered if he should bring Josette with him. He had originally hoped to find a rug in the back seat; that would have allowed him to smuggle himself out while she drove at knife point. But there was no rug, and he was left with a difficult choice. He could either lie exposed on the floor of the back seat while Josette drove—and hope the guard didn't check—or else he could drive the car out himself. His chances of success seemed greater if he took Josette, but there was another consideration: Anne. She had said Liseau would kill her if Carr escaped, and he had no doubt she was right. Under most circumstances, she would be held responsible. But if Liseau found Josette bound and gagged in Carr's room?

That was how it would have to be. Josette would arrive at ten; he would tie her up, take her keys, and slip down to the Dauphine; if he could, he would get past the gates and then to Vascard, or Gorman. But first, he had to get through the gates.

A hundred questions, possible pitfalls, flooded his mind.

Would Josette forget—or not bother—to bring her keys? Would there be a guard in the hall? Would the front door be locked? Would the Dauphine start quickly? If the Associates gave chase, would they use the Ferrari? And most important, would Anne understand what had happened, and what he was doing?

He was not able to stop worrying until after lunch, when, lulled by good food and wine, he fell into a restless sleep.

Carr had an early dinner in his room, served by Josette, who seemed full of bawdy remarks and *double entendres*. When she had gone, he found he could not touch his food. He was dizzy with tension and excitement; his stomach turned, and his knees were weak. He had a muscle spasm in his left forearm.

He examined the knife he had stolen from the kitchen. It was serviceable enough, with a solid wooden handle and six inches of slim, very sharp blade. But it gave him little comfort—a knife was not much good against a gun, and these men had guns. He knew, too, that they weren't playing games. If he were caught, he would be killed.

He hoped, if he had occasion to use the knife, that he would have the guts to kill ruthlessly. Carr had never killed anything in his life—he'd never even cleaned a fish. He had a vision of himself padding stealthily down the hall toward an unsuspecting guard. The knife would be between his teeth, or wasn't that a good place?

Anyway, he'd approach the guard, and swiftly grab his arms with both hands. Then, how do you kill him? The guard would raise an alarm. He'd have to move quickly—slit the throat? How did you slit a man's throat? He dimly remembered that there was something you had to cut—the jugular vein, or something like that. The heroes were always doing it in the movies. But where was it? In front, on the side of the neck, or where?

As the night darkened, and the wind in the trees picked up, he felt the knotting fear inside him grow worse. It was like some crawling thing in his stomach, gripping him.

He lay down on the bed, stared at the ceiling, and waited.

It was now eight o'clock. The ashtray was heaping with cigarettes; the air hung in the room, smoky and stale. He could hear cars pulling into the drive, and went to the window to see them. Three arrived within a few moments of each other: the Associates were prompt. They parked their cars in a line—two Citroëns, and a Mercedes sedan he had not seen before—and briskly entered the house. Carr noticed with a start that the driver of the Mercedes was a woman; he couldn't see much of her in the dark. He returned to the bed, emptied the ashtray into the wastebasket, and lit a cigarette.

It was not until nine o'clock that he had his idea. He was standing at the window, stretching his legs and feeling the muscles quiver, when it occurred to him. As he smoked, he looked out at the yellow light from the living room pouring out on the grass below. He heard the faint murmur of voices. The Associates were drawing up final plans for the next day.

What were these plans? He realized that he had no idea, and he could see himself going to Vascard with no proof, no shred of evidence, not even an inkling of what was going on. Even if he wanted to help, Vascard would be bound by the law. Carr needed information—and the only source was the group in the living room.

He looked again at the light on the grass; it was tempting. The Associates hadn't bothered to draw the curtains. Anyone on the lawn outside could see right in, as could anyone on the roof…

His watch told him it was five past nine. That gave him nearly an hour. He looked out his window with new interest.

For a moment, he thought it couldn't be done, and then he spotted a way. Beneath his window ran a metal trough, a rain gutter barely two inches wide. It continued around the base of the entire second story. By moving along it, Carr might be able to reach the living-room roof, since the living room, cantilevered out over the hill, was the only single-story part of the villa. The problem was handholds—the walls were glass, and offered no grip at all. Occasionally, there were bits of metal molding or short sections of brick, but for the most part it was smooth glass.

He slid open his window-wall, and placed one foot on the gutter. It bent under his weight, but held. So far, so good. He stepped fully out, holding onto the edge of the glass, and one foot slipped.

Leather soles on his shoes, he remembered—fine for dancing, but not this. He went back inside and removed his shoes, then tried again, feeling the cold metal of the gutter on his bare feet.

He pressed himself flat against the glass and edged forward toward the living room, some fifty feet away. He did not look down. He passed the length of his own room, struggling for each handhold, testing each foothold. The room next to his was a storage room—it contained an ironing board, linen, odds and ends—and he went on. He could see his breath condensing on the glass. Careful, he told himself. Slowly.

Step by step, inch by inch.

His entire concentration was on his feet and hands; he felt the cool, curved surface of the gutter, and the cold glass against his fingers, chest, and cheek.

Another room.

The light was on, and Carr paused. Should he continue? He listened for a moment, heard nothing, and decided to risk it. Edging slowly along the gutter, he saw that it was a small study, filled with books, charts, correspondence files. There was a small desk and a padded chair. No one was in the room; probably Liseau had forgotten the light. He went on.

He was stopped cold by the sound of a man whistling.

It was coming down from the lawn. He froze, not even daring to breathe.

The sound came closer. Soon he could hear the soft pad of feet on damp grass.

It was a guard; it had to be. Making rounds, probably checking the woods most carefully. At least, Carr hoped so. He glanced down and saw a burly man with a rifle slung over his shoulder; the man walked with a relaxed, easygoing gait. He was obviously expecting no trouble.

Carr hoped he would not look up. He was painfully aware of how visible he was, spread-eagled against the glass. The whistling receded, and finally the guard went around the corner.

Carr's breath came in shallow gasps; he could not breathe deeply or his expanding chest, pressing against the glass, would force him off balance. He continued on, step by step, inch by inch. He fought back his terror. The night wind blew gently in his ears. Where was Anne now?

Step by step, inch by inch.

He was coming to the end—not long, just a few yards, a few feet, a few more cautious steps...

He stood on the tar-paper-and-gravel surface of the roof and took stock of his situation. His legs no longer shook; indeed, he seemed quite calm. He looked across the vast flat roof. In the center was a drain next to the chimney, the only two objects to break the monotony of the surface. He quietly stepped to the edge of the roof and saw a tin downspout leading to the ground. That would be helpful.

With one hand grasping the gutter pipe, he lay flat on his stomach and eased himself over the side, hearing the gravel grate loudly beneath him. It seemed that someone would be sure to hear it; he waited tensely, but the low murmur of conversation in the room continued without a pause. He pushed himself farther over the side, until he was bent at the waist, with only his legs remaining on the gravel.

He was just able to see into the room.

The Associates were there, clustered around a central table, beneath the mobile. They were standing, looking at something on the table, but their bodies blocked his view. He noticed the woman standing silently in a black evening dress. She was quite beautiful, though none of the men paid any attention to her. Was she one of them?

Liseau said something, and the men nodded; a moment later, Josette entered the room with a tray of drinks. The Associates sat down, though the woman remained standing, and Carr could at last see what was on the table.

It looked like a map. A large one, done in brown and white, like an ordinance survey chart. Drawn on it was a rather free-form loop, marked out in heavy red ink. The Associates were discussing the loop, pointing to various parts of it as they talked.

What the hell was it?

His head was beginning to ring from the blood rushing to it. He wished he could hear, but the wind masked what little sound penetrated the glass. Liseau raised his drink, and the Associates rose, blocking the map once again. Carr pulled himself back up to the roof.

If only he could hear!

He looked in frustration across the roof, to the drain and the chimney. His eyes fixed on the chimney. Perhaps, he thought. He moved slowly across the roof, painfully conscious that one slip, one crunching step, would finish him. He came to the chimney, bent over, and listened.

"...are agreed then, it will be here."

"Yes. Gentlemen, a toast." Carr recognized Liseau's voice. "To Tribune R."

"To Tribune R."

"And to Herr Brauer." It was another voice; Carr did not know it.

"Herr Brauer."

The woman spoke now. "Let us come to the point—to a swift and successful conclusion of the affair."

"Spoken like an angel," Liseau said, laughing.

Carr heard glasses clicking softly, and then the wind picked up, and other sounds were lost to his ears. Damn! He went back to the edge, leaned over, and looked in. The Associates were still standing, drinks in hand, discussing the map, which Carr could not see clearly. He felt frustrated—he couldn't see, and he couldn't hear.

He checked his watch. Nine-thirty. He had better start back. Standing carefully, he returned to the rain gutter; it took him almost ten minutes to cover the distance to his room.

Once inside, he began to shake all over. He had done a dangerous thing, and he had gotten away with it. He lit a cigarette and reviewed what he had seen. It meant nothing to him—but perhaps Vascard could piece it together.

Carr leaned on his elbows, and fought to control his shuddering body. He had gotten away with it, he thought. That was something—with a little luck, he might escape as well. He could imagine Liseau's face when he was told. Amazement, briefly replaced by irritation, and then the face would go blank. Orders would be given, calmly, coldly. Carr would be hunted.

But, with luck... He told himself: All he needed was a little luck.

Someone snapped on the light in his room.

Carr whirled and saw Liseau, standing by the door. In one hand he held a gun.

Chapter XXI

"Creditable acrobatics, Mr. Carr," he said. "You surprise me. I would frankly not have thought you capable of it."

Carr said nothing. How long had Liseau been there, standing quietly in the dark?

"I came up here quite by accident, to tell you that Josette regrets she cannot be with you tonight—and to ask you please to return the knife." He smiled blandly. "Josette is a most carefully trained servant."

An engine roared to life on the drive outside.

"In fact, there she goes now to Nice." He looked curiously at Carr, as if he were unsure what to make of him. "Shall we go downstairs?"

Carr got up and left the room, feeling sick and weak, defeated, This man was ahead of him every step of the way, and he had been from the start. Carr had been a fool to try to beat him at his own game. This was no field for amateurs, he thought, feeling the gun touch him gently in the spine. Liseau was a professional—he never prodded, never shoved, never moved or acted roughly. He remained calmly, delicately, perfectly in control.

They went downstairs, and to his surprise, Carr was not taken into the living room. Instead, Liseau steered him outside to the drive. A guard was there, smoking a cigarette, and leaning against the fender of the Ferrari.

"Off the car." Liseau's voice was quiet but commanding, and the guard jumped up as if he had been stung.

"It's not a bench, my friend. Next time, lean against the

wall." He turned to Carr. "I hate to see things misused, don't you?"

Carr did not reply. He waited, passive and tired. The sight of the guard had shown him that his planned escape would have been foiled anyway—he would have never made it to the Dauphine.

"Cheer up, Mr. Carr. Things are not as bad as you think. Here are the keys to your car." Liseau held them out, glinting in the moonlight. Carr could see clearly the cross and snake of the Alfa Romeo emblem. He took the keys slowly, almost reluctantly.

Liseau grinned in the dark, showing ghostly white teeth. He turned to the guard. "Help Mr. Carr put down the top of his car." Carr looked at Liseau, who said, "Go ahead. You'll want to enjoy the air on a fine night such as this."

Carr went slowly to the car and helped unclip the black canvas top from the windshield and roll it back down behind the seat. He moved automatically, unable to think, unable to understand. He felt the cool, dewy canvas in his hands, and ran his fingers across the cold black leather of the newly exposed seats. He was confused, and he must have shown it.

"I don't want you to be alarmed," Liseau said. "I am always distressed by suspicious looks." He smiled again and pointed down the drive. "When you get to the main road, you can turn left and return to Menton. You will pick up the Moyenne Corniche after a kilometer or so, and I think you can find your way from there."

He held out his hand. Carr took it, feeling strange; the grip was warm, dry, and smooth. "It's been very pleasant," Liseau said. "I wish you a good trip back to the United States."

Carr's mind began to function. There was a catch somewhere; there had to be. "What about my clothes?"

"Oh, yes." Liseau frowned, but did not seem very concerned. "We've forgotten those, haven't we? Shall I forward them to American Express, New York?"

Carr nodded dumbly.

"Good. We'll do that then. Goodbye, Mr. Carr."

"Goodbye." He got into the car, slipped out the choke, and flicked on the ignition. The light engine started immediately, the roar booming out into the night. In his rear-view mirror, Carr could see Liseau standing next to the guard. He backed the car around and started down the drive past Liseau, who waved amiably. Carr barely noticed him; he was listening to the sound of the engine. Was there a bomb under the hood? Had they loosened the steering mechanism, so it would give way on a turn and send him hurtling off the road?

But the car felt fine, and sounded good. The exhaust was a vigorous, healthy growl. He drove slowly down the drive, and as he went, he caught a glimpse of a small yellow car pulled over into the woods—Josette's car? Then she hadn't left the villa. Who had?

The gate lay ahead, open, but a guard stood by, rifle poised. Carr tensed his muscles. They might shoot him right here.

The guard saluted, smiled, and waved him through.

Carr pulled out onto the road, turned right—he was not about to follow Liseau's directions—and headed off in second. He continued to listen to the engine, and to twist the wheel experimentally. He could detect nothing wrong. He shifted up to third, gaining speed. He was going sixty now, then seventy. The curves shot past; he took them with tires squealing.

He couldn't believe it. He was free.

Should he go to Vascard, or Gorman? Vascard would be more sympathetic, but Vascard was a policeman. He could do nothing—he would be tied to the law. Carr had no proof, and no real information; Vascard would be unable to help. But Gorman was another matter altogether. Carr had the distinct feeling that Gorman knew exactly what was going on, and precisely how Carr fitted into things.

He pushed the speedometer up to eighty. The curves grew tighter; he cut them, starting outside, slipping in toward the rock wall, then out again. The road was deserted.

Abruptly he saw headlights in his rear-view mirror. Yellow lights—a French car. The car gained.

So this is it, he thought. They'll pass me, and give me a blast from the machine gun. He should have known! Liseau would want the job done neatly, away from the villa. He increased his speed, but the headlights gained steadily. Closer, closer—and with a loud honk, the car swerved around and passed him.

It happened so fast, Carr didn't have time to react; he barely saw the white Lotus Elan as it shot past him. There were a man and a girl inside. The girl waved gaily, without looking back at him.

Carr broke into a sweat, and slowed his car. He was being ridiculous, too nervous for his own good, too jumpy. He let the speedometer dip down to fifty, and held it there. He needed a cigarette. Fumbling in his breast pocket, he found one, and pushed it between dry lips. He depressed the cigarette lighter on the dash, and waited. His hands were shaking.

Another set of headlights behind. Carr did not increase his speed, but kept his eyes on the rear mirror, trying to discern what kind of car it was. The headlamps were low, spread wide—a big car. It came closer. A sedan of some kind.

The lighter clicked out, and Carr touched the glowing filament to his cigarette. His eyes went back to the mirror.

And suddenly, he caught a glint of the curved bumper on the blunt shark-nose of a Citroën.

He stepped on the accelerator.

Behind him, he heard a *ping,* then a slow whine. Another *ping,* whine. Off to one side came a sound like paper being torn—a hissing, ugly shredding sound.

They were shooting at him.

He was momentarily gripped by fear, but he forced himself to relax at the wheel. It was idiotic, shooting from a moving car. You couldn't hit anything—the motion of the car would send your shots wildly askew. It was no wonder that the bullets were going into the road, and off to the sides.

He picked up speed.

The Citroën stayed with him, and the shooting continued. Three into the road behind, two spanging off the rear bumper. With a loud *thunk!* one passed into the trunk.

But then he remembered the Citroën suspension—the smooth, fine ride which cushioned even the heaviest bumps. No wonder they were using a Citroën: it was the finest, most advanced suspension in the world, with the axles set far apart, to get the maximum wheelbase out of the chassis, and the air–oil springing which was one of the engineering triumphs of the automobile industry. Shooting from a Citroën would be like shooting from a living-room couch.

He was painfully aware of his head and shoulders, lighted brightly in the lights of the following car. He was a simple target; his shadow was cast on the windshield in front of him. But they hadn't hit him—they hadn't even hit the glass.

Two more bullets ricocheted off the road, and another sang off his rear fender.

They were aiming low.

Why?

His car whipped around another curve, the Citroën right

behind him. Two more shots in rapid succession bounced off his fender. One more into the trunk, low.

Why?

The noise of squealing rubber was loud in his ears. He cut the next corner sharply, barely missing the rock wall, and kept going. The engine roared into the night. The Citroën squealed through the curve after him.

Why?

Two more shots into the road. He could imagine the little puffs of concrete dust, and the white streak on the surface of the road that the bullets would leave. Shooting low, shooting low.

Why?

The tires!

It came to him in a flash. He was doing eighty-five—if a tire blew at this speed, he would lose all control, smashing into the rock face, or perhaps going into the low stone wall along the edge of the road. He could see the nose of the Alfa dipping as it crashed into the wall; then the rear end would lift up, slowly. The car would raise up and over the low wall, then bounce slowly down the hillside.

But Carr would not be with it. He would be thrown clear on impact, instantly killed. No wonder Liseau had made him take the top down. It all made sense now. Fiendishly clear sense. The police would find only the wreckage of a car, and the driver, who had no doubt been drinking or had fallen asleep at the wheel, dead without a mark of unnatural violence on him. A clear case of accidental death.

It was, in a way, brilliant.

Two more bullets whanged into his fender. It was only a matter of time before they hit the tire. He increased his speed.

The road curved gently downward. It was a good road, but it had not been made for speeds anywhere near one hundred miles an hour. Carr realized it; he felt his body pulled from side to side, and he felt the sickening skids at each sharp turn. Once, he skidded too far, and banged his rear end loudly into the wall—it bounced back, he regained control, and went on.

Sweat poured down his face, forcing him to blink his eyes rapidly. His hands were slippery, and his knuckles white as he gripped the wheel.

More speed.

The Citroën dropped back slightly, very slightly. They couldn't maintain the pace, but neither could Carr. He knew it. It was only a question of which curve would catch him and finish him.

His lights illuminated the jagged rock wall, then swung out to nothing, then back onto the road. Night bugs splattered against the windshield. He maintained his speed, the wind roaring wildly in his ears, tugging at his hair.

He was putting more distance between himself and the Citroën. The big car dropped back a little more. He took another curve, and momentarily the yellow lights were lost behind the bend.

He had just one hope. A desperate, insane hope—but it might work, if he could only keep up his speed a little longer. The road continued down, the curves growing sharper, the pavement narrower. His eyes stung from the sweat; his shoulders were stiff with tension and strain. He locked his elbows and held the wheel stiff-armed; that was better.

Another twist in the road—he was cut off from the Citroën for a few seconds that time. Perhaps…

He increased his speed.

The speedometer went up to one-ten. The engine was working hard now, screaming like a tortured demon with the night wind, which bruised his ears, deafening him. He took the next curve sloppily, bouncing from the rock face to the stone wall, then miraculously back to the center of the road.

It shook him badly, but he kept his foot down. The road grew narrower still. That was good. Another curve coming up, a deadly one, sharp and blind. Good. He slowed slightly, then slammed on his brakes.

The car skidded, the rear end spinning forward. He turned a full circle, then stopped, the motor dead. The Alfa stood sideways, blocking the entire road.

He jumped out. He could hear the approaching Citroën, moving very fast. He ran over to the stone wall at the edge of the road and flung himself over.

He fell.

For a horrible moment he thought he would fall forever, but then he hit the ground, rolling, and bounced down the hillside until he was stopped by a tree that slammed into his spine. Dizzy, he groped for the trunk, clutched it, and held. He pulled himself upright. The slope was gentle and a few yards farther down, he could see the red-tiled roof of a villa in the moonlight.

Up on the road, there was a noisy metallic crash. The front end of the Citroën emerged over the low wall; broken glass tinkled down the hillside. Carr crawled up. As he had hoped, the Citroën had not had time. They had taken the curve too fast, coming hard upon Carr's Alfa. The driver had not been able to touch his brakes before they hit. The front end of the French car was bashed in horribly, and the windshield was shattered; Carr's little Alfa had been upended by the collision. Carr looked at the Citroën, looking for movement but not expecting any. No one could have survived that crash.

Suddenly, with a loud *whoosh,* the interior of the Citroën burst into flame. The entire cockpit of the car went up in bright red, silhouetting the doorposts and windows. Carr dropped down the slope again, waiting for the gas tank to go.

So that was the game. Hit the tires, force the victim's car to crash, and then pitch in a Molotov cocktail as you went by. Very tidy, very natural, very accidental—by the time the police arrived.

The gas tank exploded with a roar and a rush of hot gas.

Carr climbed slowly down the hillside toward the villa.

A white-haired man in sandals and suspenders, carrying a newspaper, answered the door. He regarded Carr with unconcealed hostility and suspicion.

"Yes?"

"My car," he said, pointing up to the road, "has been in an accident. I must call someone. May I use your telephone?"

"The garages are closed now. It is night." The old man stuck his head out the door and glanced up at the moon for confirmation.

"Yes, I know. I want to call a friend."

"Yes?" The look remained suspicious, and the man continued to block the door.

"I will pay you for the call. Please."

"Come in."

Carr entered the room, lighted softly in pink. Pink wallpaper, pink lace curtains, and light coming through a pink lampshade. In one corner, a wrinkled old lady sat in a rocking chair, knitting.

"Good evening," Carr said. The old woman looked at him

strangely. For the first time, he became aware of his clothes —streaked with dirt from the fall—and his face, which he supposed was also dirty. He must look like a tramp.

"*Voilà.*" The man pointed to a phone, resting on a lace doily next to a pink couch. "You know the number?" His tone was wary.

"No." Carr took the offered directory gratefully, and thumbed through it looking for Gorman. He found no listing, so he dialed the police. The old man's eyes grew wide as he watched.

"Nice police. *Bon soir.*"

Very pleasant, Carr thought. "Good evening. May I speak with Captain Vascard?"

"He is not on duty."

"Then could you give me his home number? It's important."

"Your name, please?"

A moment later, the number was given to him, and he dialed Vascard's home. The phone rang seven times before it was answered.

"*Allo.*" The voice was strange, muffled.

"Vascard? Roger Carr here."

"Mr. Carr." A reproving pause. "I am eating." Carr heard a loud swallow, and the voice was clearer. "You try my patience, my friend."

"You're not the only one." He glanced at his watch. "But I need your help. You'd better send somebody up here—there's been an automobile accident, and I think people have been killed."

"You were involved, as usual?"

"I'll explain later. I also need you to contact the consulate for me—I think this is a matter for them. Have somebody pick me up here."

"Where is here?" Vascard asked patiently.

Carr put his hand over the phone. "Where is here?" he asked the old man.

"Eh?"

"The address. The street."

"Ah. Villa Francine, Rue Ambrose Toine. The villa is named for my wife, Francine." He nodded toward the woman in the corner, peacefully knitting.

"Villa Francine, Rue Ambrose Toine."

"All right. That will be Menton police—I will notify them. Also the consulate. Good night, Mr. Carr."

"Thanks."

"Don't mention it, please. I have resigned myself to you."

"Ouch!"

"Oh, stop being such a sissy," Ralph Gorman said, as he swabbed iodine on Roger Carr's scraped face. They were sitting in Gorman's kitchen, in his apartment in Cimiez. Gorman wore white tie and tails; he had been called back from a diplomatic function which he had been only too eager to leave. ("Emerging nations, you know—excellent canapés, but such thin skins.")

He had fed Carr a piece of pastry, a cup of coffee, and a quick shot of brandy, and was now swabbing his cuts.

"We've been worried sick about you," Gorman said. "Really, we have. Ever since you disappeared two days ago."

"Three days ago."

"Yes, right. Three days ago. Where have you been?"

"A prisoner in a villa."

"How interesting."

"I thought," Carr said, "that you might be able to advise me on my next step."

"It sounds quite bizarre," Gorman said. "Quite extraordinary."

"I've seen a man killed. A man named Perrani."

"Astonishing."

"Is that all you have to say? Ouch! Watch that stuff."

"Sorry. Well, frankly, I don't know what else to tell you. It seems terribly complicated, doesn't it?"

Carr frowned unhappily. He was being given the run-around.

"Who owned this villa?" Gorman asked.

Carr shook his head. "No information," he said, "until I hear your side of it."

"My side of it?" Gorman put a wounded hand to his breast. "*My* side of it?"

"Yes."

"Why, I'm as much in the dark as you are."

"You make me sick," a disgusted voice said. "Tell the poor bastard what's going on. We need his help, and we haven't got all night." Vascard stepped out of the bedroom.

"Surprise," Carr said.

"*A votre service.*"

"Vascard is Deuxième Bureau," Gorman said unhappily. "You probably didn't know."

"Of course he didn't know. Quit stalling and tell him what's going on. He's been kicked around, had his nose broken, been chased down highways—and you still insist on picking his brain without giving him a shred in return."

Vascard turned to Carr. "It is well known," he said, "that the Americans know nothing about Intelligence. Either they pay fortunes and get nothing back, or they expect the world for free." He shook his head at Gorman. "Besides, you should be able to tell at a glance that this man does not care about shipments or murders. He is worried about a girl, aren't you, Mr. Carr?"

"Well, I wouldn't put it quite like—"

"A girl?" Gorman said.

"Liseau's girl," Vascard said.

"Liseau's girl?" Gorman said.

"Try," said Vascard patiently, "not to repeat the conversation. Tell Mr. Carr the problem. And let us see if we can do something about it." He turned to Carr. "I have already sent out a squad to Liseau's villa, on the assumption that we would manage to prefer charges of some sort. Would you testify to the murder of Perrani?"

"Of course."

"Good. Then that is a start. I should receive a phone call at any moment. Meantime"—he smiled at Gorman—"tell him a story."

Forty minutes later, Vascard said briskly, "Well, now that we have exchanged reminiscences, we can get down to business."

Carr had listened with complete absorption as Gorman described the mixup with Morgan, the attempts on Jenning's life, and something about the arms shipment. Carr had responded with a quick outline of the events of the past few days, including what he had heard from the rooftop.

The telephone rang, and Vascard answered it. He spoke rapidly for several minutes in French, and looked disappointed. When he hung up, he said, "That was my group at Liseau's villa. It is deserted—they left rather hastily, it seems. But in any event, they are gone."

He paced unhappily up and down the floor, then said: "This is going to be a very long night, and we had better get moving."

"Tell me again," Gorman said, "what you heard through the chimney."

"Well," Carr began, "someone mentioned Tribune R, and they were looking at a map showing a wiggly red loop, and—"

"Never mind," Vascard interrupted, putting on his coat. "You can explain it to this simpleton on the way. We have less than fourteen hours before the start of the race."

"The race?" Gorman said slowly.

"Of course. What did you think they were doing?—looking at the wiring diagram for a vacuum cleaner? They were checking the course. Let's go."

Within half an hour, Carr found himself in a darkened, stale-smelling room, smoking a cigarette and waiting for Vascard to show the first slide. The screen was blank, and irritatingly bright; his tongue was raw from too much smoking. He was very tired, with the complete exhaustion which penetrated even his bones, making them ache.

The screen was filled with blurred color, which gradually resolved itself into a picture of Le Scalpel, taken, Carr judged, with a long telephoto lens. There was considerable foreshortening. He saw three men standing in the sunlight.

"Do you recognize any of them?" Vascard asked.

"Liseau is the one on the left. The man in the middle is an Associate—I don't know his name."

"Ever seen the fellow on the right?"

Carr squinted. The picture was not very clear; the immense magnification was beyond the capacities of the film grain. "I'm not sure. He looks something like the ugly blond fellow who was trailing me all around."

"His name is Ernst Brauer. He's a German, does odd jobs. Dirty jobs."

"Brauer? I think that's the name they were toasting."

"Probably," Vascard said dryly. "Two weeks ago, he was living very high in Savona, near Genoa. Then he managed to duck us. He probably crosses the border frequently, using different passports all the time."

There was a metallic click, and another picture flashed up. This one had been taken in downtown Nice, showing a man walking out of a nice-looking flat.

"Liseau's office," Vascard said. "Know the man?"

"He's another of the Associates."

"Antoine Gerard," Gorman said. "The old devil."

"That's right. The legal arm of the Union Corse."

"Yes," Carr said. "He questioned me. They said he was a lawyer."

"He is. A brilliant one," Vascard said. His voice indicated no admiration.

Another picture. This one showed Liseau talking to a bearded man at a sidewalk café.

"Oh no!" groaned Gorman.

"What's the matter?"

"My psychiatrist."

"He's an Associate," Carr said.

"*Voilà*," said Vascard irritably. "The leak in our highly vaunted American consulate. How interesting."

Gorman sat back and said nothing. He looked as if he wanted to cry.

Another picture. Carr stubbed out his cigarette, took one of Gorman's Luckies, and looked up at the screen. It showed a man leaning against a railing with a strikingly beautiful girl on his arm. The girl was short and compact, with glossy black hair; her eyes had a fiery look. The man was much older, and looked to be in his late thirties—a vigorous, barrel-chested man with a broad smile and prematurely graying hair. He wore sandals, tan slacks, and a smug look on his face.

"Recognize him?"

"No."

"That's Victor Jenning."

"Who's the girl?"

"Number five, I believe, though it's hard to keep track. The man is irrepressibly virile," Vascard said. "This picture is two years old."

"And he's on number seven now?"

"Something like that."

"Attractive," Gorman said.

"I didn't know you were so inclined," Vascard said.

"I meant the girl."

The picture changed. Another of Jenning, with a very young girl.

"Number three," Vascard announced.

He clicked on to still another scene, taken in the Monaco port, showing Jenning holding onto the stays of a sailboat and talking to a woman.

"That's her," Carr said.

"Who?"

"The woman who was with the Associates tonight."

"*Are you sure?*" Vascard asked.

"I think so. Do you have another picture?"

"Just a minute." Vascard shuffled through his slides, selected one, and slipped it into the projector. It was a closeup showing Jenning and the woman getting out of a taxi in front of the Monte Carlo casino.

"That's her, all right," Carr said. She was tall and handsome, in a hard, rather bitchy way.

"Number seven, the latest. We don't know much about her, except that she's French Algerian, a *pied noir.* Jenning married her last year at just about this time. It's interesting —I wonder if she was one of them all along." He sighed. "Anyway, it certainly changes things."

"You know," Gorman said, "that those papers can be signed—"

"I know. We'll pick her up tomorrow, during the race. Speaking of the race," Vascard said, clicking to a slide, "here we are." It was a map of Monaco, with a heavy green loop. "The course."

Carr looked intently. It seemed to be the same loop as the one he had seen in red before.

"We use this slide to brief our men before the race—we always send a few over to help out with traffic. Now, look. As you know, the racecourse consists of public roads in the center of Monaco, cleared and converted. The circuit itself is laid out in an L-shape, running from the port up and around the casino, then back to the port. It begins here, at the port; the cars run east, then turn right up the hill and continue for a long straightaway. This is where Tribune R is located. At the end of the straightaway, there is a sharp turn, then another as the cars go around the casino. They come out to a short downhill stretch, pass three difficult turns, and emerge alongside the far end of the port. They pass through this tunnel—the Tunnel of Pigeons—and come out on a straightaway, a slight curve, then another straight stretch. Then they follow the course around to the front of the port, run one final hairpin, and return to the starting point. One hundred laps to the race, three kilometers a lap."

There was a pause.

"Mr. Carr has told us that he overheard of Tribune R, the bleachers along the uphill stretch. It is a good choice, since there are relatively few places where the drivers attain high speeds on the Monaco course. The cars will be going nearly two hundred kilometers an hour at this point—one hundred twenty-five miles an hour. At the end of the straightaway is a curve, and they must slow to ninety miles an hour to negotiate it. Barriers will be erected at that point, of course, but a car out of control would still be serious. It would probably bounce over the barriers and roll down the hillside." He indicated this on the map.

"However, we must take into account two other possibilities. The Associates may change their plans in the light of Carr's escape. There are other places where the tires could be shot with excellent effect—here, just before the tunnel, or here, just outside the tunnel. The cars will be traveling over one hundred miles an hour at either point and, out of control, would probably plunge into the water—it's happened before."

Vascard looked steadily at them. "But the second consideration is more serious. The Associates may choose to be less artful in their assassination—they may merely shoot Jenning. And if they decide to do that, it could happen anywhere along the course. Anywhere at all."

Chapter XXII

Roger Carr awoke the next morning feeling terrible. He was exhausted, cramped, and cold; his eyes hurt and his shoulders were stiff—probably from his drive in the Alfa, he reflected. His tongue was thick from smoking so much, and his nose had chosen to ache again. He sat up on the cot and looked around the cell.

It was all right, as cells went. It was reasonably large and clean, and it did not smell. He had no reason to complain. He would have complained the night before, when Vascard had locked him in, but he had been too tired to argue.

"I want you safe, my friend," Vascard had said. "See you in the morning."

He was swinging his feet onto the cold floor when Vascard peered through the bars at him.

"Good morning," he said in a grim voice. Vascard's eyes were bloodshot, and there were deep circles down to his cheekbones. His jaw was slack, his hair rumpled. "Sleep well?"

Carr nodded.

"Coffee in my office."

They went upstairs to Vascard's office. The desk had been cleared of books and papers, and a large map of Monaco set out on it. There were four coffeecups on the edges of the desk; all had cigarettes stubbed out on the saucers. A large ashtray, full of butts, rested at one corner. There had obviously been an all-night conference.

A plug-in percolator was bubbling to one side of the room.

Vascard rummaged in his desk and came up with a fresh cup for each of them. He poured the coffee, then added a shot of brandy from a hip flask into his own cup.

"Join me?"

"No, thanks."

"If you will excuse me, I need it. Please sit down."

Carr sat, holding the warm cup in his hands.

"Mr. Carr, you have been most cooperative thus far. I had originally hoped not to involve you further." Vascard shifted uneasily in his chair. "However, several things occurred during the night, and I think you should be informed.

"First, as I had expected, our check of Monaco has been fruitless. The magnitude of the problem is staggering—apartments and hotels line the course. There are thousands of windows, hundreds of possible firing points overlooking the race. Our only hope, and it was a slim one, was to stumble upon Brauer, or to find someone who recognized his description. We had no luck."

"You make it sound as if Jenning is already dead."

Vascard shrugged.

"Shouldn't we try to see him? Convince him not to race?"

"We did. Again, it was as I expected. He does not scare easily, Mr. Carr."

"What about his wife?"

"We will arrest her at the race. She is crucial."

"Why is that?"

"For the present, it is better if you do not know. However: to proceed. We have done some checking, and discovered that the girl quit her job yesterday, much to the irritation of the Palm Beach casino. No explanations, no forwarding address. Air France reports a block of four tickets sold for this evening's flight from Nice to Athens with connections to

New Delhi and Hong Kong. Three men and one woman—all fictitious names."

"I see."

"Half an hour ago, the ticket for the woman was canceled."

Carr sat up quickly. "What does that mean?"

"I'm not sure. It may mean that she will be left behind. It may mean she will leave the country another way. Or it may mean—"

"All right," Carr said. "What do you want me to do?"

Vascard spread his hands on the desk. "The problem, you see, is how the Associates may choose to leave. I doubt that they will use their plane tickets, since we know about them. They will leave the country another way. They could drive across the border into Italy or Switzerland, since the mountain passes are all open now. They could go to Spain, or north to Germany or Holland, and fly from there. They could take a yacht from Cannes; Liseau has friends. Or they could go by private plane—there's an airport, a private one, near Antibes. We can't bottle them up. It's too big a country. There are too many ways."

Carr gulped back his coffee, feeling the liquid burn down his throat. It helped wake him up.

"There is just a single hope," Vascard said. "We must find Liseau today."

"How? Where?"

"At the race, of course."

"You think he'll be there?"

"He'll be there. He's the type."

Carr nodded. "And you want me to help find him, is that it?"

"Yes," Vascard said, draining his cup and refilling it with brandy. "Better than anyone else, you know Liseau. You know his walk, his mannerisms, his gestures—and that helps in spotting a man at a distance. There will be more than one hundred thousand people at the race today. We'll need you badly."

"Why not simply look for his car? It's very distinctive."

"It is—so distinctive that the customs officers at Ventimiglia remembered it crossing over into Italy at two this morning. Liseau wasn't driving it—someone else, a skinny pale man. The papers were in order; he was allowed through."

"You think Liseau knows where Anne is?"

"He does, if anybody does."

"All right," Carr said. "Tell me what you want done."

Vascard stood. "I think I'd better explain on the way."

As they left the room, Carr took a last look at the map, with the course marked out in heavy black pencil.

The green pine-wooded hills above Villefranche slipped by beneath them. Carr looked out of the bubble cockpit as Vascard shouted into his ear, trying to make himself heard over the high-pitched whine of the helicopter. Carr had never been in a copter before, and the experience had impressed him—running up to the cockpit beneath the thumping blades, which produced a dusty wind of gale force; sitting and hearing the scream of the engines mount until he thought it could go no higher, and yet did; feeling the vibration shake the little craft with increasing force, to the point where it seemed the plane must fall apart.

Abruptly, the pilot had lifted off and headed east toward Monaco, moving fast and low, skimming the hills and little resort towns. Down below, people looked up, startled, as the shadow of the machine raced over the ground.

"One of the Associates owns an apartment block overlooking the race," Vascard was saying. "It's being searched at this moment, though I doubt we'll find anything. They're too smart for that."

Vascard's voice warbled from the vibration that shook them all. The pilot, taciturn behind sunglasses, ignored them. The helicopter came over a small rise, and they found themselves overlooking Monaco. The neat, high hotels and apartments crowded the land, which sloped steeply down to the water. Yachts jammed the port to see the race.

Vascard leaned toward the pilot and shouted something; the pilot nodded.

"We're going to follow the course. Watch carefully. It begins here, just beneath us, and runs uphill. There's Tribune R." They skimmed over a section of bleachers set along the road. Spectators were already gathering, though it was only eleven —three and a half hours before the race. "Now we come past the casino." The copter dipped and swerved left, then right. "You can see how dangerous the curves are. But after the casino, along here, are the really difficult ones."

Looking down, Carr saw a sharp S-curve which zigzagged down the hillside toward the water. "I don't think it will be here," Vascard said. "Too slow at this point to do damage. But look now—we're coming around to the tunnel. As the cars come out of the tunnel, they follow the straightaway to this slight curve—see it?—called Le Chicane." Carr saw that it was less a curve than a kink in the straight road. "Le Chicane is murderous. It's bumpy, and the cars take it fast. Anyone who went into it wrong would go right into the water."

The pilot pulled up abruptly, turning in the air. He looked questioningly at Vascard, who shook his head.

"Once is enough," Vascard shouted to Carr. "Let's land and get to work."

✿

The Grand Prix de Monaco is one of the most viciously exciting motor races in the world. It is not a fast course—not until 1964 did anyone do a lap at an average speed of one hundred miles an hour, and that was Graham Hill in a B.R.M. But it is a twisting, strenuous, dangerous track, with ten major curves to a lap, a thousand to the race. The driver is forced to shift on an average every five seconds.

At the end of nearly three hours of racing, it is not un-common for a driver's right hand to be raw and bloody from shifting. He is constantly changing from roughly 200 kilometers an hour on the straights to 50–70 in the turns, and then back. If it is a hard race for the drivers, it is sheer torture for the machines.

And the drivers take punishment enough. If it is a hot day, cockpit temperatures soar to 150 degrees, and more; a driver can sweat off ten pounds in one hundred laps. Because it is a confined circuit, hemmed in by buildings and trees, there is danger of carbon-monoxide poisoning—and the dangers of a crash. Some circuits are padded by earth embankments and grass; Monaco greets the driver with sharp-edged buildings, concrete, glass, and trees. Frogmen are always standing by to pull drivers from the waters; they did this for Alberto Ascari. Another driver was killed in 1962 when he struck a tree, and the debris of still another crash killed a track official.

These thoughts ran through Roger Carr's mind as he stood on the hill near the Royal Palace and fingered his yellow armband stamped "Presse." It would allow him to go any-where, Vascard had assured him—even down to the pits if he wanted. Vascard had one as well, and they set off in different directions.

It was eleven-thirty.

Crowds choked the streets and walked along the course, past banners and brightly colored signs erected to advertise drinks—Cinzano, Martini, Dubonnet—or automobile products—EP Longlife, Total, Antar Molygraphite, Castrol. Over the starting line hung a banner which read: *"C'est Shell Que J'aime."*

Race attendants were adjusting the last of the straw bales at the curves. The general atmosphere was one of gaiety, festivity, expectancy.

Carr watched the crowds through binoculars. He had seen the license plates of the cars coming into the city, and he knew the variety of people who had arrived for the race— Italians from Genoa, Torino, and Milano; Frenchmen with plates numbered 06 and 13, from the provinces of Alpes-Maritimes and Bouches-du-Rhône; a great many GB cars, which was to be expected, since so many Grand Prix drivers were English; a handful of Germans, Austrians, and Spaniards.

The loudspeakers on the track blared something in French; Carr couldn't understand it. The message was repeated, and then a calm British voice announced that the circuit would be closed in several minutes. Policemen were erecting barricades to keep traffic off the streets used in the race. Drivers of passenger cars got out to argue, and were turned away.

At noon exactly, the voices in French and English reported that the course had been sealed. People dressed in bright sports clothes still walked along the streets of the race, but policemen were shooing them off. A sweeper began to make slow circuits of the track.

Carr went down to the course, and was allowed onto the track by the guards. A high, frightfully loud scream burst over the chattering of the crowds, and the first of the cars pulled onto the track and came around to the pits. One by one, the sixteen competitors drove around to their respective pits.

The crews, men in coveralls and girls with clipboards and sexy expressions, clustered around the cars. So did newsmen and photographers. Carr walked over to the car which was attracting most attention, Graham Hill's B.R.M. Hill was standing next to it, in a tight-necked racing suit which reminded Carr of an intern's jacket. He was a tall man, with swept-back hair, a neat moustache beneath a rather hawk nose, and intensely serious eyes. He had qualified second in the trials.

Hill signed autographs absently as he answered the questions of newsmen. Microphones were stuck toward his face, notepads were out, pencils scribbling. "How does it feel, Graham?" "What are your thoughts just a few minutes before—" "How do you rate your chances to win an unprecedented—"

Hill answered quietly, almost offhandedly, and seemed justifiably preoccupied. He managed to ignore one little man who kept demanding in a squeaky voice, "Do you miss England? Do you miss England?"

Carr had never seen a Formula I racer close up, and his attention shifted to the car. Mechanics were removing the shell of the little cigar-shaped body, painted green with a circle of orange around the snout. Carr was astonished to see how low it was—the driver's head was bare inches above the level of the wheels. The car looked mean, low, fast.

A van drove along the track, stopping at each pit to allow men in light blue tunics to jump off and set down stretchers and first-aid kits. It added a morbid note to the proceedings. The girls walked around, talking gaily, fiddling with their stopwatches and clipboards.

Carr moved on to Jenning's pit. Jenning seemed in an expansive mood, and if he felt tension he did not allow it to show. Newsmen greeted him like an old friend, with the amity that Carr suspected was reserved for time-honored and reliable copy. Jenning's racing suit was not white, like most of the other drivers'; it was a spectacular fiery red. Carr recognized the woman in the pit as Jenning's wife—the woman he had seen at the villa the night before. She paid no attention to him, and seemed absorbed with thoughts of her own, standing apart from the crowd, smoking a cigarette held in long lacquered fingers.

An official limousine, escorted by motorcycles, came down to the red velvet box of honor as the loudspeaker announced that Prince Rainier and Princess Grace had arrived at the track. They waved to the crowd, and took their seats. It was now less than half an hour to the start of the race. Carr left the pits and started up the hill toward Tribune R.

The bleachers were temporary; throngs milled among the metal struts which supported the wooden slabs that served as benches. Carr watched the spectators carefully, pausing often to look behind him. He felt that his behavior must seem unusual, but nobody noticed him. People walked in small groups of three or four, talking animatedly, caught up in the air of anticipation which was rapidly growing to a fever pitch.

He saw Liseau.

For a moment he couldn't believe it, and stood unsure among the crowds. Liseau was dressed in a black suit, and wore his sunglasses. He was talking to a middle-aged couple about one hundred yards away. It appeared to be a friendly, inconsequential discussion—perhaps they were old patients, Carr thought, as he pushed forward. His hand reached up unconsciously to his shirt pocket, feeling the small bulge of the whistle Vascard had given him.

"Don't blow it unless you have him," Vascard had warned. "And if you do have him, blow like hell."

As Carr approached, Liseau looked casually over and caught sight of him. Seemingly undisturbed, he excused himself, shook hands, and moved off. Carr tried to follow, but the crowd seemed suddenly turned to molasses. Everyone moved so slowly!

Liseau was slipping away. Carr began to run, knocking people aside, no longer pretending politeness, but this only made his situation more difficult. The crowd, startled and annoyed, impeded him. Men plucked at his sleeve, demanded apologies. He tried to shake them off, tried to keep his eyes on Liseau, who was heading away from the bleachers, up the back streets of the town. Carr followed, falling farther and farther behind.

Liseau ducked down a street to the left; when Carr reached the corner, the man was gone.

It was two-thirty. The loudspeaker announced that the course would be opened by a series of vintage racing cars: a Mercedes 196S, driven by Juan Fangio, a 2.5-liter Lotus Climax, driven by Stirling Moss, a 2.3-liter Bugatti and a 2.7-liter Ferrari. The list of cars and drivers rambled on. Frustrated, Carr returned to the course.

By the time he had made his way to a viewing position, the antique cars had completed their lap and left the circuit. The automobiles in this year's competition were being pushed by mechanics to their positions—two abreast, for eight rows—at the start. The drivers walked along behind, waving to the spectators, who cheered wildly. Carr lit a cigarette and wondered if Liseau would reappear.

One after another, the engines roared to life. The starting line was hidden in a thick cloud of gray smoke, the noise reminiscent of a swarm of giant hornets. The loudspeaker came on.

"The starter is giving his final instructions to the drivers. He wishes them a good race, and a safe race, and reminds them that the cup is not won in the first lap." The lap was touchy, since the cars were close together, and jockeying for initial positions.

The starter, flag in hand, ran forward, leading the cars to the starting line. He reached the line, held the flag high for one dramatic instant, and whipped it down.

Sixteen cars tore forward with a cloud of smoke and a banshee scream. Tightly clustered, they came into the first turn, took it, and ran up the hill out of his view. The smell of gasoline and exhaust hung in the air. Carr's ears rang from the noise.

"A good start," the loudspeaker declared. "From our spotter at the casino, the positions are as follows: first, Jack Brabham, in a Brabham-Coventry-Climax; second, Gennaro Mollini, in a Ferrari; third, Jackie Stewart, in a B.R.M. Graham Hill got off to a poor start, and is fifth behind John Surtees of the Ferrari team."

The spectators nodded wisely at the news. Ferraris second and fourth—the Ferrari usually did well at Monaco, but rarely won. It had happened only twice, in 1952 and 1955. Still, they were fast cars, there was no denying that. Hadn't Ferraris run the fastest lap times five times since '52?

Carr idly listened to the discussion. The first of the cars reappeared at the port, engines screaming down the straight-away. Brabham led, hard-pressed by Mollini in a red Ferrari. The pack was still tight, but beginning to string out.

With whines and grunts, the cars shifted down for the final turn and came up to the starting line.

The race had begun. Ninety-nine laps to go.

He could see the drivers quite clearly as they flashed past

him, their faces stern, concentrating. They locked their elbows
and held the wheel straight-arm. It reminded Carr of the
night before, and he thought of Liseau and Anne. Did the
doctor know where she was? Was she still alive? And could
he find Liseau?

He looked up at the apartments, their rooftops and balconies jammed with spectators. Kids sat on the rooftops and
hung their legs over the side.

With a devastating roar, the cars swung around once more,
starting the third lap. He caught sight of Jenning, running
fifteenth. He was smiling slightly as he drove.

Ninety minutes later, the race was half over. Carr saw Brabham's pit crew hold out a blackboard as the cars whizzed by;
written in white chalk were the numbers 49 and 4—forty-nine
laps to go, in fourth place. Brabham, with ignition trouble,
had dropped back and Mollini's Ferrari had held the lead for
the last twelve laps. Stewart, in second place, was barely
holding his own against John Surtees. The crowd was beginning to wonder when Surtees would make his bid. And
Graham Hill, still in fifth place, three seconds behind Brabham,
was causing comment.

One car had already left the race; Connie Richards had
been forced out when his Honda developed transmission
trouble. Jenning had had one slow lap because of mechanical difficulties, but had rallied and was still in the race.

The noise was overpowering. Carr's ears were numbed;
he strained to catch the words of the announcer, often
obliterated by the scream of passing cars. He expected at
any minute to hear the news of tragedy for car 14. Brauer
bad done nothing yet—probably he was waiting until late in
the race, when Jenning would be exhausted, his reflexes slow.
That would be the time.

He looked at the crowds, and briefly caught sight of Vas-card, who waved grimly and disappeared. The cars went into the sixtieth lap.

He walked up toward the casino, and found a place where he could see the cars taking the curves. The engines growled and grunted as the drivers shifted down. The course of a thousand curves, he thought again—a circuit almost contin-uously twisting, sharp, unbanked, steeply sloping up or down. Hellish.

He did not see Liseau. He often turned up to the apart-ments and hotels, scanning the faces with his binoculars. He never once saw his man. Discouraged, he worked his way back toward the port.

Seventieth lap. Less than an hour to go in the race.

Carter Blakely crashed into the barricade at the *Virage des Gazomètres*, the loudspeaker announced. There was no word on the driver, but the car was definitely out of the race. A few minutes later, the loudspeaker said that Blakley was unhurt. Carr had been unable to see any of it from where he was standing.

Seventy-five laps.

The drivers showed the strain, and the lineups shifted twice. It was now Mollini, Surtees, and Hill running within two seconds of each other. Surtees, the Ferrari factory team leader, wanted to pass his teammate Mollini; an official waved a blue flag indicating this to Mollini, who ignored the signal for three laps. Finally Surtees took the lead. Hill, at number three, set a lap record and cut the gap between himself and Mollini to half a second.

On the eightieth lap, Jenning held fourteenth place—last place, since two cars were out. He drove doggedly, his face tense and tight-lipped beneath his goggles. The leaders had long since lapped him.

Carr kept looking for Liseau, with a growing feeling of desperation. In less than forty minutes, the race would end and one hundred thousand people would swarm down from the bleachers into the streets. Liseau would go with them. He would escape, coolly and quietly, from under the noses of the police—the crowd was his ally, and his ultimate protection.

The leaders tore down the straightaway on the eighty-seventh lap, Hill in second position behind Surtees. Carr looked down the road at the other autos as they emerged from the tunnel. Mollini was third, Stewart was fourth. All of them had lapped Jenning, who now came out of the tunnel, down the straightaway.

Without warning, Jenning's car gave a frightful roar, swerved violently, and smashed into the barricade at the water's edge. A cloud of bright yellow straw lifted into the air as the car bounced up, twisted sickeningly, and slapped upside down into the water. Spectators rose instantly; a woman screamed.

For a moment the four wheels and dirty underbelly of the car were visible above the surface of the water, and then it sank. A police motorboat churned across the port to the place where bubbles still rose. Carr waited for Jenning's head to bob up, but it did not.

"Victor Jenning, in car 14, has gone into the water at the Chicane curve. We have no word on the driver's condition."

At the pits, an official waved a white flag at the drivers, telling them an ambulance was on the course. At the scene of the accident, men were hastily sweeping straw off the track. The ambulance was parked at the water's edge, waiting, the stretcher out and ready. Two divers with aqualungs plunged in from the police boat. Carr waited, but they did not come up for several minutes.

Sickened, he turned away from the race. Liseau had won, exactly according to plan. It was all over now, all finished.

Aimlessly, Carr walked up the narrow streets of Monaco, ignoring everything around him. He felt disgusted, nauseated. As he traveled farther from the course, he came onto deserted streets, shops and cafés closed. The noise of the race receded behind him, becoming a muffled roar, like faraway ocean breakers.

He listened to his footsteps echo as he walked past the rows of parked cars. There were thousands of cars here for the race, providing transport for the thousands of people who would unwittingly help Liseau to escape. Carr noticed them idly—the expensive Citroëns and Mercedes; the occasional aristocratic Maserati; the modest little VW's and Simcas.

And then he saw a yellow Renault, with leopard seat covers. A pair of hand-tooled driving gloves were draped over the wheel.

Chapter XXIII

He reacted slowly, walking around the car in disbelief. It didn't seem possible, and yet—he was sure of it. Bending over, he quickly let out the air in the two front tires. Then he straightened and dropped back into a nearby alley.

He did not have long to wait. Within minutes, Liseau appeared at the far end of the street, walking briskly, not looking around him. He was a man in a hurry, but still cool, still confident. Liseau unlocked the Renault, got in, and started the engine. Carr stepped out and walked over to the window.

"You have a couple of flats, you know. Both front tires. Very, very flat."

Liseau looked at him from behind the steering wheel and said nothing. He appeared only mildly surprised. My God, he has self-control, Carr thought.

"How did you plan to go, Liseau? Plane, boat, what? Never mind, it doesn't matter. Let's just wait here until the police arrive." He took out his whistle. "They even gave me this little thing to speed matters along. Thoughtful of them, wasn't it?"

He raised the whistle to his lips, and felt something cold in his stomach. He looked down at the gun.

"Don't," Liseau said. "Drop it on the ground and step back."

"You wouldn't risk a shot, Liseau. They'd be all over you in a minute—and you with your hands reeking of cordite."

"That is why I am wearing gloves, and using this rubber baffle silencer. It makes no sound louder than the click of the pin against the cartridge."

Carr looked again at the gun. It was a pistol, with a long, dull black extension.

"Step back," Liseau said. "Put your hands in your pockets, and act naturally. You are taking a little walk."

Carr stepped back. "Give up, Liseau. You've had it. The race is almost over."

"Yes, isn't it?" Liseau got out of the car and pointed up the deserted street. There was nobody in sight. "It will not be a long walk, Mr. Carr. Ernst will accompany you."

Carr whirled. The German was behind him, the pig-faced one. He had come up silent as a cat.

"The park," Liseau said to Ernst. "Do it quickly." The German nodded. Liseau walked to the next parked car, a black Citroën, unlocked it, and started the engine. "How nice to have known you, Mr. Carr."

"Where's the girl?"

"As a matter of fact, I am going now to take care of her. I can't see spending the money for a plane ticket for her, can you?"

"Where is she?"

Liseau laughed. "Where do you think?" And with that, he drove off. Carr felt something push him in the back, rather roughly.

"Move," Ernst Brauer said.

They walked.

Brauer was being careful. He walked alongside Carr, not touching him, and he kept the gun out of Carr's vision. Carr didn't dare take a swing—he could not be sure where the gun was.

He tried to think of a way out. There always was one in the movies, he thought grimly.

They approached a policeman, lounging against a lamppost, obviously disconsolate that he had drawn traffic duty which kept him away from the race. There was no traffic at all.

"The gun is now in my pocket," Brauer said. "Do not speak to our friend up there. I would not like to ruin my suit, or his."

Carr kept walking. As they passed, the policeman nodded affably to them. Brauer nodded back. They continued, hearing the roar of the crowds and the cars on the slopes below.

"Where's the girl?" Carr asked.

Brauer only laughed. They came into a small, green, neatly kept park. "Sit down on that bench over there." The bench stood in a cheerful patch of sunlight. A discarded newspaper lay at one corner. Birds chirped, and the noise of the race seemed very far away.

Carr sat down.

"This is satisfactory," the German said. "After, I will put the newspaper over your head. To anyone going by, you will simply be a drunk fallen asleep. It is unusual in Monaco, but on a day such as this, some of the worst types come into the city."

"I've noticed."

"Lie down, Herr Carr."

"You'll never get away with this, Brauer." He remained sitting, his mind racing frantically, looking for a way out. Nothing came to him.

"Sit or lie—it is all the same. I will adjust your position afterward." Carr saw the finger tightening on the trigger.

"Stop!" It was a gruff voice, from the trees to the left.

Brauer turned to look. Carr jumped for the gun. It fired just as his hand closed over Brauer's; he saw the flames spurt and heard the report loud in his ears. His left leg was kicked back, and he toppled over. The gun fired again, this time into the dirt path near his face. There was another shot.

Carr rolled on the ground, saw Brauer's legs, and grabbed them. The German fell easily—too easily, Carr thought as he threw himself on the man, scrambling for the gun. It fell out of Brauer's fingers.

Carr looked down at the face. The eyes were rolled back, as if trying to peer into the skull. He was lying on a dead man.

He heard running feet on the path. It was Vascard. He came up just as Carr staggered to his feet and discovered that his left leg was bleeding.

"Nice shot," Carr said.

Vascard was panting. "Twenty meters, not bad," he said. "Is he alive?"

"No."

"Damn. That ruins everything." Vascard frowned. "Where is Liseau?"

"He got away." Carr thought—away to Anne. Liseau's parting words came back to him. Where did he think she was?

Where did he think?

More policemen were running up. Carr felt weak, giddy from his leg. His trouser, soaked in blood, clung heavily to him.

Where did he think?

And suddenly, in a burst of clarity, he knew.

Chapter XXIV

He snatched up Brauer's gun and began to run. The gun seemed heavy in his hands.

"Hey!" Vascard said. "Where are you going? You have a wounded leg!"

Carr didn't listen. He was running, trying to figure out how the safety on the gun worked. He had never fired a gun before. Well, he thought, a first time for everything.

If he was only in time.

He jumped into the first cab he saw. The driver was frightened. Carr shoved the gun in his face, and gave directions. The cabby drove.

"Faster!" shouted Carr, putting the gun behind the man's ear. The driver, shaken, stepped on the gas. They sped toward Villefranche.

If only he was in time.

Birds chirped. The flowers were gay and colorful. Carr hobbled up the gravel path. Ahead of him, the Villa Perrani—his villa, he thought angrily—was silent. A black Citroën was parked before the front steps.

His foot throbbed murderously. He had no clear idea what he was going to do. He walked forward, painfully slowly, until he reached the windows. He looked into the library.

Anne was there, tied to a chair. Liseau was walking back and forth, hands behind his back, holding the gun delicately. He was talking to her. Anne's face was white.

He went up the steps, leaving a little trail of red, and went silently inside, to the vast hallway. He could hear a soft voice through the doors that led to the library. He paused.

Roger Carr had no faith in his ability at unarmed combat. He had never won a fight in his entire life. When he was ten, eight-year-old kids had picked on him. What could he do now?

He knocked on the door.

When Liseau opened it, he would drill him. That was the answer. Footsteps were moving toward the door. The handle turned. He gripped the gun tightly. The door opened slightly, then more.

Anne.

He nearly shot her. It was only at the last moment that he lowered the barrel, firing stupidly into the wooden floor. The gun jumped out of his hand. God, it had a kick.

Anne stepped back. Liseau stood there, the gun aimed at Carr's stomach.

"How nice to see you again, Mr. Carr."

Anne screamed, and fainted.

Carr fell upon his gun.

Near his ear, he saw wood chips fly. There was no sound of a shot—Liseau was using a silencer. Carr got the gun and fired it.

He saw Liseau spin and tumble over.

Did it, Carr thought. Hot damn.

Moments later, Liseau was on his feet, blood dripping from his wrist. He held the gun loosely in his other hand. His face was tired, defeated.

"I surrender," he said.

"Drop the gun."

"As you wish." Liseau shrugged and fired quickly. No sound, just whistling air past Carr's head.

Carr flung himself behind a couch. Liseau overturned a table.

Carr heard a soft *thunk thunk* as two bullets plowed into the stuffing of the couch. He fired at the table, but missed it entirely in his excitement.

Liseau leaped for the door. Carr fired twice, but missed again. Liseau was out in the hallway. Carr heard feet running up the stairs to the second floor.

Anne came to, and looked at him through the smoke in the room. "Are you all right?" she said.

"Yes."

"You're bleeding," she said, pointing to his leg.

"Don't worry." He had forgotten all about it.

"Is Liseau…?"

"No. He's upstairs."

Carr dashed out into the hall and ran for the stairs. As he ran, a chip of marble jumped up from the railing. He dropped down. Another chip sprang up with a *whing!* He saw Liseau at the top of the stairs, and fired once.

A bullet brought a groan of pain. He'd hit something—or maybe Liseau was faking. Carr moved up the stairs, sheltering himself behind the heavy marble banister. When he reached the second floor, it was silent. Crouched, he listened intently, and heard a noise in the bedroom down the hall.

Cautiously, he went down the hall. He looked into the bedroom where he had heard the sound. Empty. And then behind him, a voice saying, "Goodbye, Mr. Carr."

Carr whirled. Somehow, Liseau was behind him. The gun was aimed directly at Carr's heart; it couldn't miss.

Click.

Carr looked at the gun.

Liseau fired again, suddenly afraid.

Click.

"Isn't that a shame?" Carr said. "Very inconvenient."

His own hand closed on the trigger.

"Please," Liseau said. "I'll pay—"

"Sorry," Carr said.

He squeezed.

Click.

"Son of a bitch," he said, and flung his gun at Liseau. The heavy Luger caught the doctor right in the mouth, and he staggered backward. Carr jumped forward. He would strangle him with his bare hands.

Liseau stood, gasping, against the wall. He reached into his breast pocket and withdrew something shiny. Carr stopped.

It was a scalpel.

"I always carry one," Liseau said, advancing. One wrist dangled limply, dripping blood. The other held the scalpel. "So useful."

Carr stepped back cautiously. Could you throw a knife like that? He didn't think so. He watched Liseau's hand.

"I will draw and quarter you, Mr. Carr. I will cut out your guts and stuff them into your mouth."

Carr moved backward. Liseau advanced.

"You will taste your own intestines, warm between your teeth."

Carr felt the wall behind him. Liseau still moved forward. Closer, then closer, leading with the glinting sharp blade of the scalpel.

"Hungry?"

Carr kicked, hard, upward. The scalpel slashed his ankle, but his foot struck solidly between Liseau's legs.

The doctor staggered back. There was a bureau nearby; bottles and tubes stood on a dresser. Carr grabbed them and threw them at Liseau. He fell.

Carr was on him.

Liseau rolled, and pushed Carr aside. He scrambled to his feet, panting. His eyes were wide, his face pale. He was losing a lot of blood from that wrist, Carr thought. He himself was dizzy and weak from his leg.

Carr got to his feet. Liseau had the scalpel again. Carr grabbed the wrist, and they struggled silently for a moment, both gasping for breath. Liseau was strong, but he had the use of only one hand. Carr was grateful.

They struggled back and forth across the room, and finally Carr tripped. Liseau came down on top of him, the scalpel over Carr's throat, slowly descending despite his efforts to keep it away. Liseau had his whole weight behind the knife; it came closer, and closer.

With a final monumental effort, Carr heaved up. Liseau rolled off, and they both got to their feet. They were moving slowly now, sluggish with fatigue and loss of blood.

Liseau held the scalpel. Carr picked up a chair and flung it. Liseau sidestepped it neatly—it skittered by and crashed into the window, smashing the glass.

Panting, they looked at each other. Liseau moved in for the kill.

"Hungry?" he said again.

Carr lunged again, and Liseau fell off balance, tottering backward to the window. He struck the glass spread-eagled, and fell through. There was a brief scream.

Carr ran to the window. Liseau lay on the steps of the villa, writhing in pain. Probably his neck had been broken. In a moment, he was still.

It was over.

Anne came into the room, took in the damage at a glance, and was about to speak when a car pulled up in the drive.

"Oh no," Carr said. He couldn't take any more, not for a minute. He was finished, exhausted, utterly tired.

Anne went to the window. "Police," she said.

He collapsed on the bed, unconscious.

Chapter XXV

Roger Carr smelled a strange mixture of starch and perfume. He opened his eyes and stared into a brilliantly colored bunch of yellow daffodils. He blinked, and heard voices. He swung his head around.

"Hello," Anne said.

Carr looked blankly at her, and let his eyes wander around the room. It was small, cream-colored, and antiseptic. The bed was neatly made, the covers tucked around him. Vascard and Gorman stood at the end.

"Hello," Vascard said.

"Hi," Gorman said. "Good to see you back."

"This place is horrible," Vascard said. "They won't let me smoke."

Anne bent over and kissed him coolly on the cheek. Carr held out his hand to her. She took it quietly.

"How did it all work out?" he said.

"Very well," Vascard said. "We got them all, except for Liseau. And the shipment will go through."

"But how? I thought that—"

"Ah, yes. But you remember I told you the wife was crucial. She was. The papers were set up so that, in the event of her husband's death, she had the power to sign the papers."

"And she did?"

"Well, she didn't want to at first, but…"

"Terrible business," Gorman said.

Anne bent over and kissed Carr again. It seemed as if she was unaware of anyone else in the room.

"Come on," Vascard said to Gorman. "Let's leave these two alone."

"I wanted to talk to Mr. Carr. I have some questions."

"Not now," said Vascard firmly, gripping Gorman's elbow. "I must apologize for my associate," he said to Anne and Carr. "He is not French; he does not understand these things. Your leg, by the way, will be all right. Nothing broken—missed that bone, whatever it's called. You can leave tomorrow if you want." He sniffed the room. "I'd want to, if I were you. Even I feel sick here." He walked with Gorman toward the door, then looked back. "Good work," he said.

"Yes," Gorman agreed. "Excellent. Very good indeed. If there's anything I can do for you, just—"

"There may be something," Carr said, "later."

"Really? What?"

"It concerns visas for aliens."

"Really? Why, I—"

"Later," Vascard said, and hustled him through the door.

Carr looked at Anne.

"How do you feel?" he asked.

"Fine. But I'm supposed to ask you that."

"Go ahead."

"How do you feel?"

"Never better." He reached over to kiss her, shifted his weight, and groaned as he felt his bandaged thigh.

Anne pushed him back. "Lie down, Samson. There's plenty of time for that."

He did. There was a long pause.

"Am I going to marry you?" Carr asked finally.

"Am I going to accept?"

"Yes."

"You take a lot for granted."

"It's a trick I learned," he said, "from a girl I know."

She kissed him gently.

The great pyramid of Cheops filled the horizon. It was titanic, a giant mass of yellow-brown stone stretching wide and high, staggering the imagination. Harold Barnaby stood near the base, in the vast shadow of the pyramid, talking to a guide.

"I want to go up," he said.

The dragoman looked at him wearily, then shrugged. "Okay, boss," he said. "I show you."

"Good."

Barnaby looked up the facade to the top. From a distance, the pyramid appeared to slope gently; up close, it seemed almost sheer. A group of tourists were coming down. They were small specks, barely visible from where he stood.

"You are alone?" the dragoman asked. He was a short fellow, very dark, wearing baggy trousers, sandals, and—incongruously—a black suit coat, on which was pinned his brass license.

"Yes," Barnaby said. "I'm alone."

"Okay, boss. We go now. You do what I do, okay? Feet like mine, hands like mine. I show you." He started off, Barnaby following closely. Barnaby would have preferred to climb by himself, but the police required a guide. Now, as they began the ascent, he understood why. The blocks were immense, three or four feet high and sometimes six feet long. In many places, there was no more than a foot of ledge between tiers, and the path had been worn treacherously smooth by the tread of countless tourists before him.

Climbing was hard work; the guide set a quick pace. He seemed adept at scrambling over the four-foot stones, but Barnaby was cautious. The ground was very far away. Taxis and camels were minuscule. As they climbed the southeast edge, he soon found that he could see all of Cairo, fifteen miles away. Though it had been stifling hot on the ground, the wind blew strongly up here, tugging at his clothes.

The guide stopped to wait for him.

Barnaby was moving carefully now, for his hands were covered with fine dry sand, and he did not trust his grip. He heaved himself up, over block after block, until he reached the guide.

"Okay, boss?"

"Sure," Barnaby said, winded. They were standing halfway up, with the desert and the Nile and Cairo spread out before them. He could not see the other pyramids of Giza or the Sphinx—the Great Pyramid blocked their view.

"Pretty, yes?"

Barnaby nodded. He very carefully did not look down. He was painfully aware that they were both standing on a narrow ledge not wider than two feet.

"Let's go on."

"Okay, boss."

They climbed.

Now it began in earnest: the wind whistled in his ears and blew sand in his eyes. He noticed the names of tourists cut into the huge stones; he forced his mind to read them, trying to forget the height. The way was steeper still, and once the guide had to stop to find the path again. Barnaby found he was sweating.

He cursed himself for wanting to do this, and paused to wipe his hands on his pants—one hand at a time, always holding onto the rock. And yet he knew that he had to climb the Great Pyramid. He would never forgive himself if he came to Egypt and did not try it.

Quite suddenly, they reached the top. Barnaby, who had resigned himself to climbing forever, was startled to see a flat space some ten feet square. The guide bent over and helped him over the final block.

He stood on top of the pyramid of Cheops, or Khufu. He felt his legs shake from relief and excitement and sat down quickly to admire the view. From his vantage point, all Cairo lay spread out at the head of the green Nile Delta. He could see the radio tower, the mosques, and the citadel. To the south, on this side of the river, were the scattered pyramid fields of Saqqara and Dashur. And behind him—he turned to see them—were the two small pyramids of Giza, the burial chambers of Khafre and Menkure.

He recalled standing atop the Pyramid of the Sun at Teotihuacán, outside Mexico City, and looking across at the smaller Pyramid of the Moon. It was a similar feeling, but this was different. Egypt imbued the view with a heavy sense of mystery and foreboding. He reached into his pocket for a cigarette, turning his thoughts to his problem.

For the first time in his life, Harold Barnaby, 41, associate professor of archaeology at the University of Chicago, was contemplating dishonesty on a grand scale.

Barnaby was an Egyptologist, and his particular interest was hieroglyphics. He was an astute linguist, a talent that had been evident from childhood. His interest in language, in obscure writings, and difficult grammars had led him in college to study the languages of the Near East—languages both living and dead. It had been the purest chance, the taunt of a fellow graduate student, that had started him on Egyptian hieroglyphics. Now he could read the characters almost as rapidly as he read English.

While a student, he had become fascinated with all aspects of Egyptian life as revealed by the writing.

And slowly, he had come to understand that much that had been translated was wrong.

It was this knowledge that had first brought Barnaby to Cairo, six weeks earlier. He had a grant to study previously translated papyri, for it was his contention that such a study would radically change all existing notions of life in the dynasties of the Middle Kingdom—an era of Egyptian history characterized by the spread of empire, fabulous wealth, and vast armies.

The day after his arrival in Cairo, he had met the proper people—the curator of the Egyptian Museum, the director of the Antiquities Service of the United Arab Republic—and had been established in a little room in an obscure corner of the rambling building. The room was bare, consisting only of a table, a chair, and a lethargic guard. One after another, the precious papyri were brought to him, and he checked the manuscripts against the translated texts. He read of the military engagements of Thutmose III, seventeen times conqueror of the Hyksos; of the court machinations of Hatshepsut; of the glories of Ikhnaton. He reviewed, like an auditor, the messages, dispatches, and bills of pharaohs dead 3,000 years. A whole new world came to his eyes as he read— he forgot the guard and his foul-smelling cigarettes, forgot the heat and dust that streamed in through the open window, forgot the clanking noise of Cairo outside.

He was completely immersed and completely happy. Until two days ago.

Barnaby had been reading a document recovered from

one of the Tombs of the Nobles, the rock-cut chambers in the cliffs of Thebes, Deir el-Medinet, across the river from modern Luxor. It was the tomb of a court majordomo, a vizier named Butehi, who had served one of the many kings who succeeded Tutankhamen in rapid succession—just which king was uncertain; the history of the period was confused.

This particular papyrus had been originally translated as pertaining to the procurement of firewood for the queen's hot baths and the disposition of slaves to attend her majesty. Now, rereading it. Barnaby was disturbed. It had been translated from right to left, which made some sense, but very little; the original translator had squeezed the grammar into his own conception of the meaning.

Translating from left to right was not much improvement. He tried reading the hieroglyphics vertically, top to bottom (the Egyptians wrote all three ways), but still no success. It was frustrating.

He began to wonder about this innocuous little passage. He was about to put it aside as not worth the effort when he had a flash of intuition, the result of long years of translating such manuscripts. He suddenly, instinctively, sensed it was important. He looked at it again and tried working from bottom to top. Still nothing.

There were no cartouches in this particular passage. That was odd. Also, the spacing of the hieroglyphs was irregular, the arrangement suggesting some kind of trick. Was it a code? If so, he was lost—it would take as long to break it as it had taken Champollion to discover the clue to deciphering the hieroglyphics in the first place.

He played with the message, rearranging the symbols, testing simple replacements. He got nowhere. He sat back, lit a cigarette, and thought about the character of the man who had caused this passage to be written. What could have been so important that it required a departure from normal writing patterns?

This man, this vizier, would no doubt have access to many secrets of the pharaoh be served. He would also be vain, as was Rekhmire, who was the vizier of Thutmose III. Rekhmire had said of himself that there was nothing he did not know, in heaven, in earth, or any quarter of the underworld; he had inscribed that on his own tomb. But the viziers were important—in their own times, they were the second most powerful men in the world.

Yes, he would be vain. And he would wish to inscribe on his tomb the deeds he had accomplished, the successful administrative acts he had managed.

Staring at the papyrus, Barnaby finished his cigarette and still had no answer. He stubbed out the butt and pushed aside the ashtray. When he looked back at the rows of symbols, he suddenly saw it, clear as day.

Diagonals.

The passage was to be read diagonally. That was what the spacing hinted at. He tried, from top left to bottom right, and got nothing. Then he tried top right to bottom left and found that it read,

> *My majesty, lord of east and west, over all things ruler, commanded*

He worked on the next diagonal, but it did not follow directly. It said something about a dwelling-place eternal, but he could not get the syntax correctly. Perhaps it was necessary to skip a diagonal and then come back.

Barnaby studied the manuscript for two hours. He found that there was no regular arrangement in the order of lines, but that the whole could be fitted together to make a reasonable statement.

My majesty, lord of east and west, over all things ruler, commanded, and I have made for him a place that may be satisfying to him therewith, forever and ever. I have built [my] majesty, my father, a rest for the heavens, a dwelling-place eternal, which no one knows and which not shall be found. My architect, my son-in-law, shall be nameless as the dwelling-place, known to no [man].

Barnaby glanced over at the guard in the corner, who was half-asleep, chair pushed back against the wall. A fly buzzed aimlessly around the room.

In deep the rock, a work of fifty men, is located the place, final rest, of [my] majesty, lord of east and west, ruler of the peoples. Not where many kings have been disturbed, but near; not so low, but high; in the north, where only by this may it be known. From the arcade of the woman-king, halfway, and north 6 iter, 1 khet, to the high cleft where fly the birds, for they draw near to [heaven] even as my majesty, in eternal rest. The fifty slaves lie near the dwelling-place, and my son-in-law watches over them. I have done this myself, and only I know the place. It was a great work that I did there, and my wisdom shall draw praise for ages after.

It was incredible. Barnaby read it again, and still again. He could not believe what he saw, though it was beyond doubt. This was the record of an official who had made the tomb of an unnamed 19th-Dynasty pharaoh and who had personally murdered all those who had worked on the tomb, including his own son-in-law. And yet, the man could not restrain from recording the deed for posterity in his own tomb. It was, Barnaby thought, typically Egyptian—kill fifty people to guard the secret, but announce it blandly for all to see on your own tomb.

But was it so bland?

He looked again at the original translation. Read right to
left, the passage did make some sense. Perhaps that was why
the vizier had felt secure—he had hidden his secret within
another statement that could be interpreted as a common-
place record. It was clever.

Barnaby stood up and walked to the window. The guard
stirred, looked at him, and relaxed again. Barnaby stared out
at the city, turning yellow-red in the afternoon light. A
streetcar rumbled past, crammed with passengers, bearing
an advertisement for Aswan Beer.

It was a staggering opportunity, he realized. With this
information, he had a reasonable chance of finding the
tomb—and there was a reasonable chance that it would still
be intact. Most tombs of the 18th–20th dynasties had been
robbed, usually a few years after the pharaoh's death. But
if the preparations had been conducted in such ruthless
secrecy, and if the official was as cunning in all things as he
had been in the manner of telling the secret, then there was
a chance.

Harold Barnaby could become famous overnight, the dis-
coverer of a tomb to rival Tutankhamen's. He could have a
full professorship in archaeology at any university in the
world. His name would become a household word, as common as King Tut's was now.

There would be secret passages, of course, and dead
ends, and a great deal of hard, dusty work, but if he were
successful....

Professor Barnaby. He tried the name on his tongue, silently. Professor Barnaby, the first man to break the seals on
the door and enter the underground sepulcher, the first man
to see the sarcophagus and the fabulous treasure stored with

it. The first man in 3,000 years to gaze at all this, as the flash-bulbs popped and the newsreel cameras whirred.

He smiled, and then his eyes narrowed, and he frowned. Something had occurred to him, something tempting and horrifying. At that moment, staring out of the window of the Egyptian Museum, the conflict was established—a conflict that was still not resolved.

It was growing late; the sun hung low and angry in the sky. It would fall quickly now, Barnaby knew. He stood atop the pyramid and beckoned to the guide.

"Okay, boss? We go now?"

"Yes," Barnaby said. "We go."

It was silent in his hotel room. Barnaby lay on the bed, smoking a cigarette and staring up at the ceiling. His mouth was dry from smoking so much, but he could not stop; he lit each cigarette from the glowing butt of the last, mechanically, his mind elsewhere.

Every instinct, every bit of training and inclination argued against him. It was so fantastic an idea that it became illogical, almost absurd. He should dismiss it outright.

He sighed and swung his feet onto the floor. He walked across the threadbare carpet and looked at himself in the mirror over the washbasin. Brooding eyes stared back at him. Forty-one years old, he thought. Most of that time spent hunched over books. In retrospect, his efforts seemed excessive, the rewards too few. Egyptology was a dying interest in archaeological circles, particularly in America. Even if he did make a world-famous discovery, he could expect nothing better than a full professorship—sixteen thousand dollars a year, perhaps. Six weeks ago such a prospect would have thrilled him beyond measure. Now, he was not so sure.

His face was still youthful, but the hairline was receding, the eyes growing weaker, the shoulders beginning to slope. His youth was departing, and he could imagine himself as an old man. He would be lonely, as he was now—he had never found time for women before. Egypt was his mistress and had been for many years.

On the airplane, coming over, there had been a girl, but he had not approached her. They had exchanged glances, and he had looked away. Timid. Afraid.

He had no idea how to carry out his plan—perhaps it could not even be done. Perhaps he was indulging himself, wasting energy on an appealing dream that could never be materialized. He doubted his own strength to carry out a feasible scheme, should he arrive at one.

He looked at his eyes. "You haven't got the nerve," he said aloud. "Stupid ass."

But nerve was only part of it. He needed contacts, finances, organization. These could only be obtained in a world that was unfamiliar to him.

Yet, there must be a way.